A Plum Job
Cenarth Fox

A Plum Job

Copyright © 2015 Cenarth Fox

First published in 2015 by Fox Plays
Melbourne Australia
www.cenfoxbooks.com
www.foxplays.com

ISBN 978-0-949175-06-9

Cover design by Ana Grigoriu

To Julie
for love and longevity

To Peter and Julie
for friendship and fun

To Jerome
for cricket and cake

Chapter 1

YOU CAN BE sacked from almost any job. You can be ignored, bullied and demoted but there aren't many jobs where you can be tortured, raped and murdered.

You can in acting; in stage acting and when acting in real-life and not many of us are good at either let alone both. Louise was.

Every actor knows you can die on stage. You can dry, miss your cue or get tongue-tied. But if you're acting in real life and fluff your lines you can literally die. It's a tough gig.

In 1923 when she was four Louise Wellesley was an English version of the soon-to-be-discovered Shirley Temple and performed for her eccentric Uncle Crispin, a cat-loving, gin-soaked aristocrat.

Louise patted the cats, checked the ribbons in her hair then entertained. To her performing was like breathing. Nobody knew the source of Louise's show business gene and certainly her parents believed the stage was no place for a refined young lady.

Who could imagine that sixteen years later in a classy brothel in Nazi-occupied Paris her toddler routine would have red-blooded men drooling? But today, Louise was Shirley Temple and got to strut her stuff.

> *A duck says "Quack"*
> *A sheep says "Baa"*
> *A happy cow says "Moo"*
> *And after all these farmyard sounds*
> *I'll sing this song for you.*
> *There's a quack and a baa and a neigh and an oink*
> *And very, very, very, long moo*
> *But the first sound every morning*
> *Is a cock-a-doodle-do.*

The applause sent a shiver up Louise's spine as she took a delicious bow then skipped to her mother. Always leave them wanting more. Louise Beatrice Wellesley, a.k.a. Plum, was a natural.

She was also a fighter and as a beautiful teenager clashed, politely, with her conservative father. In the 1930s many upper-class English families still had their daughters educated at home. Louise hated that.

'But Papa, young ladies go to school today. And there are such excellent teachers.'

'She's right, Charles,' said Victoria. Louise's mother supported her husband in public but spoke freely at home. The mother and daughter team won and Louise became the first Wellesley female to be educated at a public school.

At Roedean her flair for languages and drama delighted staff. The seaside setting was perfect. Rehearsing Shakespeare, Louise stood on a cliff top, shouted her lines at the English Channel and wondered what her parents would think of her love for the theatre and acting.

Papa would never approve. The very idea of his daughter having a job was unthinkable and as for working in the theatre, well, preposterous would be a mild reaction.

After Roedean, Louise went to finishing-school in France to be prepared for adult life. And after her sojourn in this stately chateau, she would return to England and remain at home until the right chap came along as approved by the pater and mater. *Damn.*

In France, Louise fell madly in love with the husband of her etiquette teacher. Louise knew Charlotte Brontë had a disastrous crush on her teacher in Belgium and pondered the etiquette of seducing the etiquette teacher's husband.

Louise remembered her mother's stern warnings about sex and wondered when she might encounter such situations in the flesh—so to speak.

Her fellow finishing-school students were preoccupied with marriage, body shape and clothes. The joyful exception was Matilda "Matty" Gonzales-Jones whose Spanish and Welsh parentage produced a flamboyant mixture of rebellion and *joie de vivre*. Her wild and unruly hair matched her personality and love of adventure. As a toddler her nickname was "Cheeky". In France she perfected the art of escape and Matty and Louise spent various nights wandering the nearby town.

Midnight rambles included smoking and drinking whenever fags and wine were scrounged but their *pièce de résistance* involved "borrowing" underwear from washing lines and placing said items on headstones and statues. The locals were not amused.

One night the truants' luck ran out. A priest with insomnia saw movement from his bedroom window. These hooligans must be taught a lesson so the man of the cloth crept into his churchyard. Silently he moved toward the unsuspecting females, their giggles mixing with the odd belch.

The priest sprang from behind a gravestone and roared. Matilda nearly died and Louise became Pip when Magwich grabbed the wee boy in *Great Expectations*; wee was appropriate.

The females were trapped as the priest railed against their sacrilegious behaviour. Mind you it did have its funny side.

First it was snowing down south as the priest's nightshirt poked out from beneath his hastily donned cassock. Then in his rage, the man of God grabbed a brassiere the girls had draped over a headstone and as he gesticulated about sin, the flying bra tended to undermine Father Indignation's indignation. But the dancing D-cups were not uppermost in Louise's mind. She thought of the shame of being expelled from finishing-school and of her parents' horror.

Matilda had no such qualms and sprang into action. Her French was passable but her acting was bold. She offered a sexual favour to the man who had taken a vow of chastity. Louise was stunned at the brazen antics of her friend. Could Matilda actually do that? And if so, when and where would it occur? Worse, was Louise part of the deal? And if the man of God declined, was there a plan B?

Matilda's plan failed, miserably. The priest's anger turned to fury as he added eternal damnation to his diatribe. Being Church of England, Louise feared expulsion rather than excommunication.

The priest stopped waving the bra. Both parties paused.

Matilda whispered. 'You kick his shins, I'll kick his balls and we'll run in different directions.' Louise shook her head. 'Got a better idea?' hissed Matty. Louise did have a better idea.

She stood and stepped forward. To her flawless French she added enough of the local dialect to be overwhelmingly convincing. The menacing priest froze. Anger drained from his body. Matilda's mouth opened and remained so. Louise's fluent French became intoxicating and was enhanced by her silky hand gestures and fascinating facial expressions. Finally her performance ended. She bowed.

The priest took a backward step. He replaced the bra on the gravestone and he too bowed. In humble tones he invited the ladies to attend his church. Mass times were listed on the board. He would be honoured to hear their confession. And with a blessing from his creator, the cleric departed. At 0232 hours Matilda closed her mouth.

'My God, Lou that was brilliant. And where did you learn to speak French like that?'

Louise took off. 'Come on,' she called and Matty gave chase.

'Slow down! Louise!' It wasn't until they scaled the school wall and crept up the vine into their bedroom that Louise explained.

'I told the priest my uncle was a Monsignor who worked for Cardinal Joyeuse in Lyon and they were considering our friendly friar for a senior position in Paris.'

'You what?'

'His excellent parish work has been noticed and sometime soon the Cardinal will pay our bra-brandishing brother a visit.'

'Unbelievable, but how do you know the Cardinal?'

'Matty, I'm C of E and wouldn't know the cleric from Adam, but last week I read an article about some celebrated Cardinal in Lyon. If you have a good script, perform with conviction and can throw in a powerful name, some people will believe anything.'

'*Some* people?'

Matty began to laugh. She couldn't stop. So loud were her shrieks she had to pull the blankets over her head to smother her glee. Finally, when the hilarity faded, she turned to her friend.

'And here's me thinking sex was the key. Goodnight you crazy lady. And thanks for a wonderful, wonderful show.'

In the darkness Louise smiled. *This acting caper can come in handy.* And what a buzz she felt after a live performance. But then she thought about Matilda and her convincing cameo.

'Matty?'

A rising inflexion from Matilda. 'Yes?'

'Would you really have done that to the priest?'

They started to giggle.

Louise and Matilda dreaded the end of finishing-school. They swore to keep in touch. If one was in trouble, the other would help. If one found fortune, it would be shared. They created an oath of allegiance and to respect their parents, the oath was to be declared in English, Spanish and Welsh. Choosing the English version was easy.

We swear to always love and help one another till death us do part.

The translations weren't so easy. Louise was a linguist. Her French was fantastically fluent, her knowledge of German would pass muster in any Berlin Strasse und café and her rudimentary Spanish was acceptable. But when Matilda wrote the oath in Welsh, Louise was stumped—totally.

Yrydym yn tyngu I garu a chymorth ein gilyydd tan marwolaeth wneud ini ymadael.

They sailed through the English and Spanish but ran aground with the Welsh. Matilda pronounced every syllable. Louise stumbled. Aiming for a guttural sound, she started spitting.

At first they giggled. Then they laughed. Louise spoke louder; louder still. She roared. Matilda rolled on the floor with tears streaming down her cheeks. *'Gilyydd tan marwolaeth,'* they chanted.

'How dare you!' threatened Louise. 'I would never *gilyydd tan marwolaeth* in a million years.' More shrieks from Matilda.

The cacophony was heard by the entire floor including the woman in charge of the dormitory. Normally she would have demanded silence. But as it was their final night, the unladylike pair was ignored. Most of their teachers were delighted the girls were leaving.

The young women's friendship was real. It was heartbreaking to think they may never meet again. Parents were the gatekeepers of young females from wealthy families. Soon it would be Matilda to Spain and Louise to England and ne'er the twain shall meet.

Next morning they cried, hugged and kissed. Matilda left in her chauffeur-driven vehicle and waved until she could no longer see her friend. Louise was chaperoned back to England.

Big brother Henry was waiting for her on a crowded Waterloo station. She heard him before she saw him.

'Plum!' He pushed through the crowd and hugged her. 'How's my favourite sister?'

Louise was happy. She loved her older brothers, Henry and Edmund, and reckoned if she found a husband as kind as they were she'd be truly happy. Well not completely because while marriage did have a lot going for it her heart was set on treading the boards.

On the train down to Farnham, Louise asked about Henry's career as a barrister and he asked about her feelings for Henry's chum, James "Pongo" Fingleton who was absolutely potty about her.

Louise now knew the meaning of unrequited love as she listened to her brother's enthusiastic endorsement of a man she most definitely did not want to marry. Yes he was a nice chap with perfect manners and was almost good looking but Louise had two reasons for rejecting Pongo.

First, in her he ignited no emotional electricity whatsoever and second, as Louise desperately wanted to explore life, education and the theatre, marriage was simply not an option for the foreseeable future.

Henry knew Louise was damning his friend with faint praise. Henry had a straight-shooting relationship with his sister and even though two elderly spinsters and a vicar were sharing the carriage, Henry went for the jugular.

'So if good old Pongo isn't Mister Wonderful, I believe as a practicing barrister, I can reasonably infer you have someone else in mind.' Louise smiled. Henry blanched. 'Don't tell me you've fallen for some onion-clad Frenchman?'

Their fellow travellers were terrible actors. The more they pretended not to listen, the more their fascination grew. If an ear trumpet had been available, all three would have fought for first use.

Louise lowered her voice which annoyed the eavesdroppers. 'If I tell you something, you must promise to never breathe a word to anyone.' The tension moved up a notch. 'I have a serious problem and need your help.'

Henry was unsure and worried and pretended to be joking. 'You're not angling for free legal advice I hope?' The spinsters were agog.

Louise stared at her brother. 'I need advice on how I should break my news to Papa.' The spinsters held their breath. The vicar's eyes widened.

Henry was suddenly aware their conversation was in the public domain. He edged closer and whispered. 'Look, old girl, if it's a female thingy, you should be tackling Mummy, not the old man. We chaps are not much chop when it comes to those things.'

'What things?'

Louise challenged him. Henry was shocked. What had happened to his innocent baby sister? She both looked and sounded like a woman.

Henry changed the subject. 'Did you hear old Mister McCorkingdale died?'

'What things, Henry?'

Henry was squirming. 'Plum! Behave!'

'What I want to do requires Papa's permission.'

'You *have* fallen for a Frog.'

She was almost angry. 'Will you stop going on about marriage! I've made a decision and unless Papa approves, I'll jolly well have to leave home.'

Henry's mind was racing. *What's happened to sweet, little Plum? And what on Earth is this big decision?* He spoke in a gentle fashion.

'Well, all right, tell me. I can't advise without details.'

The train slowed as it approached Aldershot. The sisters got up to depart so Louise leant back and waited. One sister took forever to collect her things. Her sibling reprimanded her about missing their station. The suspense was killing the slow-moving sister. How could she depart without knowing Louise's big decision? If only the sisters lived in Farnham.

They missed the second act and with the vicar now the only passenger, Henry pressed Louise.

'Righto, old girl, what's going on?'

Before she could reply, the vicar got in first. 'You might be able to see the road from here.' The smiling cleric pointed to the passing countryside. Louise and Henry were clueless. '*The Solitary Cyclist,*' he said.

'Of course,' said a nodding Henry who turned to face his sister and resume the inquisition.

The vicar, who always sat facing the locomotive, was up for a chat. 'It does go to prove, don't you think, that the great man did indeed entrust some tasks to his friend?'

Henry had no idea what the priest was talking about and even less desire to chat when far more pressing matters of state were at hand. He was about to say that when Louise chimed in.

'Ah, but was Mister Holmes entirely fair in telling Doctor Watson his work was remarkably bad?'

Henry was clueless. The vicar beamed. Here was a kindred spirit, a true believer. The priest was delighted.

'You know I have often asked myself that very question.' He offered his hand. 'Stanley Tripe, vicar of St Nicholas, Chawton. I'm delighted to make your acquaintance.'

Henry introduced himself and Louise and thanked his lucky stars Farnham was the next station. But if Henry was surprised at his sister's new-found maturity, he was amazed at her ability to discuss literature with authority. She engaged the vicar.

'So as well as knowing about Mister Holmes and his adventure in Farnham, coming from Chawton, I deduce, sir, you must be a lover of Miss Austen's works as well.'

6

The Reverend Tripe was in Earthly Heaven. Henry was in no-man's land and as the trainspotting trees in Surrey watched the train chug by, the two literary luminaries swapped opinions on why *The Adventure of the Solitary Cyclist* was one of Dr Watson's better yarns and whether Miss Austen had ever based any of her characters on neighbours she knew in Chawton. To this animated discussion, Henry added precisely nothing.

Farnham station was reached with Henry never so keen to alight from a train. The reverend gentleman carried Louise's case, opened the door and gave her a most wonderful blessing. He leant out of the train and the guard's whistle was not strong enough to hide the enthusiasm in the cleric's voice.

'It is not in the stars to hold our destiny but in ourselves.'

She smiled and called as the waving priest moved away. 'Farewell. God knows when we shall meet again.'

Henry looked at his smiling sister and shook his head. They walked to the family home. It was no mansion but had enough grandeur to make any passing royals feel "at home" should they pop in for high tea.

As Louise and Henry wandered along a leafy Surrey lane, he was determined to discover his sister's problem.

'I must say, old girl, I was impressed by your knowledge of literature back there. And I never knew Sherlock Holmes came to Farnham.'

'Oh he did indeed; both he and Doctor Watson.'

Henry was serious. 'I wonder if the old man ever met them.'

Louise smiled inwardly. The great consulting detective had indeed become flesh and blood.

Henry was curious. 'So how do you know so much about Sherlock, Jane Austen and the Bard? I thought finishing-school was all about flower-arranging and dinner-parties.'

Louise laughed. 'The Law has no monopoly on books.'

'Yes but even so, you seem to know so much for a girl.'

'For a girl!' Louise was indignant. It was time to tease big brother. 'But literature is not my only area of interest. I know all about that famous Chancery case of *Jarndyce and Jarndyce.*'

Henry stopped. Louise walked on then turned to see his puzzled expression.

'I've heard of that. Don't know the exact details but ...' He caught up with her. 'Don't tell me you're also reading Law books.'

Louise grinned whilst laughing inside and, having outsmarted one of her intelligent brothers, returned to her topic.

'If I tell you about my problem, you must promise not to be cruel or laugh.'

'I promise.'

'I need your advice on how and when I should tackle Papa.'

Henry looked at his serious sister. 'I promise I won't be cruel or laugh and will give the best advice I can.' They stopped. The pause lingered before Louise spoke.

'I want to go to Cambridge.'

Henry blurted his immediate response. 'But you're a girl.'

Instantly Louise slapped her brother's arm, hard. The siblings froze. Louise had slapped both her brothers before, many times, mainly when she was a child, to stop them tickling her, but this was like no other time. This was a slap of anger, frustration and disbelief.

Louise was immediately upset. She hugged her brother. This was tricky as he held Louise's case plus his own bag and briefcase.

'Henry, I'm so sorry. Please forgive me.'

Henry struggled with bags and a hug. 'Only if you let go,' he said.

She slowly released her hug. He smiled and she smiled then launched back at him. He let her cling to him before he finally spoke.

'So you want to go to Cambridge?'

She released him staring into his eyes. 'More than anything else.' She took her case from Henry. 'I can make my own way in this world, sir. Anything you can do, I can do better.'

He nodded. He knew she was no longer his "baby" sister. They resumed their journey. Louise spoke.

'I'll understand if you don't want to help but I do value your advice. You know Papa. I have a plan and ...'

'He'll never agree.'

Louise felt a pang of sadness. She longed for the slightest crumb of encouragement or, better still, some practical advice. It was too much to hope Henry would support her. Her only hope was her mother. She would calmly explain to Louise's father how times had changed, that Cambridge now welcomed female students and that Louise had a glowing report from Roedean.

'I'm going to ask him, Henry and I'd greatly appreciate your advice on when I should do so. Is there a good time? Can I soften him up first?' She paused. 'Will you support me?'

'I just don't want to see you disappointed.'

'So is that a *yes* or a *no*?'

They stopped. 'I'll help you on one condition.' Louise held her breath. She prayed a silent prayer. *Not Pongo Fingleton, please.* 'If Mother disapproves, you drop the whole idea.'

Louise beamed, stood on tip-toe and kissed Henry. 'Thank you, kind sir. I shall happily abide by your wishes.

Getting into Cambridge in 1937 wasn't easy. One needed first-class results and having a title or connection to the Establishment certainly helped. But all that applied to gentlemen. Ladies were seriously handicapped.

Louise set her heart on Cambridge as a career path. By studying Shakespeare and other dramatists, she could use that training to hopefully become an actress.

She had no theatre contacts and her parents would be horrified at their daughter's thespian ambition. Louise believed studying literature and drama at Cambridge was logically her best hope.

The first female students at Cambridge in 1869 did it tough. They were not to live at the university. They had to study subjects of a lower standard than their male counterparts. They were not permitted to sit for exams. When they were permitted they could only obtain a certificate. When they could obtain a degree that did not entitle them to become members of the university. And so on.

The initial ferocious opposition to female students had faded by the 1930s but Louise knew her stumbling-block would be Papa.

After a tearful reunion with her parents, brother Edmund, Mrs Crossley the cook and Horatio the dog, Louise went to her room. Henry had promised to warn Edmund of the possible future fireworks. Louise needed to speak to her mother alone. Getting her support was essential. With Mummy's blessing, Henry and Edmund would swing in behind leaving Papa alone in his opposition.

Not that that meant anything. It wouldn't be three votes for Louise and one against; ipso facto Louise is off to Cambridge. No, Father's word was law.

There was a knock and Louise's mother entered. Victoria and Louise were a glowing example of the claim that the most powerful of relationships is between a mother and her daughter. They thought as one, loved each other deeply and even looked alike. Both had blue eyes and neither had need of make-up as their natural beauty shone.

'My darling girl, I have missed you so much.'

'I'm so happy to be home, Mummy.'

They sat on Louise's bed. Her heart beat faster. Louise had the words rehearsed. *Mummy, I want to study at Cambridge.*

Louise knew her mother would be realistic and rather than discuss Papa's intransigence, would talk about how to win his blessing. For Louise this was one of the happiest times of her life. She was about to speak when Victoria raised a hand. Louise knew this sign. Be still and listen. A knot formed in her stomach.

'My darling, I have sad news.'

Louise barely breathed. Sad news is terrible but when unexpected it's worse. It was like a powerful surprise punch.

'Your Papa is not well.'

Louise was crushed. She knew this was her mother being gentle, preparing her for something far worse. Her father didn't have a cold or a sore thumb. And in that instant, Louise's dream vanished.

'Is he dying?' she whispered.

'He's been unwell for weeks and last month went up to London for tests. The doctors believe his war wounds have weakened his heart. He has chest pains and is taking tablets. I'm telling you this, my darling, because I know you would want to know.'

'Of course I want to know,' cried Louise.

Victoria squeezed her daughter's hands. 'Be brave my darling and as I've always said, live every day to the full.'

Louise tried to smile through her tears.

'I haven't told the boys yet so please don't mention anything until I do. And there's no need to treat Papa in any different way. The only thing I would ask is that you do nothing to upset him. But as you never do, it's silly to even mention it.'

They hugged and Louise believed her Cambridge dream was dead.

'Now,' said Victoria, 'we need to discuss the débutante ball. I've collected a few magazines with some simply gorgeous gowns.'

The next few days were pure misery for Louise. Only Henry knew of her Cambridge dream and once he'd heard the health news about the old man, waited till he and Louise were alone.

'Bad luck old girl but maybe it's all for the best. He would have said *no* anyway.'

Chapter 2

IN GERMANY cousins Max and Kurt Hartmann were catching up in a Berlin coffeehouse. Max was a soldier and Kurt a policeman. "Ripe for promotion" was an apt description of both these dashing, young men. If the police or army wanted photogenic poster boys to boost recruiting, the Hartmann cousins would have made the final cut.

They saw less of each other these days with Max serving in Lower Saxony and Kurt in the capital.

Max was always curious. 'So cousin, what wonderful feats of bravery have the police been up to this month? Have you moved on from petty criminals to joining the Nazis in harassing innocent elderly citizens?'

Kurt hissed. 'Keep your voice down. Good Germans have been arrested for a lot less. Besides the Führer does have his good points.'

Max snorted. 'I joined the army to defend our once mighty nation, not to help some warmongering lunatic.'

Kurt knew they were drifting apart and defended his beliefs. 'You know I'm not a Nazi but look at the drop in unemployment. Millions of Germans are back in work. We have magnificent autobahns and great German engineering. Hitler has restored national pride.'

Kurt's politics had veered to the right.

'National pride is fine,' said Max, 'but at what cost? You remember Herr Bruckner, that superb watchmaker our fathers went to every Christmas?' Max pushed back his cousin's sleeve to reveal a favourite timepiece. 'That magnificent watch came from Herr Bruckner. He disappeared.'

Kurt shrugged. 'So?'

'So?' Max was angry. 'I went to his shop and there was some incompetent Nazi in charge. The truth strikes home, Kurt, when the people we know are being dragged from their beds and taken away, God knows where, with their home and business gifted to the Reich. It's happening to people we know.'

The atmosphere grew frosty. 'You have a short memory,' replied Kurt. 'Remember our proud fathers after the war? They came home humiliated. They survived horrendous trench warfare to be struck down by shame. But Hitler's changed all that. The man you call a "warmongering lunatic" has made Germany and its people prosperous and proud.'

Max was worried. Some of what Kurt said was true. But their relationship was definitely changing. Max continued.

'I fear for our future, Kurt. I know from personal experience there are massive rearmament projects going on all over Germany. If ever there is another war ...'

Kurt scoffed. 'There won't be another war. The British and French aren't stupid. They see our booming economy and magnificent Wehrmacht. Germany will never be humiliated again.'

There was a pause. They were not used to arguing and certainly not over politics. They'd been close as children and their family ties were still strong. Max changed the topic of conversation.

'So how are your parents and dear sisters?'

Kurt wanted to keep talking politics but a scuffle began in the street. The shouting grew louder. The cousins moved quickly.

Two men were being arrested by some of Kurt's colleagues. Two citizens against four policemen was an uneven match until several women joined the fray. They grabbed the police causing them to pay less attention to the men being arrested who in turn fought back. The police began to struggle.

Kurt ran to the melee, drew his pistol and whipped a woman's face. She screamed and fell. The other women bent to help her and the police dragged away the two arrested men.

Kurt replaced his pistol, adjusted his uniform and turned. All he saw was his cousin's back as Max strode down the street.

Oberst Hans Reidle was a Wehrmacht officer admired by all. He was turning sixty and Max Hartmann was invited to his commanding officer's birthday party.

The atmosphere was relaxed and Max felt a sense of pride mixing with his fellow professional soldiers. Reidle tapped his glass bringing instant silence.

'Gentlemen, thank you for your attendance. I must say turning sixty is not nearly as satisfying as turning fifty but much nicer than turning seventy.' Everyone laughed. 'But I have a confession. I've invited you to not only celebrate my birthday but to consider a plan I've thought long and hard about for some time. It concerns the future of the Fatherland.' You could almost touch the silence.

'I know as professional soldiers you share my love for our country.' He raised his glass. 'Gentlemen, to Germany.'

Every man toasted the land of their birth. But there was tension in the room. Reidel was silent as if reluctant to speak. The pause seemed endless. When he continued his voice was wavering slightly as he battled his emotions.

'Gentlemen, it's obvious our great nation is being prepared for war. We see this massive build-up in arms. We play war games and read or hear the threats of aggression made by our political masters. Everything points to warfare.'

Max felt his heart-rate increase. This was not a relaxed and informal party. This was serious; no *dangerous*. Reidel continued uninterrupted.

'Having seen the horrors of the last conflict, I pray it never happens again. If it does, we soldiers know it will be catastrophic. We know the destructive power of our modern planes, ships, subs and tanks. Any future war will be disastrous even for the victor.'

Reidel paused. Nobody knew what to say. Reidel seemed to be waiting for someone, anyone to respond.

His close friend, Major Bayer broke the silence. 'Begging Herr Oberst's pardon, but are you saying Germany's re-armament is a bad thing?'

Max, everyone was transfixed. The atmosphere was electric. Where was this conversation going? Reidle paused then spoke.

'Gentlemen, a powerful nation will deter enemies and that I support. But in my opinion our present leaders re-arm not to defend but to attack. They obtained power illegally using intimidation and murder. What our leaders have done, and even to our own citizens, demonstrates what the government will do to other countries. It's obvious the Führer intends to extend Germany's borders by force and that action always leads to war.'

Max was perspiring. He felt trapped. He was scared with no idea what to do. His thoughts kept changing. *What are the others thinking? Is this some type of test? Should I say something? If I speak up will they see me as a traitor? If I walk out will they ostracize me? If I stay am I a co-conspirator? What the hell is happening?*

Reidel moved around looking deep into the eyes of his fellow soldiers. He stopped in front of Max but spoke to everyone.

'Gentlemen I have a plan to save Germany from a disastrous war. All I ask is that you listen and then, if you wish no part, please walk away and we'll never mention this gathering again. And if you do not wish to even hear my plan, please, feel free to leave and forget we ever had this conversation. Naturally I will respect your decision but I ask that you choose—now.'

Reidel turned his back and poured a drink. The room was silent, the men in shock. Max couldn't even move his eyes. He stared straight ahead. Suddenly an officer in front of him turned, brushed past him and left. Two others followed; then another. Max saw his chance. His mind screamed, *Go now. Now!* But something kept him rooted to the spot. Finally Reidel turned, smiled and spoke.

'Thank you, gentlemen; now, let us eat, drink and be merry because soon we discuss my plan to assassinate Hitler.'

Kurt Hartmann remembered his father coming home from the Great War a broken man. A teenage Kurt tried to reason with him.

'But Father, why can't Germany become great again?'

'Because our leaders are fools. We should have rejected that outrageous Treaty of Versailles. Look at our country; food shortages and massive unemployment with criminals running amok.'

Kurt wanted Germany to recover so as a young man joined the police. But being a policeman in Berlin in the 1920s was tough. Germany was chaotic. Politicians and the monarchy were despised. Violent political parties thrived.

Kurt couldn't catch the crooks. Police budgets were cut to the bone. Their firearms belonged in a museum. Forensic equipment was antiquated. Criminal gangs operated with impunity. The press attacked the police for failing to arrest criminals. Kurt was depressed.

Then things got even worse. The global recession saw the already troubled German economy collapse.

At least Kurt had a job, if you could call it that. One cold Berlin morning he was on patrol when he turned a corner and saw a thief robbing a man lying on the road.

'Hey!' yelled Kurt and raced towards the thief who took off. Kurt knelt beside the victim.

'Are you hurt?'

The victim looked terrible. He was barely alive. He tried to speak but Kurt couldn't understand the pathetic creature.

'Are you in pain?'

What ridiculous questions; of course he was hurt and in pain. The victim summoned his last ounce of strength.

'Food,' he gasped then groaned and died.

This was a first for Kurt. He'd seen dead bodies before but nothing like this. Right in the heart of the magnificent city of Berlin a man died of starvation—in the street! Kurt hated his job and with good reason. He was living in Hell.

Unemployment exploded, crime boomed and people died of starvation—again, even in the streets. Berlin and Germany were broke and broken.

Kurt and his police colleagues were helpless. Germany was in desperate trouble until the revolution began. Enter one Adolf Hitler. The National Socialists took power and thanks to Hitler, Kurt and his colleagues won the lottery.

Suddenly the police had better pay and conditions, better training, more opportunities for promotion, modern forensic equipment and the latest firearms. And it got even better.

Hitler muzzled the press ending public criticism of the police. Criminal gangs were smashed. Kurt's frustration faded and his pride in Germany grew. Everything was perfect. Well not quite.

Kurt was suddenly wary when the Nazis created a new police force, the Brownshirts. They were not your average conservative German policemen; in fact many were criminals. They bashed law-abiding citizens and trashed Jewish-owned shops with impunity. Kurt watched their mindless thuggery and did nothing. The real police had to turn a blind eye. Very few complained about or to the Brownshirts.

And if that wasn't bad enough, along came a third police force even worse than the Brownshirts. The Gestapo were the secret police and they made the Brownshirts look like choirboys. Gestapo agents arrested "enemies" of the state such as Jews, homosexuals and communists. Gypsies copped it too.

Again Kurt couldn't or wouldn't do a thing. The government made the Gestapo above the law. Criticize them and you disappeared.

So Kurt kept quiet and kept his job. And he persuaded himself that all this violence, police brutality and secrecy was good for Germany. The country's problems were so deep, radical action was justified; no pain, no gain. But deep down he was worried.

For some time he thought he was being watched and felt sick when he received a letter inviting him to a former arts and crafts building in Berlin. He had no interest in painting or pottery but knew that number 8 Prinz-Albrecht-Strasse was the headquarters of the Gestapo.

Chapter 3

IN LONDON in 1937 the débutante ball was a major event in the life of young women of a certain class. The coming-out season was highly anticipated by the débutantes and probably even more so by their mothers. Being presented to royalty gave the event, if it needed it, an added touch of class.

And just as stage mothers pushed their offspring to become stars of the stage and screen, there were many upper-class mothers who pushed their daughter's triumphant entrance into society.

Their thinking was simple. *I must allow my daughter to meet as many eligible and suitable gentlemen as possible.*

And these upper-class mothers "fought" hard to ensure their "gel" looked, sounded and moved with exquisite grace and style. The best dressmakers and the best elocution and ballet teachers were engaged. Making a curtsey to royalty required expert tuition and hours of practice.

The expression *marriage market* was outrageous but apt. As farmers fatten their livestock for market, the wives of wealthy and titled gentlemen groomed their daughters for matrimony.

Nothing was left to chance. A well-arranged marriage took exhaustive planning. Like a dedicated punter, mothers noted the names of the colts drawn to race in the Débutante Stakes. These mothers discovered the form of each horse and used codes to describe the bow-tied starters.

CE *(Chaperone Essential)* or WH *(Wandering Hands)* meant such gentlemen were definitely not to be introduced to my daughter. Other codes included VSSPQ *(Very Safe So Probably Queer)* and POMBAT *(Pots of Money but Awfully Thick).*

A POMBAT created a quandary because the mother, keen on a fortune for her daughter, needed to weigh up the boredom factor. Her son-in-law's house would be substantial but Christmas dinner with His Nibs would cause even her hair to become ill.

And all this endless discussion about dress materials and design, hairstyle, gloves, jewellery and the curtsey, the smile and proper response when asked to dance was now the lot of one Louise Beatrice Wellesley. Oh bliss, oh joy.

Louise went from what she believed would be the excitement and challenge of studying literature and drama at Cambridge to the suffocating boredom of being "prepared" for marriage. But worse was the fact that some fine gentleman would one day call with Louise the object of his affection.

How could she politely say "No"? How could she resist the gentle prodding of her well-meaning parents? How could she escape this ritual and do what she desperately wanted to do?

She couldn't offend her mother and now, could do nothing to upset her seriously ill father. It wasn't an option. She could never say the words she was thinking. *Mummy, I don't wish to attend the Buckingham Palace débutante ball. Papa, I wish to go to Cambridge.*

So she read and took the dog for long walks. She was polite and co-operative. Her parents thought that something was wrong but were in a bind. It was their duty to present their daughter to society in the way society demanded. Tradition rules.

To be fair, Louise did enjoy the elocution and curtsey sessions delighting her teachers with her winsome but powerful performances. She turned her lessons into a challenge and experimented with different moods. For one rehearsal she would be sultry and untouchable; the next her body language made her coy almost a tease. Her acting skills were honed in the least likely of places. Some girls struggled but Louise oozed confidence and her movements were rock solid yet full of grace.

Finally the day of the débutante ball arrived. Louise's father was overcome with emotion when his daughter appeared. Her beauty was dazzling and her transformation from girl to woman was breathtaking.

He wanted to tell Louise how proud he was but couldn't speak. Louise breezed towards him, kissed his forehead and squeezed his hand. Charles was dying. Nobody spoke of it. It was so quintessentially English.

Up to Buckingham Palace went Louise and her mother, to the gaiety, pomp and circumstance with the Establishment's wealth on display.

It was rude to stare but on this occasion débutantes looked over the dresses, hair and make-up of their peers. Mothers compared their daughter with other daughters. Young gentlemen, stamping the ground as feisty colts, stared intently, mentally judging which fillies they would most like to encounter in the mounting yard. Some chaps were mentally judging which fillies they would most like to mount in the encountering yard.

Louise found the dancing hard work. It seemed the skill of her parents' generation was fading. Her partners were dull even nervous. The one delightful dancer with whom she waltzed was so taken by his own image his best friend was a mirror.

It was a rotten night for Louise. It would pass and she knew she could survive but for what? No Cambridge and no theatrical career with instead just the waiting for Mr Approved-by-Mummy to commence the mating ritual. She had the gumption to stand up to her parents but not the heart.

Heading to a powder room, Louise was stopped in her tracks. 'Well I never; Miss Louise Wellesley.'

For the first time that evening Louise felt happy. Forgetting the formal nature of the occasion, she almost ran to the speaker and kissed and warmly embraced the middle-aged woman.

One of Louise's favourite teachers from boarding school smiled and enjoyed her former pupil's greeting. Louise said, 'Miss Vestey, what a wonderful surprise.'

Elizabeth Vestey had once taught Louise both French and Drama at Roedean. The two had clicked and Louise was desperately sad when her teacher departed during Louise's final year.

Miss Vestey said, 'I might have known you would grace this occasion with your usual *joie de vivre*. So is this the prologue before you launch your brilliant theatrical career?' The look on Louise's face instantly changed the mood. 'My dear child, whatever is wrong?'

The women drifted towards a corridor away from prying eyes. They sat and Louise poured out her soul. Her dream was no more. Her life was planned in fine detail and all that remained was to find the right husband. Louise became teary.

Some say getting a problem off one's chest is good for the soul. Elizabeth Vestey would have made an excellent guru under the catchcry of, "Don't bring me problems; bring me solutions".

Regarding the business of marriage, Miss Vestey spoke from experience. Forty years ago she rejected suitors gathered by her parents and plumped instead for a career. A young woman from a wealthy family, working albeit in teaching, was not common in Edwardian England. Tonight Miss Vestey was chaperone to another of her former students at Roedean whose mother had recently died.

Louise felt a flood of pleasure. Instead of discussing obstacles, Miss Vestey looked for escape routes. But one of her comments brought Louise back down to earth with a thud.

'My brother's a Don at Cambridge and I'm afraid he wouldn't support a woman being accepted at that hallowed institution. And his daughter, Molly, is most definitely in the stay-at-home-until-married basket.'

Louise explained her father's health and war service. Miss Vestey kept asking questions.

Finally she held Louise's hands. 'Let me think about this. I'll write the moment I have a plan. It's been lovely to see you again, Miss Wellesley and let's not make it as long before our next meeting.' And with that she squeezed Louise's hands, stood and went off to resume her chaperone duties.

In a corridor of Buckingham Palace, Louise felt a flicker of hope.

Driving home from the débutante ball Louise lied. 'No really, Mummy, there were one or two gentlemen I would welcome should they choose to call. I think you and Papa would approve of both.'

'And do these possibly interested young gentlemen have names?'

'Oh Mummy, you know how it works. A girl smiles at her partner and imagines he is flattered. If he finds me attractive he will write allowing you and Papa to conduct your exemplary vetting process.'

Victoria half-smiled. How could her daughter say, "If he finds me attractive"? Most of the eligible young men at the ball and almost all of the débutantes and their mothers knew her daughter was stunningly attractive.

The next morning Louise gave her father a detailed description of the débutante ball, her superb curtsey before the royals and the gentlemen with whom she danced. Charles was delighted. His health was gradually failing but his illness was forgotten with the pleasure he took from the sight and sound of his beloved daughter. She was a tonic, his best medicine.

And then letters arrived addressed to Miss Louise Wellesley. Victoria was thrilled and intrigued.

Charles felt a surge of happiness. His sons, like their father, were Cambridge graduates and now making their way in the Law. For Charles to have his daughter well married would be the crowning glory. He was determined to remain alive long enough to give her away.

At first Louise was shocked. She received invitations to house parties and requests to call and as they continued to arrive, her surprise turned to despair. The sheer number meant she would have to accept some. A weekend house party, no matter how well chaperoned, would mean participating in the ancient art of husband hunting. Even her best acting skills might not hide her distinct lack of interest.

But her heart skipped a beat when a letter arrived from Elizabeth Vestey.

Louise hid the missive from her parents and read and re-read its contents. The divine Miss Vestey had come up with a plan designed to spring Louise from her societal bind. Her dream of going to Cambridge might yet come true. Miss Vestey's final sentence was intriguing. "Stand firm, dear girl; all's well that ends well".

With each new day Louise grew more anxious when no further news arrived so was delighted when the local vicar announced that a play-reading group would begin under the leadership of a newly-arrived parishioner, Mr Beauford Nightingale. He was an actor of the old school with even his eyebrows having joined Equity. Surely her parents wouldn't object to her joining the play readers and so Wednesday evenings became an escape for Louise as a motley group of locals gathered to celebrate the spirit of Thespis.

To those who detest the theatre believing it is dominated by effeminate fops and prostitutes, Beauford "Nightie" Nightingale was proof positive of their prejudice. His use of the word *darling*, flamboyant gestures and eye-catching handkerchiefs convinced the naïve and ignorant he padded up for the other side which could not have been further from the truth. The elderly and avuncular Nightie was impossible to hide and effortlessly easy to love. He took huge delight in seeing others catch the theatrical bug.

When at their second meeting Nightie suggested the group perform a parish concert there was no more enthusiastic volunteer than Louise.

Shakespeare and Noël Coward were the chosen playwrights and Louise thought all her Christmases had come at once when Nightie asked her to play Juliet in a Shakespearean excerpt and Amanda from *Private Lives* in a Coward piece.

The young man playing Romeo was a talentless bank clerk who was instantly besotted with Louise. His class prevented any possible romantic link and the fact that the gormless dolt was christened Desmond Longbottom hardly helped. The line of local spinsters wanting their future children to be known as a Longbottom had yet to be formed.

Nightie was to play opposite Louise in the Coward scene. He was too old and she too young but Nightie knew talent when he saw it and the two would make music without singing a note of *Someday I'll Find You*.

When Mr Coward wrote the play, parts of the second act were deemed unsuitable. The fact that a divorced couple could rekindle their love and actually consummate same was deemed scandalous. The *Theatres Act 1843* gave sweeping powers to the Lord Chamberlain who alone decided if every play "is fitting for the preservation of good manners".

Private Lives was deemed unsuitable and only an appeal in person from the playwright, lyricist, composer, director and leading man—all played by Mr Coward—managed to persuade the guardian of public morals that the play would not result in the collapse of civilization. In 1930 *Private Lives* went ahead as writ.

Charles and Victoria were unaware of this saga and would certainly not have allowed their daughter to portray Amanda had they known the facts. But as Coward persuaded the Lord Chamberlain, so Louise persuaded her parents.

They sat in the church hall and were amazed. Their four year-old daughter performing for Uncle Crispin was entertaining but now their teenage daughter was breathtaking.

Her diction and emotions, her ability to become both Juliet and then the much older Amanda meant Charles, Victoria, their sons and the entire audience were spellbound. Louise was blessed with a rare and precious gift. She could act. She was superb seemingly without trying. Her expertise was effortless. Her segments were outstanding. The applause at the end of the concert was prolonged. Being an old hand, Nightie indicated he wished to speak just as the applause began to fade. He waited for pin-dropping silence then thanked all concerned. His final words were clear.

'But tonight, ladies and gentlemen, would not be complete without special mention of one performer. I've spent my entire life in the theatre but never have I seen an actress of such rare talent, grace and beauty than our own, Miss Louise Wellesley.'

The resultant applause was immediate and strong. Even those for whom the theatre meant little felt something special about this future star. Louise hesitated. She was thrilled but surprised. Nightie offered his hand. Louise stepped forward and bowed and Nightie stepped back joining the applause.

Louise smiled at her family and saw her mother and brothers rejoicing while her father was busy wiping his eyes. A loud cry of "Bravo" came thrice from the back of the hall. The Reverend Stanley Tripe was overjoyed to have made the journey from Hampshire.

At home the family gathered for a light supper. Charles sat in a newly-acquired wheelchair with a thick blanket over his knees. It was a mild night but his doctor warned against chills and the dreaded pneumonia.

Over coffee the family continued to heap praise upon the delighted Louise. The boys joked about the hapless bank clerk. His tights were too tight and his underwear should have been branded, "Not fit for purpose".

The family's laughter was on song when Louise added the punch line, 'Actually Mister Longbottom gave me a lovely floral bouquet and asked if he might call next Saturday.'

Uproarious laughter from Henry and Edmund and Charles smiled knowing his daughter was up to her usual teasing self. Victoria was taking no chances.

'I trust you put a swift end to such nonsense.'

'Tell him to join the queue,' laughed Edmund.

'Tell him he's less chance than Pongo,' laughed Henry.

Louise smiled but knew Henry was disappointed she had no interest in his friend. The laughter settled and Charles cleared his throat.

'Louise, my dear, your mother and I have been discussing your future.'

The atmosphere was instantly changed and became electric. The siblings were certain the topic was *Husband Selection*. Emboldened by her recent theatrical triumph and determined to have at least one final defiant shout into the wind, Louise interrupted her father.

'Papa, please may I say something?'

The silence became loud. From a young age the children understood the unwritten but imperative rule that once the patriarch began to speak, silence was mandatory. The brothers looked at their father. Was he too ill to become angry?

He remained calm. 'You may say something, my child, when I have finished.' A pause pushed up the tension. 'I have received a letter regarding your future from a gentleman I regard most highly.'

Louise's heart sank. It was as much shock as sadness. Her parents had settled on one of her would-be husbands without telling her. Charles held up an envelope.

Risking eternal damnation, Louise spoke quietly but with strength. 'If you'll excuse me, Papa, I believe I should be permitted to read all proposals which are addressed to me.'

The brothers held their breath. Victoria looked lovingly at her daughter. Charles remained calm.

'I agree entirely, Louise, but this envelope is addressed to me.'

Louise was crushed. Charles looked at her then continued.

'This letter arrived at an auspicious time. I believe in the acting profession it would best be described as "perfect timing". Your mother and I are of the opinion that you are not yet ready to consider matrimony and believe a time away from here would assist in your development.'

Not yet ready for matrimony? A time away from here? Louise entertained horrible thoughts. *Not another finishing-school? Did Papa just say, "Get thee to a nunn'ry"?*

With no theatrical training, Charles was making excellent use of the dramatic pause.

'Your mother and I do not wish to push you into any hasty decision regarding your choice of husband.'

Louise was in turmoil. Papa had departed from the script. He was speaking gibberish. He continued.

'If you are willing, we have received an offer for you to reside in Girton College, the finest establishment for young women at Cambridge.'

Louise froze. She lost her ability to act. Nobody spoke. In a daze Louise stumbled towards her father.

'I say, good for you old girl,' congratulated Henry.

'Bravo,' added Edmund.

Louise hugged and kissed her father tears welling in her eyes. She repeated the routine with her mother.

'Little Plum, off to Cambridge,' said Edmund with open arms. It was the season for hugs. For once, Louise Wellesley was speechless.

'Plum, you've forgotten your lines,' laughed Henry. Everyone was amused while at the same time tense. Then came more silence. Now the actress could speak with permission. It was her cue. But Louise dried. She was struggling with a thumping heart, weepy eyes and a lump in her throat. Charles broke the ice.

'I take it you are prepared to accept the offer?'

Charles wanted to continue but Louise was unable to listen. She could not stop the tears. Her joy was unconfined. Her emotions took centre stage. Victoria again embraced her daughter.

Charles was delighted to see such happiness and felt relief having made the decision to let his daughter go. Henry and Edmund were thrilled with a tinge of concern. Victoria was both proud and worried. Shunning an excellent marriage could damage her daughter's future happiness. But Victoria's loyalty to her dying husband meant she supported him with conviction. Charles spoke sincerely, convinced he'd done the right thing not knowing how, yet again, he'd been outmanoeuvred by a woman.

Still, what you don't know can't hurt you.

Elizabeth Vestey was an interesting woman. She was tall and slim with handsome even regal features. She would have made an outstanding suffragette. Her Yorkshire-based family had wealth but no title. And because of this wealth, Elizabeth's childhood was dominated by large houses, servants, a private education and travel.

Like Louise, as a young woman Elizabeth wanted to further her education and knew marriage and children would prevent that. Her parents gave her opportunities to meet eligible gentlemen then reacted with dismay and anger when their teenage daughter declined them all. Arguments became heated and Elizabeth was threatened. She ran away.

She had enough money for the train fare to London, a change of clothes and equal amounts of optimism and fear. She had an address and sometimes fortune favours the brave.

As a child, her family holidayed in Cornwall and over several summers Elizabeth became friends with another holidaymaker, Virginia Stephen. Virginia was fascinating and although they only met for a few weeks each summer at St Ives, the two girls became close friends. So when the teenage Elizabeth Vestey chose to leave home and make her way as an independent woman, the person to whom she turned was her friend Virginia Stephen.

In London, a nervous Elizabeth went to 22 Hyde Park Gate. Her fear became joy when Virginia welcomed her friend with open arms.

The Stephen household was filled with family, books, visitors and pets. Inviting Elizabeth to stay was a perfectly natural step; the unofficial family motto being, "The more the merrier".

And thus began an exciting time in the life of Elizabeth Vestey. With the help of her friend Virginia, Elizabeth studied literature and languages at the Ladies' Department of King's College in London. She found work as a tutor and became a teacher at Roedean where she met the young Louise Wellesley. Miss Vestey never married and never regretted it.

As the years went by, Elizabeth never forgot the Stephen family for their love and support and always wrote to Virginia keeping her informed about her life and activities. Elizabeth didn't need Virginia to reply as everyone knew Virginia Woolf.

Elizabeth's parents never forgave their daughter and died not knowing she had become a highly respected teacher. Her only sibling, her brother, Alfred, a Professor of Mathematics at Cambridge, had always been sad about Elizabeth's estrangement from their parents and having traced his sister's whereabouts, wrote to Elizabeth and they kept in touch. When Louise was at Roedean, Alfred wrote a special letter to his sibling.

The letter was about Alfred's dying wife. Her illness was terminal. Could Elizabeth, would Elizabeth come to Cambridge, help care for his wife and be a tutor to his daughter, Molly, Elizabeth's niece? Elizabeth would be well rewarded and become part of the Vestey family again.

Once Elizabeth would have politely declined but as the years bring change to hearts and minds, she agreed, moved to Cambridge and re-joined the Vestey family after some 40 years.

And now she faced a new and exciting challenge. How could she assist the exceptionally talented Louise Wellesley obtain her father's blessing and enter Cambridge University?

Elizabeth prepared. Of all her ideas, one stood out—*noblesse oblige.* An English gentleman well understood the obligation of nobility. Alfred Vestey and Charles Wellesley were steeped in the concept.

Elizabeth discovered all she could about Louise's father then approached her brother. Alfred was under stress. His wife was dying and his darling daughter watched the slow and painful death of her mother.

Elizabeth asked for Alfred's guidance. Oh the wisdom of the woman. Here she was controlling the situation yet allowing her brother to believe he was indispensable. Elizabeth painted a picture.

Charles Wellesley is a gentleman; Eton, Cambridge and a successful law career. He volunteered for service in the last war, was promoted to Lieutenant-Colonel where his courage in battle stamped him as a selfless and wounded hero. His two fine sons are graduates of their father's alma mater. But now his health is in jeopardy. Charles is dying a slow and painful death. Alfred was never more in sympathy with any man as he was with Charles. *Noblesse oblige* was alive and well.

Then Elizabeth described Louise. A brilliant student, a wonderful linguist and actress and a loving and devoted daughter who brought honour and pride to her parents but who now was living at home watching her beloved father die. Louise became Alfred's daughter, Molly.

So having created the scenario, Elizabeth described her predicament and asked for her brother's wise counsel. What a magnificent pitch.

What could Alfred suggest to help this brilliant young woman and relieve the terrible pain being suffered by a dying father?

There was no need for tears or melodramatic music. Alfred, who believed a young woman's place was not at university, immediately discarded his conservative beliefs and wrote two letters. The first was to the Mistress of Girton College some two miles from his Cambridge home.

The second was to Charles Wellesley Esquire. Alfred respectfully urged his former fellow soldier to allow his daughter to avoid watching her beloved father die. Alfred would be honoured to watch over Louise's progress should Charles allow his daughter to enter his alma mater.

These thoughts were contained in the letter held by Charles when he asked Louise if she would accept an offer from Girton College. Both men believed they were doing the right thing; Alfred in writing and Charles in changing his mind. But the happiness both fathers felt was but nothing to the joy Miss Vestey and her former pupil soon entertained.

And that was how Louise Beatrice Wellesley, a.k.a. Plum, began her undergraduate life at Cambridge University.

Chapter 4

WHAT AN ENORMOUS change awaited Louise. No parents, siblings or chaperone to rule her life. She would soon be free to do whatever, wherever and whenever she fancied.

She told Nightie Beaumont her news. He was thrilled, gave her his blessing and advice.

'Learn as much as you can about Chaucer, Shakespeare and Shaw but always remember acting is very much a doing thing. Nobody ever learnt to act by reading a book.'

Saying goodbye to her parents was extremely difficult. In recent years she'd spent time at Roedean and in France but now there were new and powerful emotions. Her father's health weighed heavily as she knelt beside him.

Both were thinking this may be the last time they would ever see one another yet neither mentioned it.

'I don't know how to thank you, Papa.'

He stroked her hair and whispered, 'Shhhh.'

Louise stood, kissed her father then spoke softly in his ear, 'I love you so much, my darling Papa.'

She found it very difficult to look into his eyes. She and her mother hugged for a long time. Not a word was exchanged but many thoughts and much love passed between them. Louise fondled the ears of Horatio the elderly black Labrador.

A baggage-carrying Henry called, 'Come on, Plum. We'll miss our train.' Edmund was to drive them to the station. Louise stopped at the door, turned and blew a kiss to her parents then left wondering who might be there when she returned.

Charles insisted that Henry accompany his sister to Cambridge and so the two siblings shared another rail journey. On the train Henry teased his sister.

'I suppose you know your jolly Girton College is a million miles from Cambridge.'

'I think you'll find it's about two.'

'But do you know *why* it's so far from the University?'

'No, but I'm sure you're going to tell me.'

'It's to keep you safe, old girl, safe from all those male undergraduates desperate for female company. When they chose your college, the Victorians knew a thing or two about separating the sexes.' Henry winked and Louise raised an eyebrow.

After a while, Henry decided to make his big brother speech. 'Now look here, Plum, if you ever find yourself in a spot of bother, you just tell them that Henry Wellesley is your big brother.'

'Oh and that will save me, no doubt.' Louise grinned but Henry feigned seriousness.

'Listen, Miss Wellesley, there are at least three Law Dons who swear I was the best opening batsman they ever saw and having won a Full Blue in rowing, let me tell you my name counts for plenty.'

Louise smiled and patted his arm, 'My hero.'

Henry smiled. 'Oh and I looked up that legal case of *Jarndyce and Jarndyce.*'

'Really?' replied Louise with an even bigger grin and slapped his arm. Henry joined her laughter.

They changed trains in London and from Kings Cross travelled down to Cambridge. Their compartment was crowded and despite this both wanted to talk about their father.

'Plum, about the old man ...'

'I know,' interrupted Louise. 'I can't bear the thought he'll die and I'll be in Cambridge. Promise you'll telephone the moment you have any news—promise.'

Henry squeezed her hand. Both were unsure how they would handle the death of their father. The train pulled into Cambridge and Henry took his sister's belongings.

They wandered along the crowded platform with Henry looking for a taxi. He didn't fancy taking a bus out to the sleepy village of Girton. Then a cockney voice was heard calling.

'Taxi for Miss Louise Wellesley. Taxi!'

No taxi or driver could be seen. And what was a Cockney cabbie doing in Cambridge? Louise thought it was one of Henry's pranks but he looked blank and shrugged.

Then the driver stepped into view. Elizabeth Vestey wore a double-breasted dust coat, a flat cap and a big grin. The women embraced with Henry nonplussed. Then his ego took a beating when he discovered Miss Vestey had borrowed her brother's Austin Ten to deliver Louise to Girton.

It did look comical with Elizabeth and Louise in the front seats and Henry and most of the luggage squeezed into the rear. He used a hatbox to hide his face as they drove past many of his old Cambridge haunts. A chap has a reputation to protect.

Girton College was, by comparison with other Cambridge institutions, almost brand new having only been built in the 1870s. It sat in spacious grounds in a tranquil rural setting.

The car purred up the College drive with Henry feeling ever more redundant. Big brother was reduced to station porter as he traipsed inside with Elizabeth making all the introductions.

Soon Henry saw he was in the way. He caught Louise's eye and she moved to him. He said, 'Look old girl, you're in good hands. I'll pop along and leave you to it.'

Louise could see his embarrassment and kissed him. 'Thank you, Henry. I'll write often, I promise. And don't forget to phone with any news of Papa.'

They hugged and he waved to Elizabeth and began to leave. She moved quickly to join him.

'Oh Mister Wellesley, please, you must allow me to drive you back to the station.' Henry politely declined citing the excuse of wanting to call on an old professor who lived just up the road.

Henry waved and left. There was no old professor just up the road but a chap does have his pride.

Louise was in love with the Girton library, dining-hall, gardens and chapel. She loved her eccentric teachers and the company of her fellow students. She loved the ancient village of Girton and the ancient city of Cambridge with its history and architecture and music and students; students on bicycles, on foot and on song. This was a world apart for Louise and a time and a place she adored. She dived in head first.

At Girton she became friendly with the girl in the room next door. Emily Fraser was demure, quietly spoken and as introverted as Louise was extroverted but opposites attract and the two women became pals.

Emily was a scientist with a burgeoning knowledge of chemistry and mathematics. She knew little about the theatre and even less about sex. Partying was not an agenda item. Louise would lie in bed thinking about Matilda and their escapades in France; no chance of that with Emily.

A fortnight after she arrived at Cambridge Louise received an invitation from Elizabeth Vestey to take tea next Saturday. If she could accept, Miss Vestey would collect her at 4pm. Louise was delighted but declined the offer of transport as she was now mobile. Many Girton women caught the bus into Cambridge but Louise joined those hardy students who took to the road on their own two wheels.

There are some who believe Cambridge and Oxford were chosen as university sites simply because of their cyclist-friendly topography. It's an interesting theory until one discovers the universities pre-dated the bicycle by several centuries.

The Vesteys lived in Cambridge, a short walk from the University colleges. Louise rode along thinking happy thoughts when a loud car horn blasted from behind. She looked back, lost her balance, tried to correct and fell off her bicycle. A grassy landing helped so only her pride was hurt but her temper was raring to go. The car pulled over and its two male occupants strolled back towards her.

'All right, Miss?' asked the driver. 'You might learn to ride that contraption.' Louise was furious. She had been riding safely and sensibly.

True, her mind was miles away but how dare they speak to her like that and surely a gentleman would show some concern.

The second gent was blatantly offensive. His accent was smeared with Welsh cream. 'Bloody women; they want the right to go to university yet can't even learn the road rules.'

Louise fumed and struggled to speak. Without thinking she blurted out the Welsh oath Matty had taught her in finishing school. 'Yrydym yn tyngu I garu a chymorth ein gilyydd tan marwolaeth wneud ini ymadael.'

Because her Welsh accent mingled with her fury, the words took on a sense of authority and venom. The motorists were shocked.

'My God, Gareth,' said the driver, 'she's a bloody Blodwyn.'

'Now I've seen everything,' smirked Gareth. 'Not only women at Cambridge, but Welsh women!'

Both men laughed, walked back to their car and drove off. Louise checked her bicycle and herself, gingerly mounted and resumed her journey. As she cycled along her mood improved when she realized she'd convinced her latest audience, including a boyo from the valleys, that she was Welsh. Without trying to play a role she'd done just that—naturally.

Then she remembered her Welsh lesson with Matilda and smiled.

At the Vestey home Elizabeth introduced her brother Alfred and his daughter, Molly. Louise had already written to Professor Alfred Vestey expressing her immense gratitude. Now, meeting the Don in person, she explained again that without his letter she would not be here today.

Alfred said. 'Elizabeth tells me you're interested in the theatre. Have you had time to join any performing clubs?'

'Not yet, sir, but I've heard there are several groups.'

Molly was keen. 'I belong to an amateur group here in Cambridge. You'd be most welcome to join.'

Louise was bubbling. Her ego-battering tumble and the rudeness of the men in the car were a distant memory. She savoured the scrumptious high tea, thanked the professor and his daughter and felt she'd found a new family. Elizabeth walked Louise down the drive and spoke kindly.

'Thank you for being so sensitive about my dear sister-in-law. Alas her health is failing and having your smiling face certainly helped Alfred and Molly to think of more pleasant things.'

'You know I'll never be able to repay you, Miss Vestey.'

Elizabeth laughed. 'Oh I do wish you'd stop calling me Miss Vestey. Please, call me Elizabeth.'

Louise feigned mock surprise.

'Call my teacher by her Christian name—whatever next?'

They laughed. Louise leaned in and kissed her mentor, hopped on her trusty bicycle and rode back to Girton.

Life could not be better; new friends, possible new theatre opportunity, a kind if somewhat unusual fellow student in the room next door and literally all was well with the world.

28

But that was about to change. There was a letter on her pillow and its contents had news to make Louise suddenly feel ill.

She picked up the envelope. It was from Spain and addressed to her home in Surrey. Louise's mother had re-addressed the envelope to *Girton College, Cambridge University.*

Louise had only been at Cambridge for three weeks but a twinge of homesickness came over her as she thought of her parents and father in particular.

Two miles away Molly Vestey was living with her mother who drifted towards death. Had Louise been still at home she would have faced a similar situation. But those distressing thoughts were pushed aside when she began to read Matty's letter.

Dearest Louise

How I have missed you. Your smile, your wonderful acting, your friendship, your brilliant mind, your terrible Welsh accent; I miss them all more than I can say. How I wish we could meet every month, every week, every day, and do crazy things as we did in France.

How are you? Married? Surely those dreadful débutante balls will have given you the best selection of thoroughbreds in England. How are your riding skills?

Louise smiled. She could hear Matilda speaking these words.

My darling, I have news. Are you sitting down? Good because, believe it or not, I am to become engaged! I wanted you to be the first to know. And yes my beautiful friend, you must, must, must be my bridesmaid. Mother wants my boring cousins but I've said there will be no wedding without Miss Louise Wellesley. How's that for standing up to the folks? And just to make you jealous, I've enclosed a photograph of my handsome husband to be. Father wanted a Spanish suitor but I told you about Welsh females—women who don't know the meaning of surrender. So a Welsh husband it is. I do hope you like him. Write soon with all your news.

Love and kisses

Matty

Louise opened the envelope and removed the photo. She suddenly felt ill. The man looked familiar. He should have; it was Gareth, the brutish passenger who, with his equally rude driving companion, ran Louise off the road that very afternoon.

In shock Louise read Matty's writing on the back of the photograph—*Gareth Llewelyn, husband and doctor to be.*

So Mister Rude Welshman, presumably reading medicine at Cambridge, was to marry my dear friend Matilda.

29

What could Louise remember of her cycling incident? The driver enquired if she was injured. The passenger, Gareth, the man in Matilda's life, was a cad. Surely Matty would never marry such a man. She was intelligent, witty and kind and would never fall for an arrogant oaf.

So should Louise warn Matty? And if so, say what? Perhaps Gareth was really a nice chap who was just having a bad day.

Louise's natural impulse was to tell the truth. But what was the truth and could she base a character assessment on a momentary experience?

She decided. To help her friend she would investigate the future Dr Llewelyn. After all, Louise was to be part of the wedding party.

But she needed facts and the words of the consulting detective sprang to mind. *I cannot make bricks without clay.*

And of course she must investigate anonymously. This was new—Louise Wellesley the spy.

Chapter 5

MANFRED FABER worked in the Berlin postal service. He was Herr Average but managed one spectacular achievement. He changed the language. Not many people get to invent a word.

In Nazi Germany the secret state police were called the *Geheime Staats Polizei*. This new government enterprise handled correspondence. Mail was sorted, stamped and sent on its way and the key to a good stamp is brevity. But squeezing *Geheime Staats Polizei* onto a single stamp was tricky.

Manfred Faber had an idea. He chose letters from each word— **Ge**heime **Sta**ats **Po**lizei—and so the stamp read *Gestapo*. Did Manfred ever know how hated and reviled his invented word would become?

In Berlin the architecture at 8 Prinz-Albrecht-Strasse had a sense of grandeur. Internally there were spacious corridors, high ceilings, wide staircases and grandiose rooms ideal for executive officers. In the basement were storerooms perfect as cells and torture chambers.

Victims in this house of horrors did not need operatic training to project their misery. Pedestrians heard the horrific screams coming from the bowels of the stately pile.

So Berlin police officer Kurt Hartmann was naturally nervous when he received a letter inviting him to attend Gestapo headquarters. Kurt knew police officers who'd joined the Gestapo. They were proud card-carrying Nazis. Kurt was not like that—yet.

He thought about the times he and his cousin Max had discussed Germany and its Führer. He knew Max's politics. But what would Kurt think if he knew his cousin in the Wehrmacht had recently joined a plot to assassinate Hitler?

Being German, Kurt automatically arrived at 8 Prinz-Albrecht-Strasse on time. Having an appointment with the Gestapo made even his punctuality punctual. Wearing his police officer's uniform, he entered the building and approached a receptionist. The man looked at Kurt's uniform and smirked. He held out a hand and Kurt gave him the Gestapo letter.

The receptionist pointed and said, 'Wait there'. Kurt picked up his letter and moved to one side. The receptionist spoke briefly on a telephone. Kurt heard footsteps. He refused to look. He thought about his parents and if he should have written to them.

A man in a suit arrived. 'Come with me.' They climbed the expansive main stairs, walked along an expansive corridor then entered an expansive room in which several people sat working at expansive desks.

Kurt came to an expansive door. The man knocked and a voice was heard. 'Enter.'

As he entered a sumptuous office with the biggest desk he had ever seen, Kurt thought that this was not the way to an examination or inquiry; not even to an interview. So why was he here? A bespectacled man in shirtsleeves was kneeling on the floor.

'Kurt Hartmann from the Prussian State Police, sir,' said Kurt's guide who left.

'Ah, Hartmann, over here. I've lost a camp. Come and help me find it.'

And so Kurt's first task as a Gestapo agent was to crawl around the floor of the Gestapo's second-in-charge's office looking for a small wooden hut from a model concentration camp which had fallen from the vast map on the vast desk in a vast office at 8 Prinz-Albrecht-Strasse.

It didn't take much persuasion for Kurt to change jobs. He willingly swapped his police uniform for a smart suit, hat and black leather coat. He was conservative and approved of much of what the Nazis did. Would he approve of all their activities?

Today he was their latest recruit and instantly acquired great powers.

Max couldn't sleep. Three days ago he'd agreed to be part of an unknown plan to assassinate the Führer.

Max had sworn allegiance not just to the Weimar Republic but to the Führer himself; a personal oath. Even thinking about disloyalty in Germany was dicing with death.

Since the events at Oberst Reidle's party, nothing had happened; no message, no order, not even a secret code. Had the others gone ahead without him? Was he no longer a part of the plot? Surely he'd know if there'd been an attempt on the Führer's life.

When he rubbed shoulders with the men who remained behind that night he looked indirectly then directly at them; nothing.

He was returning to barracks and bumped into Erich Klug who had left the infamous meeting early.

'Klug, how are you?' asked Max.

Klug lied. 'Fine. And you?'

Max lied. 'I'm well, thanks.' He wasn't well and it showed.

Klug paused. He was nervous. 'Can we talk?'

Max saw anxiety in Klug's eyes but nodded and they strolled with each wanting the other to speak first. Finally Klug began.

'Do you think I'm a coward for walking out the other night?'

'No, of course not.'

'I'm not fishing. Believe me I don't want to know what was said after I left.'

'You weren't the only one to leave.'

'They say you don't know how you'll react when faced with action in war. Well I faced a peace time decision and bottled it.'

'No you didn't.'

'I swear on my mother's life, Hartmann, I'll never breathe a word.'

'Nothing happened.'

Klug was dumbfounded. 'Nothing?'

Max continued to lie. 'Nothing.'

'But what about Reidel's plan to save Germany from a disastrous war? What about his blatant criticism of our glorious leader?'

Max shrugged. 'The whole thing was just a test of our loyalty.'

Klug was devastated. He'd refused some treasonous plan which didn't exist. It was a simple loyalty test and he blew it. The real question was, "Gentlemen, will you follow me into battle without question"? Klug squibbed it. 'Oh this is worse,' he moaned. 'I *am* a coward.'

Max put his hand on Klug's shoulder. 'Klug, listen to me. If war comes, we'll both have the chance to prove we're loyal Germans. Herr Oberst is a patriot as are we. Head up, man; head up.'

The two soldiers looked at one another. Klug was desperate for the truth. Was Hartmann lying?

Max stared at Klug and spoke with conviction. 'You are not a coward.'

Silence lingered then Max broke his gaze and walked away. He wasn't sure why he told such a monumental lie about Reidel's plan. Deep down he wished he'd joined Klug and had walked out of that treacherous birthday party.

Five days after Reidel's unusual social gathering, Max walked into a packed briefing room. Ever since he agreed to be part of the plot to kill Hitler he'd heard nothing. Oberst Reidel entered the room and everyone stood.

'Gentlemen, be seated.'

The briefing was to explain their next series of war games. The word *blitzkrieg* hadn't yet been invented but all manoeuvres were based around speed, surprise and short, sharp attacks. It was smash-and-grab warfare. The exercises were explained then suddenly Max froze. This new exhibition of German firepower was to be observed by the top military brass including the Führer. What?

Max twigged. His heart took off. His commanding officer was revealing details of the planned Hitler assassination. It was brilliant. A terrible miscalculation on the training field would see the watching VIPs "accidentally" slaughtered. Hitler and his inner-cabinet would be wiped out in one horrific, military blunder—a planned military blunder.

The military top brass would be eliminated leaving a vacuum. How could you blame an entire army? It was a tragic accident. And those who would seek revenge would all be dead.

Max's body did strange things. Reidel was behaving as if this was a simple everyday operation. To the vast majority of officers and men it *was* a simple everyday operation.

Max was sure his cohorts from the birthday party meeting were all thinking alike. What a brilliant plan. Every soldier at this meeting was unwittingly involved.

In any inquiry, each man would say everything was perfectly explained. Assassination didn't come into it. Nobody is to blame.

The meeting ended and Klug slapped Max's shoulder. 'Our commanding officer is a genius, yes?' Max smiled and nodded. 'Next week we'll have a chance to show our Führer just how powerful his army really is.'

Max was thinking. *Yes my friend; more than you can ever imagine.*

When Berlin policeman Kurt Hartmann joined the Gestapo in 1937, he joined a smooth-running machine. The major lines of business for the Gestapo were spying, arrest, torture and murder.

Millions of Germans were a potential enemy of the state. Fear was the tool to keep them in check. And the Gestapo were good at fear. They used spies, ordinary people turning neighbour against neighbour, worker against worker. They even copied Sherlock Holmes with his Baker Street Irregulars as the Gestapo too enlisted juvenile spies.

As part of his training, Kurt worked with an experienced agent, Klaus Weber. He was an excellent teacher. In a Mercedes-Benz 260 D Weber drove Kurt to a Berlin suburb.

'An easy task to get you started,' said Weber, 'nothing too difficult for the new boy.'

'I am an experienced policeman,' replied Kurt and immediately regretted saying that.

'Rule number one, Hartmann; forget your past. Rule number two; fear is your greatest weapon.'

Kurt vowed to remain silent. The car stopped. It was late and dark. Weber shone his torch to check the house number and then strode to the front door. He knocked hard and spoke harder.

'Open the door. Now!'

A light came on in the hallway. 'Hurry up!' More door banging. Slowly the door was partly opened. Weber forced it open and a woman in her nightdress fell back.

'Frau Steinberg?'

'Yes,' said the terrified woman.

'You are under arrest.'

'Arrest? What for?'

'Get your children.'

'My children?'

'You have two minutes. Now move!'

The woman ran to find her daughter, 12 and son, 9.

Finally Kurt spoke. 'Should I know the charge, Herr Weber?'

'See what I mean by Rule Number 2, Hartmann. Fear is your greatest weapon.'

Kurt was getting a good lesson in Gestapo tactics. Arrive unannounced in the dead of night. Give the victim as little time as possible. Be violent, intimidate and terrorize. Oh, and tackle the weak.

The pathetic looking woman came into the hallway with her two terrified children.

'Please,' begged Frau Steinberg, 'take me but leave my children.'

'Take the boy,' yelled Weber as he dragged the screaming daughter outside. Kurt looked at the young lad and saw pure fear. He pushed the child outside. The distraught mother ran after them. The lights in the house remained on with the front door wide open.

The trio of "prisoners" was bundled into the back seat and clung to one another as Weber and Kurt drove back to Gestapo headquarters.

Kurt completed his first secret police exercise and succeeded with flying colours. It was slightly easier than arresting a blind nonagenarian. Kurt felt a tiny sliver of pride when Weber congratulated him.

Kurt decided to risk speaking his mind. 'I must admit I did not think women and children were a threat to the Reich.'

'There's a method in our madness, Hartmann. The husband of that woman and father of those children is a traitor to Germany, a coward who has fled to Switzerland. We've tried to kidnap or kill him and failed. Now we offer him the opportunity to return of his own free will in order to save the lives of his dear wife and children.'

Kurt's heart went cold. IIe was about to ask, "You would kill them if he doesn't return"? but stopped and stared at Weber. The experienced Gestapo officer observed the new recruit.

'Remember, Hartmann, mercy equals weakness.'

Gestapo agent Hartmann didn't know it at the time but he'd just passed his first test.

Chapter 6

LOUISE COPIED a method of detection used by Sherlock Holmes and disguised herself. She invented a tale becoming a young Frenchwoman, Mademoiselle Forgeron, seeking her younger sister who had left Paris to be with her lover, a Cambridge medical student.

Of course Mademoiselle Forgeron could not be Louise. Matilda's bridesmaid must be a complete stranger when she meets the groom.

The cyclist Gareth briefly met was an angry Welsh woman. The lovely Louise is an English rose. Mademoiselle Forgeron is Gallic to the core.

Louise borrowed some of Emily's drab clothes and covered her beautiful curls with a beret. She borrowed old-fashioned spectacles from an old-fashioned librarian, gave herself an unpleasant facial mole, too much garish lipstick and carried a walking stick. She told people she was preparing for a play which wasn't a million miles from the truth.

She limped to the Girton bus-stop. Two students she knew from the dining-room ignored her. Louise was pleased. In town, she limped through the closest set of College gates and knocked on the porter's door.

'Good afternoon, Miss. Can I help thee?'

In her French accent, Louise turned on the charm. 'Oh pardon, Monsieur. Can you please 'elp?'

'Foreigner, eh? French or Belgian?'

'I am from France, Monsieur and looking for a gentleman who is a medical student.'

'We've got a few young gents reading medicine. What would be his name?'

'I believe 'e is from Wheels.' Louise was overdoing the accent.

'From Wheels, Miss?'

'No Monsieur, Wales.'

'Oh he's a Taffy. Sorry Miss. All our medical gents are English. But you could try Trinity. They take all sorts in there.' He raised his hat.

Louise limped away. Trinity could wait. She looked at her list and shuddered. If her parents even thought their daughter would enter a public house there would be one almighty row. For her to do so unaccompanied was beyond the pale.

She was about to open the pub door when a young student overtook her. 'Not here, Miss. You want the *Ladies* next door.'

She walked down the street and entered an empty room. She could hear rowdy male drinkers next door and wondered if one was a particular Welsh medical student.

A middle-aged woman poked her head around the corner. 'Hello dearie, wot can I get you?'

'Ah, could I 'ave a cognac, please?'

'Sorry, luv, no such 'fing in 'ere. 'Ow about a sherry or a nice G and T?'

'Sank you. I would like some sherry.'

'Sweet or dry?'

'Pardon?'

'I'll make it sweet. Won't be long.'

Louise was despondent. This routine was a great opportunity to work on her acting skills but as an exercise in helping her friend avoid a possibly horrendous marriage, it was a budding disaster. The woman returned with the sherry.

'On the 'ouse, dearie. You look as though you could do with a stiffner. Penny for 'em.'

Louise opened her handbag. 'Only za penny?'

'No, no, no, the drink's free. I was askin' about y'troubles. I can see you've got a few.'

Louise seized the opportunity and explained her missing sister's situation. She described Gareth in detail. The barmaid nodded.

'Oh I certainly know that fella. 'Dat particular gent is Gariff Llewelyn, and a right pain 'e is an' all. Tall beggar, over six foot, built like a rugby player, 'as brown wavy hair and a really 'fick Welsh accent.'

Louise was excited. 'Oh oui, zat is 'im, Monsieur Llewelyn.'

The barmaid gave Louise chapter and verse on Matilda's intended. The stories went from disturbing to outrageous. But were they true?

According to Doris of *The Eagle*, Gareth ran up a tab in another Cambridge pub, the *St Radegund* and was barred.

It was common knowledge he'd had his wicked way with a young shopgirl and tried to perform the termination himself. The girl disappeared and some reckon she'd met with foul play. But his *piece de resistance* was in fooling everyone into believing he was an upstanding gentleman as he began courting the Mayor's daughter, his current young lady. *What!? He's about to become engaged to my best friend.*

Louise acted superbly. She was horrified that an evil man would attempt to seduce her sweet and innocent sister. 'Oh Madame, sank you so much. My family will be most grateful. Now I must find my sister and take 'er back 'ome to France.'

'Well be careful. You is 'alf 'is size and the man's a brute.'

Louise thanked Doris and hobbled away.

What a disaster. What a predicament. Should Louise reveal Gareth's sordid secrets? Were any of them true and, if so, how could she save her friend from the appalling Mr Llewelyn? What did the Bard say? "I must be cruel only to be kind".

Louise was lying on her bed thinking. How could she rescue Matilda from a marriage to a very nasty man? How could Matilda fall for such a monster? Was it parental pressure?

Emily walked past clutching books. Louise's door was open and Emily stopped. 'Goodness Louise, I wish I could lie around all day doing nothing.'

'Well hark at you, Miss Swot.'

'You won't get through on your natural talents.'

'Thanks for your concern, Miss Fraser, but fear not. I shall read and re-read all my jolly texts.'

The women, who were total opposites, had become firm friends. Louise hopped up and followed Emily into her room.

'What frustrates me,' said Louise, 'is that discussing the great dramatists is not nearly as enjoyable as performing them. I want to act, Em.'

Emily unpacked her books. 'So now you want to change the curriculum. I was over the moon winning a place at Cambridge and I'm going to take full advantage of it.'

'Yes all right, guilty as charged. But I'm going out tonight and won't be in for supper.'

'*Again?*'

'The local theatre company has invited me to their dress rehearsal. Hey, why not come? Free show and who knows, you might meet some handsome Scottish scientist.'

Emily threw a cushion at Louise who squealed as it hit her.

'Louise, a plain, bookish girl like me, doesn't see the world as does a beautiful and talented girl like you.'

Louise was upset. 'Oh Emily, that's not fair.'

'We come from different worlds. You have the looks and talent and men line up to open doors for you. That's just not me.'

Louise went to speak but Emily held up a hand. 'Please, I'm ever so grateful for the way you try and get me involved but I'm happy just going to class, working in the lab and singing hymns on Sundays.'

'Well I'm not going to stop asking, so there,' she said throwing the cushion back at Emily who made a meal of catching it.

'But I also want to say,' said Emily, 'That I think you're a very kind and generous person and I couldn't be happier with you as my friend.'

They hugged then Louise headed for the door and called as she left. 'Don't wait up for me, Mother.'

She caught the bus into Cambridge and walked to the Vestey home where Molly opened the kitchen door. Alfred and Elizabeth were visiting Molly's mother in hospital.

'Just in time, come in, come in. What are you like at cooking?'

'Close to hopeless, why?'

'Well you can stir the soup while I go over my lines. I play Veronica, the vicar's daughter. I have the smallest part and I come in on page 12. Iain McTavish is my suitor.'

Louise held the script in one hand, stirred the soup with the other and read aloud the lines of a play she'd never seen.

'*Do you mean to say ...,*' began Louise.

'He's Scottish,' said Molly.

Louise immediately spoke with a strong Glaswegian accent. '*Do you mean to say your daughter is not welcome to the idea?*'

'The other character is my father, the Reverend Alderney,' said Molly. 'He's Cornish.'

Louise was thrown in at the deep end. With what she thought was a cross between a Cornish fisherman and a tin miner's accent, she began. '*God moves in mysterious ways, Mister McTavish. Ah, here comes my daughter now.*'

'That's me,' said Molly and began speaking as her character. '*Good day to you, kind sir, ...*'

'Wait, wait, wait,' said Louise neglecting the soup. 'Your accent is Irish.'

'Yes, I'm from Limerick. And please watch the soup.'

Louise returned to stirring. 'So you're Irish, your father's Cornish, and your suitor's a Scot?'

'Yes and my mother's Norwegian.'

'But the play's in English?'

'Well of course. How else could we understand one another?'

'That was going to be my next question.'

They returned to rehearsing Molly's lines until the soup was ready. They enjoyed the hearty broth with some crusty bread and a pot of tea. Then, wrapping up well against the cold autumnal night, they set off for a dress rehearsal of *The Interlude of Humanity* by F.N. Crumpley.

En route Louise tactfully enquired after Molly's mother. The fact that Molly just shook her head and increased their walking pace said it all.

In Cambridge the St Peter's Players troupe was a group of well-meaning amateur thespians with considerable enthusiasm and somewhat less talent. Their founder was the diminutive but portly Miss Audrey Finchley, 75, who was quicker to jump over than run round. Her abilities as a director were limited to start with and reduced even further due to her ever increasing deafness. In giving notes to performers, her main response to questions and remarks from the actors was, "What's that, dear"?

Molly led Louise into the hall and announced, 'Everyone, this is my friend Louise.' There was much hand shaking and Audrey spoke.

'It's lovely to see new members. You're very welcome, Denise. Have you done any acting?'

'Just a little.'

'What's that, dear?'

And so Louise became an honourary member of the St Peter's Players as well as their Prompt.

After what seemed an age, the various lighting, set and costume problems were sorted, the curtains closed and the dress rehearsal began.

The audience consisted of Audrey the director, Clive the costumier and Geoffrey the lighting operator. Oh and Louise who was given a chair, a script and a torch with the instruction to "Call out if anyone gets lost".

The curtains opened and the play began in darkness.

'Geoffrey,' cried Audrey.

'Just a minute,' replied the prickly lighting operator and suddenly the stage was flooded with light.

'That's Act Two,' called Audrey.

'All right, keep your wig on.'

'What's that, dear?'

Louise smiled and thought about her own theatrical experiences— reading the classics at Cambridge, performing in plays at Roedean, and with Nightie and his group in her family church, and going to the West End to see wonderful actors in wonderful plays. The St Peter's Players troupe was in a league of its own.

Finally the dress rehearsal got under way and immediately Louise was curious as to the casting. The actor playing the Scotsman McTavish was from Somerset while the actor playing the Cornishman was Scottish. As they were a similar age Louise wondered why the director had cast them so. Particularly as both actors had trouble maintaining their accent and often slipped back to their regional dialect. When Molly's stage mother, a woman with a strong Liverpudlian accent, came on playing the Norwegian Heidi Engelstad, the cultural mix was complete. All it needed was for Molly to enter on page 12 speaking pure blarney all the way from Limerick and the play *The Tower of Babel* would be complete.

One unfortunate fact was that *The Interlude of Humanity* was a drama. It had a theme of family conflict with raw emotion.

But as the actors became angry, frustrated or distressed, their accents swapped regions. Even Molly moved from Limerick to Belfast and back to Limerick via Cambridge. Surely the audience would not be able to suspend disbelief if this happened when the play opened. The drama became a comedy. Opening night beckoned.

Louise thought about her neglected studies. She vowed to change. She'd been the Prompt for both dress rehearsals of *The Interlude of Humanity* but now, on the afternoon of the play's opening night, was hard at work in the Girton College library. She had to choose a theme in a Shakespearean play and then compare a recurrence of that theme in another of his works.

The final dress rehearsal with the St Peter's Players saw a marked improvement and with tickets sold for tonight's opening, Louise found her mind drifting towards *The Interlude of Humanity*. It might be an ordinary production of an unknown play but it was live theatre. Studying the works of great dramatists was fascinating and hard work but Louise preferred to act. She wanted to study by performing.

She was making notes about Orlando and Rosalind from *As You Like It* when someone approached her table. She looked up surprised to see Elizabeth Vestey.

'I'm so sorry to barge in on you like this, Miss Wellesley.' Louise had declined Elizabeth's invitation to call her former teacher by her Christian name and so she, Elizabeth, had decided to continue calling Louise, Miss Wellesley. There was genuine affection between the two women.

Louise was concerned. 'Is something wrong?'

Elizabeth was sombre and sat beside Louise. 'I'm afraid so. My dear sister-in-law, Molly's mother, passed away this morning.'

The two women clasped hands. 'Poor Molly,' said Louise. 'The Professor and you must be devastated. Please accept my condolences and pass on my deepest sympathy to them both.'

'Thank you, I will,' whispered Elizabeth.

'I suppose, in one way, it'll be a relief for your family. Missus Vestey was ill for a long time and must have suffered greatly.'

'Your wisdom does you proud, young lady. And as sad as it is, a blessing is a good way to describe it.'

'Oh no!' gasped Louise. 'Molly has her opening tonight. How can she possibly go on?'

'She can't. The poor girl is overcome with grief.'

'But what about the play and all that work? Can they postpone it or ... surely they won't cancel?'

'The show must go on, Miss Wellesley. You of all people should know that.'

Elizabeth placed a large envelope on the table and looked at Louise.

'Is that what I think it is?' asked Louise.

'I have spoken with Miss Finchley and Molly and they have asked me to ask you to step in and play Molly's part tonight—please.'

'But ...'

'You would use the script, of course,' said Elizabeth patting the envelope.

Louise looked at the envelope then at Elizabeth. Louise nodded. 'I would be honoured to help Molly and Miss Finchley and especially you.' Elizabeth squeezed Louise's hand.

Elizabeth stood. 'Well if Miss Wellesley would deign to prepare, her car will arrive at 6.45pm sharp. I'll bring Molly's make-up case and I'm sure her costume will suit a treat. And on behalf of Molly and everyone, thank you ever so much. Till tonight.'

Elizabeth blew a kiss and left and Louise stared at the envelope. She closed her Shakespearean tome. *Sorry Professor, I was unable to complete my essay due to unforeseen circumstances.*

Back in her room Louise was lying on her bed reading the script when Emily came in to return a scarf she'd borrowed. She was disappointed. 'Oh Louise,' cried Emily, 'you promised you'd spend the afternoon in the library.'

Louise explained the situation and Emily was most upset. Before long she was holding the script and hearing Louise go through her lines.

'How can you remember all these words?' asked Emily.

'I'll tell you later. What about my accent? I'm supposed to be from the south of Ireland.'

'Sounds fine to me but you could ask that Irish lass in Second year.'

'You know a girl from Ireland?'

'She's reading science and we meet in the laboratory. She's upstairs somewhere.'

'Let's go,' said Louise.

They found Brianna O'Connell from Wexford and she was delighted to be a part of something so exciting. Twenty minutes later, Brianna pronounced Louise's Irish accent to be almost like that of a native.

The tension was building. Louise, who rarely got nervous before going on stage, began collecting butterflies. She knew why; insufficient quality rehearsal time.

Emily was excited. 'I wouldn't miss this for the world,' she said.

'Oh please don't feel you have to come,' said Louise.

Emily ribbed her friend. 'You keep telling me how much you prefer to perform than study; well here's your chance to prove it.'

Louise rehearsed alone in the chapel. She gave herself small targets, one speech, two speeches and then a whole page. She'd hold the script and read the lines of the other actors then lower the book when it was her cue. Anyone coming into the chapel would have been highly entertained by this energetic Irish woman pacing about in front of the altar.

After two hours, Louise collapsed on the front pew taking deep breaths. She'd never felt like this before. Performing was what she loved but always after careful and solid preparation. This was different. Louise felt the fear of possibly falling flat on her face.

She looked at her watch and nearly died. It was half past six.

The dressing room for the St Peter's Players was basic. It normally housed hymn books, choir robes and Sunday school material. During a play season, a sheet was hung across the room affording the females some privacy. Louise was greeted like the long-lost daughter. Everyone wanted to give the fill-in actress advice. Talk about too many cooks.

Miss Finchley fussed as Louise tried on her costume. Clive the costumier, who was born on the wrong side of the blanket, was now on the wrong side of the sheet. He enjoyed manhandling Louise's costume with Louise inside it with a little too much hands-on activity.

Miss Finchley gave Louise explicit instructions. 'Now stand by the settee, Denise, and speak with as loud a voice as you can.'

'Yes, Miss Finchley. I'll certainly do my best.'

'What's that, dear?'

Louise explained. 'I think I'll be okay with Act One and I've made some cue cards for Act Two.'

'Lift your arms,' said Clive.

'Where is your script?' asked the producer.

'There,' Louise pointed.

Miss Finchley offered it to Louise. 'Molly has marked her lines so you should be able to follow things.'

'Thank you but I hope I won't need it, Miss Finchley.'

'What's that dear?'

Louise took the script and smiled. Finally the stage manager called, 'Beginners for Act One.' The others left and Louise was alone.

Suddenly the audience hubbub died as Miss Finchley stepped through the curtains and addressed the audience.

'Good evening, ladies and gentlemen. A warm welcome to you all but I'm afraid I have some very sad news. The mother of our wonderful young actress, Molly Vestey, passed away today. Of course Miss Vestey is unable to perform but in maintaining the tradition of "The show must go on", we have asked our newest member, Miss Denise Wallsey to step in at the last minute. She's a very brave young lady and I'm sure you'll treat her with every kindness. Oh and please stay for a cup of tea after the performance.'

Miss Finchley tried to exit the way she entered but couldn't find the gap in the curtains. Her fumbling was entertaining until she finally departed. Then a scratchy recording of the National Anthem began and the audience numbering forty-three and a dog stood. The pooch was a monarchist. Suddenly the music stopped mid-anthem as the needle was scratched across the record. Miss Finchley re-appeared.

'I do apologise. I forgot to say that the vicar has asked me to remind you to please leave by the side door as he's having trouble with his drains.'

She made another stop-start exit then the hall lights went dark, the curtains opened and *The Interlude of Humanity* began.

Louise watched from the wings. She was doubly worried. The play had reverted to the standard of the first dress rehearsal. Accents skipped borders; actors changed character. The audience was hooked. Was this a drama or a comedy?

But why were the actors struggling? Did they think the inexperienced Louise would fail? Would she wreck all their hard work? Louise's nerves came out to play.

The Interlude of Humanity by F.N. Crumpley

McTavish	Oh sir, kindly do not judge me, for I am a wronged man.
Alderney	It is abundantly clear, Mr McTavish. You will know them by their fruits.
Mrs Ald'y	In my country, sir, no man would ever do such a thing.
McTavish	But I never doed it, done it, oh, I, I mean I didn't doed it.

Now the cast became tongue-tied and it was catching.

Alderney   Oh come, Mr McRadish, your denials are all in vain.

The actor playing the Reverend Alderney had just called McTavish McRadish. There was a pause. Would someone laugh? The Norwegian with the Liverpudlian accent kept going.

Mrs Ald'y   We can only believe in what we know, sir.
McTavish   Yes but it's all a lack of pies.

Lack of pies? Come in Spooner. McTavish went as red as a McRadish. The actors watched their performance slide off the stage and into the arms of an audience teetering on the brink of uncontrollable laughter.

Finally someone in the audience did laugh making a strange sound. That set off others and guffaws erupted. People had been bursting to laugh for some time and when given the chance they let rip using both barrels.

Louise looked at the horrified actors. The play stopped. The actors had no idea how to continue their drama which was now a rib-tickling comedy. For the cast this was a nightmare. Without thinking, Louise entered and boldly spoke in a strong Irish accent.

Veronica   Mr McTavish! How dare you speak to my parents thus.

Everyone stopped. The actors were dumbstruck, the audience fell silent. A hat pin crash-landed on the floor and the sound reverberated around the hall. Miss Finchley gasped. The dog pricked its ears.

Gliding effortlessly centre-stage, Louise had invented a line just before her proper cue. She then reverted to the script. The other actors remained stupefied. Louise knew that her stage father should speak the line, *My daughter, have you finished your bible studies?* Without missing a beat, Louise smiled at her father and said, *Father, I have finished my bible studies.*

Her stage mother understood.

Mrs Ald'y   We were discussing Mister McTavish's proposal. Kindly return to your room.

Louise was word perfect and spoke with an intensity the other actors had never heard from Molly. Louise added depth and colour to her character. Veronica came alive. She inspired Mr McTavish. She angered her father and gave pride to her mother. The play changed in an instant. Louise brought it to life. Miss Finchley exhausted her supply of gasps.

When the curtains closed at the end of Act One, the audience clapped with feeling. A buzz erupted. St Peter's Players had a first—a hit.

Backstage the actors fell over themselves to congratulate Louise. Everyone was in the female half of the dressing-room. Louise was ecstatic. On stage she had been concentrating like never before. Now she was having trouble remaining calm. Her adrenal glands ran out of hormones.

Miss Finchley came in beaming. 'Oh my dear young lady, that was absolutely wonderful. However could you remember all those lines?'

Louise muttered something. Now she was muttering. She was less confident with Act Two and wished everyone would go away so she could cram some more memory exercises. The stage manager appeared. 'Five minutes everyone.'

The second act was a blur for Louise. She'd developed mnemonics to help remember her main speeches. She read small cue cards when she was off-stage or surreptitiously when there was a break in her dialogue. She was in a hair-raising, heart-racing situation and she loved it; the greater the challenge, the greater the risk, the greater the reward. Not using the script was risky but the adrenalin rush was amazing.

A major benefit of Louise's acting was the inspiration she gave to the other actors. Their accents became stable, their movements natural and the story began to shine. The audience suspended disbelief. The final scene was quite moving and when the curtains started to close, the audience was already enthusiastically clapping.

For the curtain calls, the applause went up a level. The actors beamed.

Backstage the dressing-room was buzzing with happiness. Actors changed their clothes and removed their make-up not caring who was here or there. Miss Finchley was clapping and kissing.

Geoffrey, the lighting operator, who always sneaked out for a beer and a smoke after the show, was backstage in the middle of everything. Clive the costumier looked like the cat from the Cambridge dairy. The stage manager and the vicar crowded into the room. The St Peter's Players had stuck gold.

Why was *The Interlude of Humanity* a hit? Clearly Louise's acting had inspired the others and as their confidence rose, so did the standard of the performance. And because the audience had seen such an ordinary and error-strewn production in the first scene it was obvious why it dramatically improved. Louise Wellesley had turned the play on its head.

Not one of the forty-three audience members or the dog left after the final curtain and it wasn't the tea and cakes which made them linger. Everyone wanted to meet the girl from Girton.

In the dressing-room, Miss Finchley was in a joyous mood. 'Ladies and gentlemen, your public awaits.'

Louise was congratulated, kissed, hugged and thanked by almost everyone. Some came back for seconds. She joined the cast and crew in the hall. Miss Finchley's neighbours, Mr and Mrs Bird were in charge of the supper. When the actors made their appearance, applause broke out.

Louise found herself surrounded. Elderly parishioners were overjoyed to see not just a new face but someone who could actually act. The vicar forgot his drains and lost his stutter. Louise had tea and cake thrust upon her from delighted theatregoers who couldn't stop fussing. Friend Emily and dialect coach Brianna were bursting with pride.

Finally Elizabeth Vestey appeared but as both women were juggling a cup of tea, they found it impossible to embrace.

'Well Miss Wellesley,' said Miss Vestey. 'Why am I not surprised?'

Before the two could chat seriously, Louise was whisked away. Outwardly she was happy. Inwardly she was ecstatic.

Miss Finchley received compliments, smiled, laughed, and never once said, "What's that, dear?"

But many thoughts were nagging Louise. *What about tomorrow? Would Molly go on? Would she want to, knowing I've received such high praise? What would Elizabeth recommend?*

Gradually the crowd began to leave. Having thanked so many people, Louise found smiling to be mildly painful. Finally alone, she took a sip of tea and found her hands were shaking. She placed the cup in its saucer and it rattled.

'I can recommend the cakes.' Louise turned to smile yet again and say "thank you" but stopped when she looked at the speaker. She had to look up to see his smile and that was what gave her pulse rate a jolt. She held onto her cup and saucer even harder.

'I'm serious,' said the man. 'My aunt baked them and believe me, she is the Cake Queen of Cambridge.'

Louise was struggling. The actress who convinced people she was French, who could remember all those lines and who had just pulled off a minor theatrical triumph was suddenly tongue-tied.

'I'm Tom,' said the man. They shook hands. 'And just like everyone else, I thought you were absolutely marvellous.'

'Thank you. You're very kind.'

'My wife used to drag me off to the theatre in London all the time.' Louise felt flat. 'But since she died, I hardly ever go.' Louise felt less flat. 'Is it true you stepped in at the last minute?'

'Yes, this afternoon.'

'Well I reckon that makes a fantastic performance even better. But if you'll forgive me, you seem far too young to be a professional actress.'

Louise was finding it difficult to remember anything about tonight's triumph, about her role as a young woman in love or the topic of her essay requested by her literature professor. She vaguely remembered it was about love. Let's see now. That was love between a man and a woman; romantic love, physical love, hand-trembling and heart-fluttering love. Why on earth was she thinking about love? Tom continued.

'I'm just here for the weekend and I only came tonight because my aunt and uncle dragged me along. They're the couple in the kitchen. And I have to say, it was a night I'll find very hard to forget.'

For Louise, the word *ditto* sprang immediately to mind.

Molly was far too distressed to even think about performing in any play so Louise reprised the role.

The Cambridge grapevine was in full bloom meaning extra chairs were required to accommodate expectant patrons. Even the dog came back but, having seen the play already, chose to sleep through the final performance.

In some ways Louise felt her acting lacked the opening night sparkle. Perhaps the fact that she'd already climbed the mountain took away her nervous energy. But she was still in fine form and the happiness of the cast and crew and the enthusiastic audience response capped off one of the best seasons ever for the St Peter's Players.

Before the final performance Louise found herself thinking about the caterers' nephew. Tom or, she guessed, Thomas, had the voice of an actor, the eyes of a hero and the charm of a gentle man. His smile was bewitching.

Mixing with the large audience after the final performance, Louise kept glancing around hoping to see the man who caused her rapid heartbeat. Alas, no Tom.

She found it interesting that in the midst of so many well-wishers she felt sad. The speech from Miss Finchley, who finally got Louise's name right, and the gifts from the cast and others were overwhelming. As things wound up, Louise popped into the kitchen to thank Mr and Mrs Bird. Well, she did have an ulterior motive.

'I just wanted to thank you for those heavenly cakes.'

Mrs Bird smiled, a bit like her nephew. 'Oh you're very welcome, young lady.'

Mr Bird was just as sweet. 'But we're the ones who should be saying "thanks". You stole the show, miss; a proper star of the stage you be.'

Louise smiled and murmured her thanks then continued with her subtle fishing. 'Your nephew told me you are the Cake Queen of Cambridge and I can confidently say he's right.'

'Oh now don't you believe anything young Tommy tells you,' laughed Mrs Bird wiping the bench. 'He's got the gift of the gab, has that lad.'

He certainly has, thought Louise, *and a lot more besides.*

But try as she might, Louise couldn't bring herself to ask anything personal about "young Tommy". Like, where does he live? Will he be coming back to Cambridge? What does he do for a living? Is there a wife number two on the horizon?

So sans information she hopped into the Vestey Austin Ten and headed home to Girton. En route Elizabeth was up for a chat.

'So Miss Wellesley, now that your latest thespian triumph is o'er, how go the studies?'

'Oh don't ask,' sighed Louise.

'It's almost the end of term, young lady. All this acting's well and good but you *are* here to learn.'

'You sound just like a teacher I knew at Roedean.'

The women laughed. It had been a memorable weekend.

But Louise was well aware she was at Cambridge to study and with Elizabeth's message ringing in her ears, she climbed the stairs to her room and flopped on her bed. She found it hard to sleep and was still awake when there was a soft tapping on her door. It opened and in the darkness, Emily's voice was heard.

'Can I have your autograph, Miss?'

Chapter 7

EVEN THOUGH German soldiers had trained in Lower Saxony for decades, under Hitler some 70,000 acres were set aside solely for the military. Thousands of German citizens were forced to leave their homes and army barracks, a hospital and other buildings were erected.

And it was here that Max and his Panzer Division went through their paces. It was dangerous being a squirrel in the Bergen-Hohne Training Ground.

The latest military exercise was to find the best route from A to B, travel fast and strike hard at a stationary target. This was war simulation. Everyone had to achieve their goal without delay or failure. With the Führer and top military brass observing, the stakes were high.

Max was quiet. 'A pfennig for your thoughts, Oberleutnant?' asked his driver.

Max nearly died. If he was seen acting strangely before Hitler's assassination, this would be reported at the inevitable inquiry.

'Oh, nothing;' he said. 'I was just thinking about a girl I met last week.' His driver laughed.

Max pictured the Gestapo questioning his driver. "Did you notice anyone acting in a strange way? Who? Oberleutnant Hartmann? How was he behaving?" Max immediately tried to be one of the boys.

It was raining; perfect weather for mass murder. Cue the Wagnerian music.

The tanks made their way to Point A. Max's thoughts were on the "minor" matter of Hitler's impending death.

But how would it happen? How could a shell land with pinpoint accuracy on the VIP observation post and look like an accident? And what was Max's role? Would this be his finest or final hour? He looked at his watch. The rain got heavier. He felt sick. Sixty seconds to start time.

The tanks rolled and not far away the cream of the Wehrmacht's leadership took shelter in their military observation post. None was expecting to die today.

Max struggled to concentrate. Was he about to assassinate Hitler? Was Max about to die? The rain was relentless and visibility poor. Reidel's tank was leading.

Max knew taking the established roads was the long way to the target. Speed was vital and there was a short cut. But if Max took the short cut and got stuck, particularly in this weather, his shame would be known throughout the Wehrmacht. He decided to risk it.

Reidel had the same idea and just as Max prepared to turn off the forest road, Reidel's tank beat him to it taking the same short cut. Max followed. He chose to drive his tank on this particular exercise. He wanted total control but for what he wasn't sure.

He was lucky. Reidel's tank was a battering ram as it raced along the old woodcutters' track. Tree branches snapped like matches as the powerful Panzers ploughed ahead. There was no chance to pass and Max drove hard keeping close to Reidel who was pleased another tank was with him.

Ahead Reidel saw the trees were thinning. His tank broke free of the forest and swerved hard left. Max ploughed after him but was too aggressive, missed the turn and took precious time steering back to firmer ground. By now Reidel was well ahead and driving fast. Their target was close without being visible.

Max's crew member was worried. Why was Oberleutnant Hartmann driving so erratically? Speed was important but this was a training drill, not a suicide mission.

Suddenly Reidel swerved right heading towards the target. Max strained to see through the rain and then to his amazement saw another Panzer approaching from another direction. This third tank had gone outside the training ground and was driving straight at the target.

Then panic struck Max. The third tank suddenly opened fire. Whoosh. A shell exploded. Climbing a rise, Max saw a pillbox, the observation post. The third tank was presumably firing at the target but with the observation post in its direct line of fire. Max had crazy thoughts.

Had the war games turned lethal? Was the rogue tank really aiming directly at the observation post? Was this the Hitler assassination?

Max was dicing with panic. All three tanks were travelling at their maximum speed. The rough terrain had them "riding the waves". Max's driver was yelling at him. Max yelled back and ordered him to take the controls. 'What the hell is happening?' screamed his driver.

'Just drive,' screamed Max.

Then Reidel fired, not at the observation post but at the rogue tank. He missed. Trees splintered. Max's brain was spinning. The third tank continued towards the solid concrete observation post. A Panzer could obliterate that shelter. Those inside the OP were confused with their concern running to catch up.

Reidel's plan was working. He knew the commander of this rogue tank was a fanatic. Reidel had subtly encouraged the madman to become a hero and save the Fatherland. And once the plan was 'live' Reidel knew how to ensure it worked. He would fire at the rogue tank but deliberately miss. This fake attack from Reidel would drive the madman to succeed.

Reidel was racing parallel with the rogue tank. He wanted to get a better "pretend" side-on shot. Max refused to follow Reidel and ordered his tank to drive straight at the rogue machine. It was making better speed. It fired again and only just missed the target. The occupants of the observation post were now terrified. Max's driver panicked and kept screaming at him.

50

Reidel fired again at the lunatic Panzer but again deliberately missed. The rogue commander hadn't considered that other tanks would be present let alone attack him. His plan was under fire—literally. He changed tactics. Forget firing shells at the observation post; just ram the damn thing. The rogue commander switched to a suicide mission and set his Panzer to crash into the OP.

The rogue tank was only fifty metres from its target and heading straight for it. In a few seconds it would smash into the OP and kill the military hierarchy. Hitler was about to be assassinated by a suicidal Wehrmacht officer. Reidel fired again and missed again. Max took aim. There was a blinding flash and Max fell back in his tank.

Hitler avoided many assassination attempts. He was being driven to the observation post in Lower Saxony when he ordered his driver to turn around. His sixth sense worked again. Mind you, even if he had been inside the OP he would have survived.

The rogue tank was driven by Hauptsturmführer Franz Bruer. He was deeply religious and a strong believer in the monarchy. To him, Hitler was no Kaiser, not even fit to clean the boots of the German monarch. Weeks earlier a quiet word from Oberst Reidel planted a seed in Bruer's disturbed mind. And when God sent him a message to wipe out the imposter Hitler, then Bruer knew his duty.

His tank was only metres from the OP when it exploded. The Wehrmacht hierarchy were terrified but alive. Hitler insisted on everyone involved being shot. Reidel, Max and their crews were arrested.

That night Max stared at the ceiling of his cell. The fact that his shell was the one which destroyed the rogue tank and thus saved the top brass meant nothing. Max's father and grandfather were decorated soldiers but he was about to be shot. His cell door opened.

'Out!' barked a man in a suit. Max's heart sank. Gestapo. He was marched upstairs and entered a room where a man stood with his back to the others. No-one spoke. Max had never been in trouble before and certainly not with the Gestapo. He wondered when the torture would start. They say it's the bravest who scream the loudest.

Just being kept waiting was a kind of torture. The man with his back to Max turned and Max was looking at Heinrich Himmler. Not quite God but close.

Himmler sat, began working on papers and spoke to Max without looking at him.

'Why?' That's all he said. Max added confusion to his fear. A Gestapo officer punched Max hard in the kidneys. He cried out and regretted his response more than the pain.

Himmler kept working, his voice low.

'Why did you attempt to assassinate the Führer?'

'With respect, Reichsführer, I ...' Himmler looked at Max for the first time. Unlike Hitler, there was no rage, just a quiet voice.

'Do you think we are stupid?' Pause. Max was unsure. 'I asked a question.'

'Of course not, Reichsführer.'

'Then why did you attempt to assassinate the Führer?'

'Again with respect, Reichs ...'

'Oh come now Hartmann. You are about to be shot. At least let us have the truth before you die.' There was another pause. Without warning Max felt intense pain as the second Gestapo officer kicked Max's knee.

He knew of no specific plan to assassinate Hitler. He was about to die so perhaps should invent some wild tale. Himmler walked to the window with his back to Max.

'Did you attend Oberst Reidel's 60th birthday celebrations?'

Max was stunned. Another punch smashed into his kidneys.

'Yes, Reichsführer.'

'Did you stay in the room when Reidel asked those who would join his scheme to remain?'

Max's head was spinning. What did they *not* know? He spoke quickly to avoid more pain. 'Yes, Reichsführer.'

Himmler smiled and returned to his desk. 'You see, Hartmann, we are not stupid, murderous thugs.' Himmler paused. 'Do you not agree?'

Max was silent expecting more pain. Himmler continued.

'I admire your bravery, Hartmann. Unfortunately the world will never see it. Take him.'

Max was dragged away and thrown into a cell. He cowered on the floor and was savagely kicked and beaten. The Gestapo agents then stepped back, drew their revolvers and took aim at Max. He froze.

'Bang,' said one Gestapo officer. They laughed, retreated and slammed the door. Max lay still hoping the pain would fade. It didn't and then he discovered he'd evacuated his bowels. Trying to clean himself with his bare hands was the least of his worries.

That day Max's cousin Kurt was relaxing with several colleagues after an arduous torture session. He'd become a dedicated Nazi who believed in the Gestapo and all the "perfect" goals of the Third Reich. Suddenly a Gestapo agent burst into the room and shouted.

'Someone's just tried to assassinate the Wehrmacht High Command!'

The room erupted. Agents yelled questions. Others couldn't hear the answers so yelled at those who were shouting questions. Finally the news bearer got a chance to be heard.

'There was a military exercise in Lower Saxony. All the top brass were there. Hitler was supposed to join them.'

'Was the Führer there?'

'Apparently he turned back.' More hubbub.

'So what happened?'

'On one of those lightning war exercises, tanks were sent to destroy a fixed target but some rogue tank broke free and attacked the observation post with the High Command sheltering inside.'

The hubbub became feverish.

'The rogue tank then came under fire from other tanks.'

Kurt was hooked. Which Panzers were involved?

'The assassin's tank finally made a suicidal charge at the OP and just as it was about to smash into it, the tank exploded.'

'The rogue tank exploded?'

'They say another tank destroyed it with a single shell.'

'And the top brass are all okay?'

'Okay but on the warpath. I don't fancy any of the Panzer commanders who were even remotely involved.'

When he heard more details Kurt was staggered. *Cousin Max, patriotic Max; it can't be true. Yes he despised Hitler but Max was a loyal soldier. He followed orders. Max assassinate the Führer? Never.*

Kurt immediately went to his commanding officer. It was risky and Kurt knew he was playing a deadly game. He felt compelled to discover the truth about Max and the incident in Lower Saxony. He could never face his father or uncle if Max was executed and he, Kurt, had done nothing. But what would happen if he did do something?

This was seriously dangerous. If Max was guilty then being associated with him was potentially fatal for Kurt. He could lose his chance at promotion, his job or even his life.

Kurt arrived at Gestapo HQ and was granted access to the commanding officer. Kurt was humble but bold.

'Herr Kriminalkommissar, I have known my cousin since birth. We grew up together and his family and mine have long and distinguished military careers serving the Fatherland.'

'Get to the point, Hartmann.'

'May I be permitted to see my cousin, sir?'

'Of course; we're not barbarians.'

'Thank you, sir.' Kurt saluted and started to leave but stopped when spoken to.

'But understand, your cousin will be shot in the morning.'

Kurt nodded. He went downstairs, surrendered his revolver and followed the guard. He stepped inside a cell and struggled to adjust to the dim light. The cell door slammed and Kurt focused on the prisoner. His stomach lurched.

Max was slumped on the floor. His face was puffed with splashes of dried blood. He'd been tortured by the Gestapo and Kurt knew all about that. With Max there'd been no attempt to hide the torture. He'd be dead soon enough.

'Kurt?' gurgled Max. His swollen lips made speech difficult. His saliva was streaked with blood. Kurt knelt beside his cousin trying to make him even slightly more comfortable. From his coat pocket Kurt took a flask of beer and two tablets of Pervitin, the soon-to-be-released Wehrmacht so-called wonder drug.

Kurt helped Max drink and swallow the tablets. The wretched man coughed and groaned. Kurt lifted his cousin onto the "bed". Using rags he made a next-to-useless pillow then placed Max's coat over his cousin to provide a little comfort.

Max slowly regained his ability to talk. In faltering sentences he told Kurt everything from the party in Oberst Reidel's rooms to the events of the tank battle. Kurt was stunned.

'But that means you fired the shell which destroyed the rogue Panzer. It was you who stopped it crashing into the OP. Your action saved the lives of the top brass.'

Max nodded and mumbled. 'Perhaps Reidel was genuinely surprised. Perhaps he took advantage of the situation and deliberately missed the rogue tank. I just did what I thought was right.'

Kurt was pleased. He knew the love he'd had for Max was still strong. And knowing the truth, Kurt was determined to help his cousin. He rose to leave. Max raised his arm, the one which wasn't broken.

'Kurt,' he spluttered. 'Promise me you'll say none of this to anyone. Tell my father I died a proud German and that I love him, my mother and sisters. Promise me.'

Kurt knelt and kissed Max's bloodied forehead. 'I promise, cousin. God bless you.'

Kurt called the guard then hurried upstairs. He'd made his cousin a solemn promise. But Kurt was in the Gestapo and their promises were worthless.

He returned to the senior Gestapo officer who was curious. 'You again? Has the traitor confessed?'

'He has indeed, Herr Kriminalkommissar.' The leader was interested. 'I discovered the truth, sir, not by torture, but because Max Hartmann is a proud German and doesn't wish to die in vain.'

'This had better be good.'

Kurt spoke with passion and explained how Max had saved the lives of the military top brass. Kurt delivered his final pitch.

'Germany needs men like Oberleutnant Hartmann. He has skills and courage and besides, killing the man who saved the lives of the General Staff and, had the Führer been present, the leader of the Third Reich, would send a powerful message to the men in the Wehrmacht, the SS and the Gestapo. The message being that military heroism is *not* rewarded, it is punished.'

The commandant was furious. But Kurt's passionate defence continued; in for a pfennig, in for a Reichsmark. He made the attack personal.

'I admire you, Herr Kriminalkommissar. You may go down in history as the officer who executed the man who saved the life of the Führer. I congratulate you on your brave decision.'

Kurt finished. His sarcasm lingered. It was time for a second Hartmann to face the firing squad.

'Get out,' barked the senior officer. Kurt hesitated. He was wound up, carried away with the strength of his convictions and love for his cousin. *Had my superior officer called for my arrest? What did he actually say?* The pictures on the wall shifted in fright when the Kriminalkommissar repeated himself.

'Get out!'

Kurt saluted and left. Only outside in the street did he notice he was trembling. How many Gestapo agents had given a senior officer a dressing down? Or rather, how many had done so and lived? If Kurt survived, at least he could tell Max's father that his son had died a brave and innocent man.

Max was confused. His body was pain writ large and any movement was agony but despite this he felt reasonably bright. His mind was actually alert.

Then he remembered Kurt's beer and pills. Max didn't know that German scientists had been instructed by Hitler to produce chemicals to help German fighting men remain alert and push through pain. Kurt got wind of such developments and obtained samples. They did little for Max's physical pain but his ability to think clearly and remain alert was surprisingly good.

It was early when Max heard footsteps. The cell door opened. A dawn execution; such is life. He hated the fact he could barely walk and reeked of vomit, faeces and sweat. Two guards lifted him onto a stretcher. The pain was exquisite. Was Max being carried to his execution?

They went along a corridor and into a courtyard. A van was parked with its rear doors open. Max was slid into the van. Two heavy blankets were carefully placed on him. Max was bewildered. The van drove out of the courtyard.

It was a long journey where every bump and turn put Max's pain threshold to the test. Finally the van stopped. The rear doors opened and two orderlies carefully lifted Max. He was about to enter hospital. Hospital? No firing squad for Max Hartmann which alas was not the case with Oberst Hans Reidel.

He refused to co-operate despite horrendous Gestapo torture. When confronted with the facts about his birthday party chat to kill Hitler, Reidel hid his alarm. He was brave but dead.

There were informers in every part of German life. Why should the Wehrmacht not have its own spies?

Max was helped into a hospital bed with the freshest and whitest sheets he had ever seen. Was he dreaming?

Kurt's impassioned speech had prompted drastic action. Max dodged several bullets; literally. Away from Berlin he received the very best of care. One day he was being tortured and sentenced to death. The next he was reprieved and receiving the finest medical care his country could provide.

He sat in a comfortable chair on the veranda of the private hospital in its idyllic forest setting. It was chilly and an orderly produced a blanket. Max was impressed. Then his elderly doctor appeared and spoke reverentially to Max.

'And so, young man, I have here your report and it makes for good news.'

'Thank you, Herr Doktor.'

'From the accident in your tank, you have sustained a number of serious injuries.'

Max was struggling. In the tank battle he copped a whack on his head and used up a lifetime of adrenalin. His new injuries had nothing to do with the war games. *Does my doctor think otherwise?*

'Your broken arm and badly bruised leg are healing but I fear you will never be as handsome as before. You can show those scars to your grandchildren.'

Max smiled but hid his concern. He wondered if his doctor was part of some Gestapo scheme and if he genuinely believed Max's injuries were the result of a tank battle. Perhaps the doctor was involved in some brainwashing operation to convince Max the Gestapo torture sessions never took place. Or was he just incompetent? The medico continued.

'I have to admit, Oberleutnant, some of the burn marks on your body are peculiar.'

'Peculiar, Herr Doktor?'

'Men trapped in a burning tank usually have large burns over their body. Your burns are very specific. Can you remember your tank catching fire?'

Max hesitated. Should he explain that his broken limb, bruising, burns and scars were all from Gestapo torture? Was Max being tested? Was the doctor really a doctor? Max decided to tell the truth.

'No sir, I cannot remember my tank catching fire,' he said.

'Thank God,' said the doctor as he scribbled some notes then touched Max gently on the arm. 'Good luck, young man. You are a credit to your country. Heil Hitler.'

'Heil Hitler,' replied Max and watched the doctor walk inside.

Max ate a nutritious lunch but with an arm and leg in bandages, dining was difficult. His broken arm and badly bruised leg were on opposite sides of his body; typical Gestapo barbarity and perverted humour.

Other diners at Max's table were a motley mix of Wehrmacht officers who gave away nothing and Max responded in kind.

An excellent cheese board was being passed around when a uniformed officer entered and fairly roared.

'Achtung!' Every diner was upstanding and silent.

This was easier said than done. Those with their lower limbs in good working order were fine. Max floundered. His walking-stick was on the floor and he struggled to pick it up. At this rate he would be the only person in the room not standing. The officer with the extremely loud voice continued.

'Heil Hitler!'

'Heil Hitler,' responded the dining-room although Max, in his haste to try and salute, managed to drop his walking-stick. It made the traditional sound of wood on wood but when such a sound happens just as your Commander-in-Chief enters a silent room, that sound tends to hog the limelight.

Max had his back to the entrance and couldn't see the guest. The faces of his fellow diners told Max that someone in the Deity class had just arrived.

Not a sound. Then footsteps. They sounded close to Max. They *were* close to Max. He dared not look. As a soldier he knew how to stand tall, face front and speak only when spoken to.

The footstep-making person stopped by Max, bent and picked up the walking-stick. The failed Austrian art student spoke.

'Yours, I believe, Oberleutnant.'

Max knew the procedure. He'd been spoken to. But he was expected to reply keeping his eyes straight ahead. If he fumbled for his stick and missed or dropped the damn thing again or, horror of horrors actually touched the Führer, how would that go down in the annals of the Third Reich? Which section of military law covered "goosing the guv'nor"?

Without pausing, Hitler clasped Max's good arm guiding the walking stick into Max's hand. There now, what was all the fuss about?

The official party left. No guesses which topic of conversation ensued over the cheese platter.

Ten minutes later the walking megaphone re-entered and read aloud a list of names adding, 'All those officers will assemble in the driveway in fifteen minutes. Heil Hitler.'

Max's name was on that list. Not wanting to be late, he went to his room, washed his face, combed his hair and adjusted his bandaging to give his uniform as much exposure as possible. He hobbled off to the front of the building.

He arrived to find most of the other men already there. Conversation was limited. Trust was an unknown commodity.

Then suddenly the official party appeared unannounced simply walking around the drive from the side of the hospital. They ambushed the waiting officers who immediately sprang to attention. There was no fanfare. No raised voices. No salutes. It was just a commanding officer congratulating some of his men.

Hitler's behaviour was ordinary. At the far end of the line Max could barely hear let alone understand the brief conversation Hitler had with each man. The Chancellor drew closer. Max thought of his father and grandfather. Their son, their grandson was being personally addressed by the Commander-in-Chief.

Then Hitler was speaking to the man next to Max. When Hitler finished each "chat" he saluted by raising his right hand against his shoulder whereas the officer to whom he spoke would give the whole nine yards with straightened right arm at a good 45 degrees. Max suddenly realised that with his right arm in a sling, any form of salute was likely to look disrespectful. He might as well offer the Führer a two-fingered gesture. Then it happened. Adolf Hitler arrived. He wasn't frightening to look out, almost short, and his voice was restrained.

'Congratulations Oberleutnant. I believe you risked your life to save your commanding officers. Your bravery does you proud.'

'Thank you, my Führer.'

'With men like you, the Third Reich will last for a thousand years.'

Hitler placed his hand gently on Max's good arm. 'Congratulations, *Oberst* Hartmann.' Hitler saluted and before Max could respond, the leader walked away, climbed into his car which drove off. Max was in a daze. He'd just had a one-to-one chat with the Führer and been seriously promoted. So it really *is* true. If you want adventure, join the army.

Max recovered from his Gestapo beating, from the shock of his firing squad reprieve, from the magnificent treatment in the hospital in Bavaria and from his encounter with Herr Hitler. To be congratulated by the man he had agreed to assassinate was surreal. Now Max had been promoted and congratulated by the Führer himself. This Christmas he would not be short of a good tale. Pity he'd taken a vow of silence.

Christmas 1937 drew near and Max's family was overjoyed to see him. The incident in Lower Saxony remained secret. The men who died were buried without ceremony. Those who were a party to Reidel's plan were executed and their families told their loved one died in the execution of his duty; "execution" being appropriate.

Max's mother noticed the scar on his neck which came courtesy of some Gestapo torture.

'And what is this, Maximilian?' she asked examining her son. When he was in trouble, Max was always Maximilian.

'Now Mother, I am too old to have my fingernails inspected.'

They both laughed but Max saw his father's face. Max might be able to deceive his mother but not his former soldier father.

Max was aware of his extraordinary luck. Without Kurt pleading his case, Max would not be celebrating Christmas with anyone. He'd been given a second chance at life and went out of his way to really enjoy the festive season. But across town Kurt's family was unhappy. Unlike Max, Kurt chose to work. He could have taken leave but Kurt had other fish to fry. He wanted recognition and promotion and the sooner the better. Besides, rounding up Jews, homosexuals and communists was far more entertaining and important than family feasts and presents.

Chapter 8

THE PLAY with the St Peter's Players was over and Louise threw herself into her studies. Her literature professor had a dry sense of humour.

'I must say, Miss Wellesley, you write as if you have first-hand knowledge of the Bard's characters. Are you perhaps a time traveller?'

'Thank you, Professor. Actually I *am* a time traveller but only every other Tuesday.'

He smiled, wrote *Outstanding work* in his flowery hand and returned the essay. 'Going home for Christmas?'

'Yes sir; and very much looking forward to seeing my family.'

'Well in-between the plum pudding and bonhomie you might try a little prep. Here is a list of reading material for next term.' He handed Louise a list of texts. Her eyes widened. University was demanding. Thank goodness she had nothing else on her plate.

Ah, not quite. She had yet to deal with Matty's future fiancé, the two-timing Welsh medical student. She still needed a plan to expose the rotter and save her friend.

Cycling through Cambridge she saw a notice in a shop window and the words *Lord Mayor* caught her eye. Wasn't fiend Gareth courting the Mayor's daughter?

The notice advised that this Saturday His Worship was to open a new infant welfare centre as part of the Cambridge Hospital. *Would his family be present? Would Gareth be there?* Louise suddenly had an idea. She cycled to Miss Finchley's. She beamed.

'My dear young lady, it's so lovely to see you. I can't tell you how many wonderful comments I've had about the play.'

Louise spoke clearly and with added volume. 'Thank you, Miss Finchley, but I actually wanted some help with a costume.'

'Oh how exciting. What's the play?'

'I'm giving a presentation in my literature class. Would you have anything Shakespearean I might borrow?'

'Of course I have. Follow me.'

Miss Finchley led Louise through the house. Dr Livingstone would have become lost here. They entered a room filled with costumes on racks. There were boxes with labels such as *Hats Gentlemen, Hats Ladies, Collars and Cuffs, Jewellery, Bow-ties* and *Ribbons*. It was an Aladdin's cave for a thespian.

'My goodness,' exclaimed Louise. 'What an amazing collection.'

'Now there's more in the spare room and outside in the garden shed.'

'I don't know where to start.'

'What's that, dear?'

'May I have a look for something suitable?'

'Of course. I'll pop the kettle on. You take what you like.'

Louise waded through the racks of dresses and found an ideal period piece. When she eventually found her way to the garden shed she discovered exactly what she wanted. She hid a pantomime outfit inside the large Elizabethan dress and went back inside.

Now while obtaining a costume was her primary goal, discovering anything about Tom came a very close second. Mr and Mrs Bird were neighbours. Locating the Bird house would be a start. No harm in asking about the supper couple.

Louise got chatting. 'You're so lucky to have neighbours like Mister and Missus Bird to help with the play group.'

It was a brilliant line, fishing at its finest. It was innocent and the perfect prompt for Miss Finchley. She would agree wholeheartedly then divulge the location of the Bird residence next door or across the road. That would mean Louise could think of some excuse to call on the Birds and hopefully discover something, anything about that fascinating man.

Louise expectantly awaited Miss Finchley's fulsome reply.

'What's that, dear?'

Oh well, at least Louise had her costume.

Mr Mayor, his wife and daughter discussed the forthcoming event.

'It's all right for you,' said Mrs Mayor, 'you have your robe and chain. I have to constantly come up with something suitable and new.'

'Suitable I understand but new?' groaned her husband.

'Oh, so you would enjoy reading that the wife of His Worship the Mayor wore a charming light blue suit with matching coat but the *same white hat and gloves she wore last month!*'

Mr Mayor shook his head; bloody women. His daughter, Miss Mayor, joined the fray.

'And Daddy, those new all-in-one trouser suits are just divine. I simply must have one.'

'Trousers!' Mr Mayor's colour matched his red robe. 'Ladies please, you are only required to stand quietly in the background while ...'

In parrot-fashion, the women completed his oft-made remark. 'I deliver my memorable speech.' His Worship was being mocked by his family—again. He fired back.

'At least Gareth Llewelyn, never fusses about his clothes.'

Miss Mayor replied. 'Yes but he's a man, Daddy.'

'Not quite, he's Welsh,' murmured Mrs Mayor, who was far from pleased with her daughter's beau. Mr Mayor rehearsed his speech.

When the official party arrived at the hospital, plastic smiles were in abundance. Mrs Mayor had reluctantly agreed to her current outfit on condition Mr Mayor subsidize her imminent visit to Cambridge's finest boutiques or one fine London establishment—he could choose.

Miss Mayor looked a picture of youthful femininity. Her partner, the dashing Welshman, Mr Gareth Llewelyn, was all teeth and tumbling locks. He was a cross between handsome and interesting and, years before graduation, had already perfected a seductive bedside manner.

The official opening of the new infant welfare centre was about to begin. Many new mothers with their offspring were present.

'My Lords, ladies and gentleman,' began the Mayor. This was wishful thinking. His Worship had long hoped he might one day receive *any* form of recognition from Buckingham Palace. That was never going to happen.

On and on he droned. A simple, "I declare the centre open" was out of the question. Mothers rocked their grizzly bubs. Many were thinking, *Come on, Sunshine; just cut the ruddy ribbon.*

Just as His Worship began to run low on pomposity, a disturbance began at the back. A mother with a pram pushed her way through the crowd. Other mothers moved to protect their precious infants.

Everyone turned to watch. His Worship moved from irritation to anger. *Latecomers! How dare you interrupt me! Don't you know who I am?* The photographer from the local paper awoke from his slumber.

The mother with the pram stopped in front of the Mayor. She was not your average Cambridge mummy. Her bobbing curls were blonde and she was dressed in the traditional costume of Wales—a cloak or bedgown, striped flannel underskirt and large black hat. But this was no eisteddfod nor was it St David's Day. The woman faced His Worship and waited for the stunned speaker and onlookers to fall silent.

Then in a voice which reeked and even leeked of the greenest Welsh valleys, she poured forth her woes.

'Oh Gareth,' she wailed. 'How could you? The babi is crying and wants his Tad. Come home, Gareth, come home to Wales. Llan Ffestiniog is calling!'

A Welsh male choir would have been the icing on the pathos cake.

The photographer snapped and snapped and snapped again.

His Worship suffered a near-fatal injury; he was rendered speechless. Mrs Mayor and Miss Mayor clung to one another for succour. Gareth Llewelyn was coming to the boil.

In his mind there was something about this woman. He'd heard her voice; but where? *Was it on the Cambridge road with a woman on a bicycle? No, she wasn't a blonde and certainly not with child.*

He stepped forward to denounce the Welsh mother. 'Who is this woman? I don't know her. I've never met this woman before, ever!'

These denials turned the spurned maiden into a bawling, blubbering Blodwyn. Her fit of the vapours incited the crowd.

A hospital official barked orders. Two kindly mothers moved to comfort their motherhood sister. The Mayor berated Gareth who gave as good as he got.

On cue, six babies bawled in sympathy with the abandoned bub in the Welsh ma's pram. The photographer felt pain in his clicking finger.

In short, the infant welfare centre opening was a circus and the local rag did very nicely out of their front page even garnering additional funds providing some London dailies with a scoop from the sticks.

In the hullabaloo, the Welsh mother, her pram and its contents—a doll as it happened—disappeared without trace as did the prospects of the Mayor's political fortunes and young Gareth's romance rating.

Oh dear.

Louise was brilliant as the unwed Welsh mother. Her audience believed that the Celtic bounder had lived up to his new name of Gareth the Bastard and had abandoned the poor girl and her bub.

Several events flowed from the incident. The press had a field day. Mr Mayor lost whatever slim chance he had of a gong. Mrs Mayor was stuck with the same wardrobe. Miss Mayor was looking for a new boyfriend and Gareth got his comeuppance in a way he could never have imagined.

Louise worried about being discovered. Unlike her role as the Frenchwoman, her Welsh mother routine was a very public performance.

She'd borrowed a blonde wig from a fellow student and the Little Red Riding Hood costume and doll came from the pantomime collection in Miss Finchley's garden shed.

The pram was a last-minute addition. Louise planned to carry the doll into the ceremony wrapped within her cloak. When she arrived there were empty prams the mothers left in the foyer. Louise helped herself.

Having the pram meant she parted the crowd with ease. Her speech over, Louise made a speedy exit, taking her "baby" and leaving the pram where she found it.

The photos in the local press concentrated on the apoplectic Mayor and his outraged entourage. The photos of the Welsh mother were dominated by her large black hat, her blonde curls, a large beauty spot, granny glasses and the tears and smudged make-up on her cheeks.

Nobody knew who she was but half of Llan Ffestiniog used up their annual gossip quota trying to identify the young lass who had strayed from the straight and narrow.

Louise waited a few days before returning the costumes to Miss Finchley. She arrived bearing chocolates and flowers and while the hard-of-hearing theatrical director popped the flowers in a vase and made some tea to have with the chocolates, Louise replaced the costumes.

Anna Walters, the student who supplied the blond wig, was thrilled to hear Louise had caught the bounder *in flagrante delicto* and Louise's invented tale was not all that far from the truth.

So her secret was safe but her problem remained. Matilda knew nothing of her two-timing future husband and Louise now had to tell Matty that Mr Wonderful was really Mr Woeful.

It was so hard being the bearer of bad news to someone you love. *Write that letter, Louise and do it now.*

But speaking of bad news, Louise was about to discover some of her own. As she tried to concentrate on her studies, Emily came into Louise's room holding a Cambridge newspaper.

'Louise, have you seen this?' Louise read the front page.

Cambridge Student Murdered

Cambridge University medical student, Mr Gareth Owen Llewelyn, was found dead last night by a man walking his dog beside the River Cam. Police suspect foul play.

Mr Llewelyn, from Abergavenny, Wales, was in the news last week when confronted by a Welsh woman at the opening of the new infant welfare centre.

Police have made no arrests but wish to interview two women who may be able to assist with their enquiries. The Welsh woman, pictured below, is a possible witness, as is a Frenchwoman wearing a beret and walking with a limp who was seen in Cambridge on the 14th of last month. Both women are asked to come forward.

The picture was definitely a disguised Louise Wellesley although only she could tell that. It was time to call on all her acting experience as she spoke. 'What an awful thing to happen to such a fine young man.'

'You knew him?' exclaimed Emily.

'No, no, no. It's just that he had his whole life ahead of him. And think about his poor family.'

Louise was performing with a new brilliance. Internally she was a mess. Externally she exuded calm.

She thought of Matty. *Perhaps I should tell her an edited version. What you don't know can't hurt you. Send a simple condolence card with no mention of the adventures of Casanova Llewelyn.*

But Louise's mind was in overdrive as she re-read certain sentences.

Police have made no arrests but wish to interview two women who may be able to assist with their enquiries.

Both women are asked to come forward.

That's me.

Chapter 9

WITH CHRISTMAS approaching, the St Peter's Players were preparing to stage a short nativity play and Miss Finchley asked Louise to take the role of Mary. The girl from Girton politely declined citing university commitments but suggested Molly and was delighted when the young woman accepted Miss Finchley's offer.

'It's the least I can do,' said Molly to Louise at a rehearsal. 'You stepped in for me and now I'm proud to step in for you.' Louise enjoyed seeing Molly getting stuck into life after her mother's death. Louise liked Molly but as with friend Emily, neither girl had anywhere near the get up and go of one Matilda Gonzales-Jones.

After Gareth's murder, Louise sent Matty a condolence card and a long letter about how dreadful the terrible murder was and how this fine young man had his life snatched away. Louise went on about how Matty should hold her head high, how life was too short to worry and all that "be positive" malarkey.

Being so far apart, Louise could only guess how distraught her friend might be. Then, on the day before Louise left for Surrey, a postcard arrived. She recognized Matty's handwriting.

> *Plenty more fish in the sea!*
> *Love*
> *Matty*
> *xxx*

Louise laughed out loud. Who else but Matilda would or could write a response like that?

Louise left a Christmas card and small gift on Emily's bed and went downstairs. She planned to catch the bus into Cambridge, pop into the Vestey home then catch the train to London. She rugged up well and was walking through the foyer when she heard a familiar voice.

'Taxi, Miss?' Louise smiled. Elizabeth Vestey walked towards her. 'We can't have Cambridge's leading actress slumming it on public transport. Your carriage awaits, Madame.'

Louise spent a lovely hour with Professor Vestey, Elizabeth and Molly. This family had played a significant role in her life. If she had to spend Christmas in Cambridge, Louise knew she would enjoy a grand time with these wonderful people.

But there was sadness in the room, it being the first Christmas without Molly's mother. Deceased loved ones are particularly missed on birthdays and at Christmas.

Louise found it natural to give Professor Vestey a hug as she left. Without his letter to her dear Papa, Louise would not be here. Elizabeth and Molly went to the station with Louise. They wanted her to spend Christmas with them. Their farewell was warm yet sad.

On the train Louise was thinking about three topics.

Her father was poorly and may be facing his last Christmas. The police wanted to talk to her about a murder. And Tom, nephew of the Cambridge Queen of Cakes, was often in her thoughts.

Her train pulled into St Pancras where brother number two was waiting. Louise was desperate for news of her father. Edmund was insensitive but never intentionally cruel. He called a spade a spade.

'Seriously Plum, I think the old man refuses to die until he sees his darling daughter happily married.'

Louise grimaced. It could well be an unusual Christmas.

Louise and Edmund arrived home to a sombre household. The patriarch was poorly. Victoria took control and led Louise towards the library.

'Your father's been asking all day when you'd arrive.' They stopped at the door and Victoria whispered. 'Don't be alarmed, my darling. Your Papa is growing old.'

That warning did little to prepare Louise for the shock of seeing her father. He'd lost weight, his eyes were sunken, his neck too small for his collar and his skin was pale and blotched. He sat in his wheelchair and despite obvious discomfort, smiled as he'd not done for months. Louise moved quickly to him. She was worried that too strong an embrace would possibly hurt or distress him. His feeble hands reached out to her.

'My darling girl, how wonderful to see you. Let me look at you. Yes, even more lovely and almost as beautiful as your mother.'

'It's wonderful to see you, Papa.'

That was all she was able to say as the tears flowed and she knelt beside him while he stroked her hair. Silence took over and lingered for some time before Victoria spoke.

'I think it's time for Papa to rest. You'll have lots of time to catch up over dinner.'

Louise stood, kissed her father's brow, squeezed his hand then left the room without looking back. She felt intensely sad.

Victoria smiled at her husband. 'You haven't looked so happy in ages. Your little girl's come home for Christmas.'

But it was a Christmas like no other. It takes patience and skill to successfully walk on eggshells.

Louise was desperate to talk to Henry about the Cambridge murder but chose to wait. Seeing her father dying reminded her of Molly Vestey's mother. If Louise had not gone to Cambridge she'd be in Molly's situation; living at home watching a dear parent slowly fade away.

The day before Christmas, Louise went to see Nightie. When she told him the saga with the St Peter's Players and the characters swapping accents, he laughed uproariously; and when she explained how she'd stepped in at the last moment and rescued the production, he applauded with gusto.

She gave a highly redacted version of her off-stage acting as both a French and a Welsh woman explaining the performances as being part of a drama exercise. Nightie's magnificent eyebrows came alive.

He asked about her studies and university life. Louise found it easy to talk to Nightie. He genuinely took an interest in her life but suddenly shocked her with a question.

'So, Miss Wellesley, tell me about your love life? Have you met the man of your dreams in historic Cambridge?' Louise was thrown and Nightie seized on her hesitation. 'Ah, I see that Cupid's arrow is in flight and the matter is, as yet, unresolved.'

Louise smiled and shook her head. 'You are a very interesting man, Mister Beauford Nightingale.'

'Flattery will get you everywhere, darling.'

'But I never saw you as a fortune-teller. How on Earth could you possibly know about my love life?'

Nightie smiled. 'It's observation, dear girl. The best actors look into their fellow actors' eyes, the window of the soul. When I mentioned romance, your heart beat faster and your eyes told me so. When you failed to elaborate, I deduced that things are still in a state of flux.'

'Well sir, on matters thespian, I willingly defer to your superb talent and generosity. But alas, in matters of the heart, I shall keep my own counsel.'

'Hmmm,' said Nightie. 'This sounds serious.' They laughed loud and long.

Back home Louise entertained her father with tales about her studies, fellow students, the Vesteys and Girton College. He loved hearing about the old buildings, the students on bicycles, the Dons, the pathways and even the *Keep Off the Grass* signs. Charles was now so proud his daughter had followed in his footsteps. His original objection was long forgotten.

Because of his failing health Charles and Louise spoke frankly as never before.

'And are you happy, my girl?'

'Papa, I am blissfully happy at Cambridge but desperately unhappy to see you so ill.'

'Ah, it's nothing but a cold,' he said feigning a cough. He smiled but they both knew his levity was postponing the truth. Louise took his hand.

'I would rather you spoke frankly, Papa. I think I can be brave if I know the truth.' He paused then nodded. 'Are you dying, Papa?'

Charles squeezed her hand. 'You've always been brave. Anyone who can sing and dance for old Uncle "Misery-Guts" Crispin deserves a medal.' They looked at one another then Charles accepted her challenge.

'I'm afraid, Miss Wellesley, your dear old Papa is not much longer for this world.' Louise gasped. Charles was upset. 'Oh, now look what I've done. I've frightened you.'

'No,' protested Louise. 'I want to know. And I've decided I won't return to Cambridge and leave you like this.'

Charles changed instantly. He found new strength. There was a sliver of anger in his voice. 'Now that is the most ridiculous thing I have ever heard. You fought tooth and nail to persuade me to let you go there and now you're turning it down?'

Louise looked at him. She remembered Nightie's words about the eyes being the window of the soul. Her father's eyes blazed with determination.

'Thank you,' she whispered and rested her head on his blanket.

Christmas lunch had its usual fine fare but everyone was sadly aware of the patriarch's poor health. Louise kept her family entertained with tales about her cycling expertise, her acting for the St Peter's Players, Miss Finchley's hearing and the comment *Outstanding work* scribbled on her essay.

But it was Henry who stole the show when he announced he'd met a girl. Everyone stopped eating. In a most unladylike performance Victoria dropped her dessert spoon.

'Well somebody say something,' protested Henry. 'Anyone'd think I'd just confessed to murder.'

Charles and Victoria were delighted, Edmund was surprised and Louise was desperate for details. But having spilled the beans, Henry retreated into his shell.

'Well at least tell us her name, Henry,' teased Louise. 'I hope it's not something awful like Hortense or Duplicitous.'

'Ask her to come down for the weekend,' said Victoria.

'Oh Mummy, please be sensible. With Father not well it's hardly fair on him or Georgina.'

'Ah, Georgina,' beamed Louise. 'I shall call her Georgie. But will I like her? Is she fun?'

Henry stalled. 'I think she's wonderful,' he said before taking another mouthful of plum pudding. There were smiles all round with Henry the last to join the laughter.

Henry's news was a welcome distraction from the wretched health of the head of the family. Louise was tempted to speak of her love interest then realised there was nothing to say.

But exciting news is difficult to hide so Louise decided to tell her mother about Tom. Mummy would know why Louise was thinking about him at odd times, frequently, every day.

Late that night the fire was dying and the men had retired. Henry was writing a letter to his lady love and Edmund had turned in ready for his ride with the local hunt on Boxing Day.

Louise said, 'How strange that Henry found it hard to tell us about Georgina.'

'No more strange than you not telling us your romantic news.'

Louise looked at her mother. How could she know? She couldn't. She was guessing, fishing. No, that wasn't Mummy. It was simply another example of their unique relationship. They both smiled and Louise drew a breath before opening her heart. She was about to speak when they heard a commotion. There were heavy footsteps in the hall and then Henry came racing into the room.

'It's Father. I think he's had a stroke!'

So much for the mother and daughter chat, Henry's love letter and Edmund's early night.

Waiting for an ambulance on Christmas night wasn't considered. Henry and Edmund carried their father to the family car. In the back, Louise and her mother sat either side of Charles with the two boys in the front. They drove as quickly and as carefully as possible having first telephoned the hospital.

Everything happened quickly. Charles went straight to emergency care. The family waited in a small room. Time dragged. They suspected Charles was dying but even with a warning, when that dreadful moment arrives, it's both painful and harsh. No-one wanted to say "Merry Christmas". Of course people died but on Christmas Day?

Eventually a nurse arrived. 'Mister Wellesley is resting and the doctor says you may visit him for a wee time.'

The family entered the room. Charles looked serene. Louise gasped when she first saw her father thinking he was dead. But her shock was even greater when the doctor standing beside the bed turned around.

She was staring at Tom, the nephew of the Cambridge Queen of Cakes. Louise was in unchartered waters. Different emotions roamed around inside her body.

Two hours ago she was about to tell her mother about a widower called Tom. Then her father's health crisis killed that conversation. Now she stood in a hospital room staring at that very same widower. She could hardly say, "Mummy, this is the man I wanted to tell you about, oh, and by the way, is Papa dying"?

There was a pause, that moment when people who have met, meet again. Tom smiled.

'Good evening, Miss Wellesley.'

'Good evening,' was the best Louise could muster. She was in shock and an actress without a voice is rare. Tom looked at Victoria.

'Missus Wellesley I presume. How do you do; I'm Doctor Curzon.'

'How do you do,' replied a stressed Victoria. 'These are my sons, Henry and Edmund.' All three men nodded. 'And I gather you've already met my daughter.'

'I have indeed had the great pleasure of seeing Miss Wellesley perform triumphantly upon the stage.' Victoria, ever elegant, wished to dispense with the niceties.

'Please, Doctor, how is my husband?'

'He's as comfortable as possible. I can let you stay for a short time and I'll be outside when you wish to speak to me.' And with a nod to Louise, Tom left the room.

The family surrounded the bed and gazed at the beloved patriarch.

'We're here, Papa,' said Louise leaning in and kissing her father. His eyes were open but barely moved.

Victoria adjusted the bedclothes a tiny amount. 'Rest, Charles. You are in the best of hands. And even your doctor is a great admirer of your daughter.'

A tiny movement of the patient's lips indicated he understood. There was no limit to his daughter's talents. Henry and Edmund each kissed their father then stepped back. Henry took Louise's arm and signalled to Edmund. The siblings left.

Outside, Tom was speaking to a patient in a wheelchair. Henry spoke softly. 'So, Plum, is there no end to your list of beaus?'

Louise was struggling. Her grief took over. 'Papa looks terrible. He looks like he's dying.'

'He *is* dying,' said Edmund. Henry and Louise wanted to rebuke their brother but knew he spoke the truth. They fell silent. What was the etiquette when waiting in a hospital with a loved family member at death's door?

Victoria joined them and daintily blew her nose. She wanted to cry but the presence of her children plus her upbringing kept her emotions in check. Tom approached them.

'Thank you for your kindness, Doctor,' began Victoria. 'My children and I would appreciate your frankness at this time.'

Tom smiled. It was a smile of friendship, of caring and sensitivity. 'Of course,' he said.

Henry was impatient. 'Has my father had a stroke?' The women cringed. Yes, they wanted the truth but please at least ask for information in a tactful way.

Louise knew Tom was sensitive. She was not surprised to learn that the man who impressed her greatly had devoted his life to caring for others.

'Yes,' began Tom. 'Mister Wellesley has had a stroke which makes speaking difficult.'

Edmund was his usual blunt self. 'Will he recover?'

Tom was calm. 'Possibly, over time; but I fear he has another problem.' The others held their breath. 'Mister Wellesley has contracted pneumonia and given his age and war wounds, then ...'

'How did you know about his war service?' asked Victoria. Even she had forgotten her basic manners.

69

'There are records of course but I was intrigued by the results of an x-ray we took. His pneumonia is quite pronounced but so too was a small piece of what I can only guess to be shrapnel in his abdomen.'

'He's had that inside him for twenty years,' murmured Henry.

'Perhaps longer,' added Tom.

'So what is the treatment for pneumonia?' asked Victoria.

'There are serums which have recently been developed in Germany and America but sadly with mixed results. We can of course keep Mister Wellesley comfortable and warm and provide pain relief whenever it is needed. He really is in the best place.'

Tom didn't mention a Scottish doctor currently working at St Mary's in London. The medical world had heard of his progress with a new drug he called penicillin. Dr Alexander Fleming was a brilliant scientist and this new drug would one day help patients with diseases including pneumonia.

Louise was anxious. 'Is there another drug, another treatment you could try?'

Tom paused. He looked at Louise. 'I wish I could be more optimistic. And you're welcome to have another doctor examine Mister Wellesley. We can help him rest and remain as pain-free as possible but I think you should prepare for the worst.'

That killed any conversation. Silence dominated. It's not every day you're told your husband or father is about to die. Finally Victoria asked what nobody wanted to ask.

'In your opinion, Doctor Curzon, how much time does my husband have? Will he die tonight?'

Tom paused. 'I never like to answer that question.'

Louise spoke up. She placed her hand on Tom's arm. 'I think we would all like to know your opinion ... please.'

How could Tom refuse? He spoke calmly.

'Mister Wellesley's lungs are infected. If this infection progresses, he will have difficulty breathing and his blood flow will be restricted. I think he has days rather than weeks but doctors are only human and we've been wrong before.'

'I would like to stay, Mummy' said Louise. 'It's Christmas and the thought that Papa might die without any of his family by his side is unthinkable.'

'Thank you, darling,' said Victoria.

'I'll stay,' said Henry. 'Eddie and I can take it in turns and you ladies can come back in the morning.'

'I'm staying,' said Louise in a quiet, determined voice. 'You boys take Mummy home and come back after you've had some rest.'

Victoria was struggling. 'Louise, I'm not sure ...'

'Mummy, I've been away from home for months. Papa wants to know about all the things I've been doing.'

Victoria was never so proud of her daughter and nodded then turned to Tom.

'Doctor Curzon, might I prevail upon you to keep an eye on my daughter as well as my husband?'

'Of course, Missus Wellesley, and if there's any change with Mister Wellesley, I'll telephone immediately.'

And with that, the family went in to say goodnight to Charles who seemed at peace. Louise kissed her mother and brothers who left. She pulled up a chair and sat beside her father. Tom came in with a couple of cushions. Louise was more than grateful.

Tom spoke quietly. 'I'll just be outside. Call me for any reason. Goodnight.'

He smiled and she smiled and their eyes meet and they held each other's gaze. Tom broke the spell and quietly left. Louise looked at her beloved father then moved in close to him. She kissed him then whispered in his ear.

'Papa, have I told you about the man I'm going to marry?'

Charles sighed.

Tom was right about his patient. Fleming's new wonder drug, penicillin, was just around the corner. But Charles succumbed to pneumonia the day after Boxing Day. His wife and children were by his side. The children kissed their father and left Victoria alone with her husband. She spoke from the heart.

'Charles Wellesley, you have made me the happiest wife in Christendom. In all the years we've been together, I would change nothing. Do you hear? Nothing. Your children adore you and rightly so. I've always loved you and will go on loving you until I breathe my last. Thank you, my darling man ... thank you.'

Her tears flowed freely. She ignored them, squeezed his hand and cried the more.

The funeral was impressive. Victoria wanted something simple because she knew Charles would hate fuss. But former comrades in arms would never allow a fallen soldier to be buried without their solemn attendance. Folk from near and far remembered a kind and generous solicitor who freely gave advice to anyone in need and failed to send accounts to those who struggled. Charles was respected or loved or both. There was no way this was going to be a small funeral.

Asking the aristocratic older brother to attend his younger brother's funeral was never an option. Crispin was now the recluse of the century.

The vicar had known the family for decades and could genuinely speak about Charles. Henry was to speak on behalf of the family. The arrangements fell into place until Louise asked if she could speak.

'Please, Mummy,' said Louise.

'I'm not sure my darling,' was Victoria's gentle reply.

'Men's business, Plum, old girl,' said Henry.

71

Louise paused. She had her mother's wisdom and was learning how to win an argument.

'Do you think Papa would want me to tell the world just how wonderful a father he was to his only daughter?'

Rhetorical questions are rarely subtle. Edmund cracked first.

'Oh come on, in for a penny. Father allowed Plum to break all the family traditions, to go off to Roedean, to turn her back on the marriage market and trot off to Cambridge. Surely he wouldn't stand in the way of his darling "gel" popping into the pulpit.'

'And we know she can speak better than any of us,' added Henry. 'She's clearly the finest actress in the country.'

Louise was stunned. The old-boys' club, of which her brothers were life members, was in disarray. Victoria saw the cause was lost.

'I'm not sure what the world is coming to,' said the head-shaking widow.

Edmund sealed the deal. 'I think the old man'll be seriously chuffed to hear what Plum has to say.'

And so it was that Louise Wellesley spoke at her father's funeral. The church was packed. In the porch and even outside, the overflow crowd stamped their feet and blew steam on the cold January morning.

Louise had never prepared as well as she did for this service. She wrote her speech, polished it and knew it by heart. But she couldn't control emotion and had no idea how she would react standing beside the coffin. Knowing her script was one thing; being able to control her feelings was something else. On stage she had to pretend to be angry or sad or afraid. Here she wasn't acting. She prayed she wouldn't disappoint her family and especially her father.

The Wellesley family arrived together, entered via a side door and sat in a front pew. This wasn't an occasion to look around and wave to your chums. Louise had no idea who was present. Then from the pulpit she looked out at a sea of faces.

The Vestey family, the Professor, Elizabeth and Molly were there. Fellow-student Emily had come from Scotland. Nightie was there with members of the play-reading group. Some girls she knew at Roedean were there. The Rev Stanley Tripe from Chawton and Miss Finchley from St Peter's were there and seated beside the theatre director was Tom. Doctor Thomas Curzon was dressed in a black suit with a white shirt, black tie and black overcoat.

Louise had never been in such a play as this. There were distractions galore. She could see the faces of the people in the audience. Her mind was filled with many thoughts. Nightie's face shone with expectation and love. It was her cue and with a gentle nod towards her father's coffin, Louise gave the performance of her life. There was no acting technique. This was a performance from and of the heart.

When the service ended and the coffin was carried down the aisle, Louise took Edmund's arm and followed her mother who took Henry's arm. They moved to the churchyard. The gravedigger took ages to dig the grave and even broke a pick-handle attacking the frozen ground.

Louise was concerned her Papa would be cold and wished he had died in the summer. Then she wished he hadn't died at all and she could invite him to see her perform on a West End stage and have him give her away when she married Tom and then show Papa her first child, a boy called Charles. Louise wept without restraint.

She recovered at the wake. It was mainly a temperate affair with tea, sandwiches, cakes and crackling fires.

Louise was overcome to see the Vesteys. They knew exactly how she was feeling. Emily was a saint and Nightie squeezed her arm. 'You made an old actor very proud, dear girl. God bless.' He kissed her and went in search of more sherry.

Louise felt tired having spoken to people she knew, didn't know and thought she knew. Then it happened just like the first time.

'I can recommend the cakes.' Louise turned to see Tom holding a plate. 'Courtesy of Miss Finchley, they come from the kitchen of the Cambridge Queen.'

Louise was struggling to speak. What was the power this man had to command the actress to fall silent? Her grief mingled with her romantic emotions. Finally she spoke. 'Thank you for everything, Doctor Curzon. You've been simply wonderful.'

'Doctor Curzon? All my friends call me Tom and we are friends are we not?' Louise smiled. Silly question. 'I'm sorry I never got to know your father. He must have been a remarkable man.'

That was the tipping point; her father's death, his funeral, her family and friends and now Tom. Suddenly Louise wanted to cry. Tom saw her distress. He put the cakes aside, gently took her arm and helped her to sit. He brought another chair close and sat facing her. Louise couldn't stop the tears. Tom placed his handkerchief in her hands and she pressed it to her face. Finally she recovered, felt foolish and offered the handkerchief to Tom.' He spoke.

'The tears of the famous actress; I shall sleep with them under my pillow.' She smiled. 'Perhaps some fresh air might help.'

They went into the hallway. Louise was nervous. She'd thought about this man for weeks and imagined the sorts of things she might say. Now, when she had the chance, her mind and tongue refused to co-operate.

'Louise,' said Tom, who himself was nervous; 'I know this is not the right time but I've long wanted to say something to you.'

Louise was suddenly alert. Her grief was real but something else had crept in and it definitely wasn't sadness.

'Please don't be embarrassed but ever since we met back in Cambridge, oh about ...'

'Six weeks and two days ago,' Louise said quickly.

They looked at one another. Both wanted to speak. Tom paused. He hoped his words would come out the right way.

'I've wanted to tell you that since we met, all those weeks ago, I haven't been able to get you ...'

Suddenly the front door slammed and a shriek was heard. It sounded like a person who didn't know how to behave at a funeral. It was a person who wore their heart upon their sleeve.

Matilda Gonzales-Jones was wearing the largest fur hat and the most stunning fur coat Louise had ever seen. The two women froze then ran at full pelt towards one another. They hugged, kissed and cried.

Victoria and her sons came into the hall as Louise greeted her long-lost pal and, after pausing, Tom quietly slipped away.

Late that night it was just like old times as Louise and Matty shared a room. There was no climbing out of the window for a midnight frolic but the all-night banter was in fine form when suddenly the chatterboxes were interrupted by a quiet tapping on the bedroom door. Immediate silence. Victoria's head appeared.

'I'm so sorry, Mummy.' Matty added her apology.

'No Missus Wellesley, it's my fault. I should have the decency to show respect for your late husband. Please forgive me.'

Victoria wasn't angry. 'Goodness I wasn't thinking of that for a moment. Of course I know you mean no disrespect. But it's so late and you both have packing and travel plans in the morning. Your father would expect you to be ready for the new term, my dear.'

'Sorry, Mummy, but ...'

'I know, you've got so much to catch up on.' Victoria started to leave. 'Oh and it's lovely to hear some laughter in the house again. Goodnight.'

The young women chorused "goodnight" and made faces. Louise whispered. 'Now tell me the real story about your late-lamented lover.'

'I've told you; it's all water under the bridge, he got what he deserved.' Louise wanted more so Matty continued. 'Look, his mother and mine go way back and they fixed the whole thing. Still, he's no longer on the scene.' There was a pause and Matty stared at Louise. 'What?'

'There's something I need to tell you,' said Louise.

And she did. It took a pretty good yarn to render the garrulous Matty speechless but mute she was. Louise described the bicycle tumble, the rude car occupants, the limping Frenchwoman, the unwed Welsh mother and the tales of Gareth's philandering. When Louise produced the newspaper report about the police looking for two women, Matty's eyes grew bigger. She looked at her friend.

'Say nothing,' said Matty.

Louise was stunned. 'Nothing?'

'You had nothing to do with his murder.'

'Matty,' said Louise in an angry whisper. 'Of course I had nothing to do with it.' Matty held up her hand stopping Louise in her tracks.

'But I know who did.'

Louise was poleaxed. 'What?'

'I have a Welsh friend, Carwen Hughes. We lost contact when I moved to Spain but caught up last year and Carwen told me she loved Gareth.'

'Don't tell me. He seduced her too.'

'Are you psychic?'

'And she was pregnant?'

'No, no, just devastated.'

'Matty, how could you marry a man like that?'

'Oh, Louise. We both know that money makes the world go round.'

'Money!'

'Families have always arranged marriages. Gareth's family owns half of South Wales. Add those to my father's Spanish estates and you've got a marriage made in Threadneedle Street.'

Louise shook her head. She knew about arranged marriages but couldn't believe Matty would marry a brute she didn't love.

'But what about Gareth's murder?' asked Louise.

'I'm coming to that. When Carwen's father heard Gareth had deflowered his daughter, he had his three rugby-playing sons kick Gareth into touch with touch being the River Cam.'

'They murdered Gareth because he seduced their sister?'

Matty shrugged. Louise stared at her. It was hard to sleep that night. Next morning feelings were muted. Their farewells were affectionate but restrained. Edmund drove Matty to the station. Girton beckoned for Louise. It was sad and strange not having her father at home to say goodbye. Her brothers travelled up to London with her but from there she journeyed alone.

It was wonderful to find the cockney cabbie and Molly waiting at Cambridge. The three women went to the Vestey home for tea.

'You spoke so well at the funeral,' said Molly. 'Your dear father would have been so proud.' Tears welled in Louise's eyes. Molly was upset but Louise waved her away.

'Please, I'm okay.' She wiped her eyes. 'It's funny. I was fine during the funeral but afterwards it really hit me. And just now I can see Papa as if he were here in this room.'

'More tea, Miss Wellesley?' said Elizabeth lifting the pot. 'And I must say we've all missed you terribly.'

'Hear, hear,' said Molly.

Elizabeth drove Louise out to Girton. She climbed the stairs and was unpacking when Emily burst in.

'Louise, did you see them?'

'See who?'

'The police; they've just arrested that second-year girl, Anna Walters.'

'Arrested her?'

'Yes, for the murder of that Cambridge medical student.'

Anna owned the blonde wig Louise wore to the hospital.

Chapter 10

A WEEK AFTER Louise and her family buried their beloved patriarch, Kurt Hartmann was called to a special Gestapo meeting. Germany was to annexe Austria making it part of the Third Reich.

'We're sending you to Vienna, Hartmann. You'll deal with the Jews.'

Kurt was thrilled. His early concerns about Gestapo tactics were long forgotten. He was now a firm believer in Nazi policy and desperate to please his superiors. Harassing, arresting and deporting Jews had become his favourite job. The fact that an Austrian holiday was part of the deal made the posting even better.

Needless to say Austrian Jews didn't share Kurt's enthusiasm. Stories of Jews being brutalized in Germany had crossed borders. The annexation may have been good news for some Austrians but it was a potential death sentence for others. Kurt simply saw this task as a chance to boost his profile. He craved positive publicity.

He arrived in Vienna and demanded Jewish business owners tell the world they were Jewish and close their shops whenever requested.

Kurt dragged an elderly tailor into the street and stood over the man as he painted *JEW* in large letters on his front window. A tailor of distinction, a hard-working Austrian grandfather with ancestors going back several generations was branded because of his birth.

Kurt was not satisfied with the size of the letters. 'Larger, make the bloody letters larger,' he yelled punching the tailor in the back.

Once the word was painted, Kurt spoke to an Austrian policeman. 'Stand by the door and eyeball anyone who wants to enter. No need for any violence. We'll starve the Jew of any trade and see how he likes that.'

Job done, Kurt set off for his next little Jewish *tête-à-tête*.

Cousin Max was progressing too now moving in exalted circles. His promotion to the rank of Colonel meant he had access to planning meetings with some of the Wehrmacht's most senior ranks. Today he was listening to a lecture given by a Generalleutnant.

'Gentlemen, today's warfare involves tanks, armoured vehicles, mobile infantry and the Luftwaffe all working as one.' The high-ranking officer was an evangelist and Max was hooked. 'We will perfect the art of lightning war and this tactic will wreak havoc on our enemies.'

I believe you, thought Max. The Generalleutnant continued.

'Lightning war means you move and keep moving at speed. You strike with might then leave to hit the next target while the enemy is still in bed. You give them the best wake-up call, ever!'

The officers laughed, their excitement contagious. Max felt powerful. So did his cousin Kurt but for different reasons.

In Vienna, Kurt stood amongst a huge crowd as Hitler arrived in an open-topped car. Delighted Austrians waved flags. Hitler waved back. It was spontaneous. After all, Adolf was an Austrian old boy coming home.

Kurt's assignment in Austria went well but he wanted new challenges. Back in Berlin he reported for his next assignment.

'I'm happy to serve wherever I'm needed, Herr Direktor.'

Heinrich "Gestapo" Müller wasn't impressed by sycophants. 'Hartmann we are about to liberate the German people in Czechoslovakia.'

Kurt was buzzing. Join the Gestapo and see the world. He was ready for any challenge. Austria, Czechoslovakia, anywhere. But suddenly he got bad news. His next task had no foreign travel.

He wasn't expecting this assignment. He wanted to say, *You want me to do what? That's not a promotion.* It sounded almost boring but Kurt could never imagine his new task would create headlines around the world. He listened to his commanding officer.

'Liberating our own people in foreign countries is one thing but here in Germany, not only are we overcrowded with German Jews, we even have hordes of Polish Jews. It's time they left. I don't care how you do it, Hartmann, but within weeks I don't want a single Polish Jew in Germany. Do I make myself clear?'

'Perfectly, Herr Direktor.'

'Heil Hitler.'

Kurt returned the salute. He considered the benefits of his new task. In Vienna he'd been responsible for small parts of the city. Now he was to be responsible for the whole of Germany. What a chance to outdo his fellow Gestapo agents and impress his superiors.

It would be easy to locate most of the Polish Jews in Germany. Many lived in the same cities and suburbs. For them trouble was brewing; their worst nightmare was about to become real.

Of course deportation was terrible but surely their homeland would welcome them back. Alas, no. Germany told them to "get out" and Poland told them to "keep out". Kurt couldn't care less.

When he was given the task of ridding Germany of its Polish Jews, *precision* became his byword. His planning was fanatical. Many in the Gestapo noted this. The slave-driver ruleth.

In 1938 every Polish Jew in Germany was paranoid.

If Kurt knew of this fear, he would have been dissatisfied. It wasn't enough. Having Jews afraid was good but having them dead or deported was better. The campaign to remove Germany's Polish Jews was ready to roll with Kurt Hartmann the man in charge.

Chapter 11

LOUISE WAS UNDER pressure. Things were getting out of hand. She couldn't hide her involvement any longer. It was time to confess. She decided to tell the police everything. She had nothing to do with Gareth's death but her conscience demanded she tell all.

Elizabeth was the only person she trusted. Louise told her everything and so the two women found themselves in the Cambridge police station seated opposite a smiling Inspector Williams. He was middle-aged, middleweight, middle class and of middling intelligence.

'Ladies, I believe you have some information about the death of Mister Gareth Llewelyn.'

'We do, Inspector,' said Louise, 'I'm the two women you are seeking; French and Welsh.'

That certainly got his attention and off she went. Inspector Williams had never heard anything like it. When Louise finished he sat there with mouth open. He paused. Did he think this was a joke?

Elizabeth Vestey came to Louise's defence. 'I can vouch for everything Miss Wellesley has said, Inspector. I taught this young lady at Roedean and can assure you she comes from an outstanding family.'

'Thank you, madam.' He smiled at Louise. He couldn't be angry, he was smiling. But did he believe her? 'Tell me, Miss Wellesley, have you ever auditioned for the Arts Theatre here in town?'

Louise was stunned. *What about Gareth's murder? What about my confession?* 'Ah, no, Inspector, I haven't.'

'Opened a couple of years ago, financed by Mister Keynes, that economist chap. The wife dragged me along last month. Damn fine show it was too.' He stood. Surprised, the women stood too. 'Well thank you for your most interesting tales and you can safely leave the police work to us.' *Was that it?* 'And I look forward to seeing you on stage Miss Wellesley. Jolly good luck to you.'

Non-plussed, the women walked to the Vestey residence. That was not the expected outcome. They agreed a pact of silence.

Louise was glad she'd finally come clean. If Anna, the girl who owned the blonde wig was involved in Gareth's murder, then there was nothing more Louise could say or do.

She threw herself into her studies but missed performing and thought about joining the St Peter's Players as a way of making contact with Tom. *What was he about to say to me at Papa's funeral?* But all that had to wait. She'd been given the chance to study at Cambridge and was determined to succeed.

Mind you, when Elizabeth sent a note about attending a matinee at the Arts Theatre next Saturday, Louise jumped at the chance. And oh what a change it was from the church hall and the St Peter's Players.

The repertory theatre at 6 St Edward's Passage had a narrow almost plain frontage but my, what a theatre lay inside. There were hundreds of plush seats in a magnificently raked auditorium. The proud stage seemed to be calling to actors, singers and dancers. Louise was like a child in a sweet shop.

The play was good but the venue and atmosphere sent shivers down her spine. Inspector Williams and Elizabeth had thrown out the bait. Were they a part of some conspiracy?

Coming out of the *Ladies* Louise bumped into a young woman, the Mayor's daughter, looking as if the whole world knew she'd been humiliated by a dead Welshman.

The women's eyes met and for a second they knew they were not strangers. Miss Mayor was sure she was looking at ... no, it couldn't be.

Back at Girton, Louise went to enquire about Anna of wig-borrowing fame. She was in her room and free as a bird.

Anna knew of Gareth the Cad and, after his murder, made some silly remarks about him getting his just deserts. These were reported to the police who took Anna in for questioning. But with a solid alibi for the night in question she was soon released without charge.

Louise was hoping Gareth's murder would be solved quickly and her secret performing life forgotten. Little did she know the murderer would soon be holding her hand.

The Lent Term ended, Louise went home for Easter and really enjoyed sleeping in her own bed. The sadness of the patriarch's death was slowly fading. Louise enjoyed being with her mother and brothers. She talked non-stop leaving out the secret bits but prodded the others for their news.

'Georgina's arriving tomorrow,' said Henry.

'At last,' said Louise. 'We'll have some good old-fashioned girls' gossip. And what about you, Eddie; when shall we meet your latest sweetheart?'

Henry laughed and Edmund shook his head. 'Confirmed bachelor, old girl; I'll leave the marrying to you and Henry.'

They went to take coffee in the sitting-room and Louise got a strange expression from her mother.

Henry's intended, Georgina, was perfectly polite, pretty and possibly the world's most boring person. Louise was lumbered with a ventriloquist's doll. If you saw a photograph of Georgina you might be impressed by her femininity and deportment. Some might call her beautiful. But if you met her and she opened her mouth you might be almost alarmed.

Louise was keen to speak. 'Now, Georgie, would you like to hear about Henry's bad habits or his *really* bad habits?' Louise had a twinkle in her eye. Georgina didn't do twinkle.

'Oh I cannot believe Henry would ever behave in an ungentlemanly manner. And please, my name is Georgina, Miss Wellesley.'

Miss Wellesley? Georgina was born years after Queen Victoria died but was clearly living in the last century.

She changed the luncheon mood. Jokes and teasing vanished. Henry discussed the weather. Victoria took the hint and added refined sentences on the early arrival of daffodils. Louise despaired.

Georgina said, "Thank you" twice and Edmund called his sister Louise. Why do people change when a stranger enters their midst? Louise wanted to scream. *My name is Plum!*

After luncheon Louise found her mother alone and reading a letter.

'Mummy, what's going on? Georgina's an absolute drip.'

'Shhhh, keep your voice down.'

Louise whispered. 'Oh Mummy, Henry's made a terrible mistake.'

'Calm yourself, my darling.'

'You cannot allow him to throw away his life by marrying that nineteenth century figurine.'

'Her father's a judge.'

Louise was struck dumb. She wanted to make some derogatory comment but simply shook her head. She thought of Matty agreeing to marry Gareth to combine vast estates in Wales and Spain. Was this the same thing with Henry marrying Georgina to further his legal career? Victoria continued.

'And don't forget your brother will one day inherit the title from your Uncle Crispin. Henry too is a good catch.'

Louise fell back in her chair. *Am I in the wrong world? Do my feelings for Tom count for anything? Was love ever a part of marriage?* But if Louise felt awful now, she was about to feel much worse.

Victoria picked up her letter. 'Do you remember Sir Anthony Wilding? He was a very good friend of your Papa's.' Louise was suddenly worried. 'Sir Anthony and his sister have invited me to stay with them in Wiltshire for a week or two. I think it'll be good for me to have a break.'

Louise remembered Sir Anthony as a kind man who was as dull as ditch water. He spoke to children as if they were simpletons. Why was her mother accepting an invitation from this man? Victoria continued.

'Oh and another thing, my darling; please don't tease dear Edmund about his latest lady friend. Let him live his life the way he chooses.'

Louise was stunned. *Does Mummy have an admirer and is Edmund homosexual?*

It was a difficult time and Louise returned to Cambridge as soon as possible. With her mentor driving her from the station, Louise opened up to Elizabeth about her domestic news. Once she'd let it all out, Elizabeth responded.

'I do believe, Miss Wellesley, it's time to put your head down and concentrate on those studies.'

'Thank you, Miss Vestey. Goodness, I nearly called you Elizabeth.' They both laughed. Elizabeth continued.

'Of course, in-between your studies, you might care to attend a play audition.'

Louise was immediately interested but chose the polite reply. 'Thank you, again, but I really don't think the St Peter's Players and the wonderful Miss Finchley are really my cup of tea.'

'Who said anything about Miss Finchley?' Louise looked at Elizabeth. 'There are open auditions next week at the Arts Theatre and I've booked you in on Wednesday at 3.'

Louise squealed and grabbed Elizabeth's arm. She took fright and the car swerved then suddenly stopped. Both women were momentarily afraid. They recovered quickly, smiled then laughed. Plum was buzzing with excitement.

Louise couldn't sleep the night before the audition. This was a professional theatre company. *Could I get a part? If I do, how will that affect my studies?* On the day of the audition Elizabeth drove Louise into Cambridge.

They walked to the stage door. Inside a man crossed off Louise's name. The two women sat and waited.

Suddenly they heard sounds coming from the theatre then a young woman burst out in floods of tears. Louise and Elizabeth exchanged glances.

'You're on, Miss,' said the man. Elizabeth squeezed Louise's arm then the actress walked into the theatre. The stage was well lit but the auditorium was dark. An unseen man called from the rear.

'Downstage centre, face front and speak up.'

Louise moved confidently DC, turned, looked out into the darkness and paused. It was the count, the beats before she began which gave her an edge. She built anticipation and kept them waiting just enough before becoming Juliet and reciting her favourite Shakespearean speech.

> O Romeo, Romeo! wherefore art thou Romeo?
> Deny thy father and refuse thy name;
> Or, if thou wilt not, be but sworn my love,
> And I'll no longer be a Capulet.
>
> 'Tis but thy name that is my enemy;
> Thou art thyself, though not a Montague.
> What's Montague? it is nor hand, nor foot,
> Nor arm, nor face, nor any other part
> Belonging to a man. O, be some other name!
> What's in a name? that which we call a rose

By any other name would smell as sweet;
So Romeo would, were he not Romeo call'd,
Retain that dear perfection which he owes
Without that title. Romeo, doff thy name,
And for that name which is no part of thee
Take all myself.

Silence lingered. Then murmurings came from the back of the stalls. *Do they want more; something else perhaps?* Then a woman called.

'Do you have an Equity card?' Louise froze.

'No, not yet,' said Louise, dying inside.

She could hear the man speaking to the woman.

'There are exceptions in some regional theatres. They start then get their card later.'

The woman walked from the back of the theatre and onto the stage. 'Hello, I'm Laura. Relax it's all over. You did very well.'

Louise felt fantastic then terrible with Laura's next question.

'How can you work in rep when studying fulltime at the University?'

Louise replied. 'There are the holidays and I'm lucky to have an understanding professor who loves the theatre.'

'Good answer,' said Laura extending her hand. 'Welcome to the Arts Theatre.'

The next few minutes were a whirl. Louise was given a contract, told to take it home and read it, then, if happy, sign it and return it tomorrow. If she didn't have an agent, she was advised to get one. And she was told that union membership was essential. A contract? An agent? Equity? She suddenly felt giddy and light-headed. Laura was worried.

'Are you okay?' Louise wasn't. 'John,' called Laura and the man sprinted from the back of the theatre, leapt onto the stage and he and Laura caught Louise just as she fainted. Had it been a scene in a melodrama, the audience might have swooned.

Elizabeth was summoned and entered in trepidation. When Louise recovered, the two old Roedeanians strode out into the Cambridge sunshine, stopped and looked at one another. They hugged then, holding hands, skipped around in a circle. Locals going about their business stopped and stared. It was some celebration.

Many moons ago Dr Tom Curzon left the Wellesley home with mixed emotions. He was pleased he spoke with the young woman who had occupied his thinking ever since he first saw her on stage in Cambridge. He found her intoxicating.

He was disappointed his speech at the funeral wake had been interrupted and wondered if he should have stayed and tried again. But funerals are a time for grieving and trying to woo the daughter of the deceased at such a time was hardly gentlemanly behaviour.

He thought about Louise and his work. He thought about his promise to his late wife. As young medical missionaries—he a doctor and she a nurse—they went to Africa to serve the sick. His wife contracted malaria and died in his arms. At the time Tom made her a promise that he would dedicate his life to help those in need.

Back in England Tom worked as a doctor in Surrey. It was serendipitous, although a very sad occasion, that he again made contact with the young woman he so admired.

Tom decided to tell Louise she'd made a lasting impression on him but when his speech was interrupted, he withdrew.

Sir Francis Drake got an attack of nerves when trying to woo Queen Elizabeth, and she, annoyed, had a window etched with the words, *Faint heart never won fair lady.* Sir Francis and Dr Curzon were like two peas in a pod.

Tom thought about writing to Louise but didn't. In the summer he went to Cambridge for a weekend with his aunt and uncle.

They were delighted to see him and made the usual fuss. Tom could hardly wait to ask about the St Peter's Players and a certain young actress. He didn't need to weave Louise into the conversation as his aunt did it for him.

'Do you remember Louise Wellesley, the young girl who performed for the Players last year?'

Tom was no actor. He pretended, badly. 'I think I do.'

'You think?' queried George. 'Good lord man, she was such a bonny lass you'd have to be blind not to remember her.'

'You're right,' smiled Tom. 'I do.'

'She's in a play this weekend,' said Marjorie.

'Well I guess I should come and support the Players; oh and of course to enjoy your delicious cakes, Auntie Marj.'

'She won't be at the church,' said his aunt. 'She's in a professional play in the new Arts Theatre in town.'

Tom was thrilled. He drove his aunt and uncle to the theatre. He perused the programme and found the photo of Miss Louise Wellesley. She looked enchanting. She was to play the role of The Maid. It was one of those linking parts, a role where there are enough words and bits of business to fail but not enough to shine. Louise's diction and humility were perfect and Tom, obviously biased, thought she was a star.

She was the least experienced but looked right at home. At the final curtain Tom applauded The Maid with pride.

The Birds and Tom gathered in the foyer and his aunt got chatting with Cambridge folk. Tom re-read his programme and looked around waiting for Louise to appear. George nudged him.

'She won't come out here, young man. You need to go round to the stage door. We'll be chatting a while yet,' he said and winked.

Tom smiled and left. He walked towards the sign *Stage Door* where several patrons were gathered. Some actors emerged and were greeted by friends or autograph hunters.

Tom grew anxious. Then Louise appeared and looked around. Tom tried to make eye contact. He raised a hand and waited for her response. Suddenly two women stepped in-between him and Louise. Elizabeth and Molly embraced the actress and arm-in-arm the trio walked away and Tom did a Francis Drake all over again.

Life changed for Louise. She loved her mother and brothers but, as often happens, people grow older and drift apart; even close family members. When the academic year ended and her brief professional play season finished in the summer of 1938, Louise was not keen to return to Surrey but she did.

It would be unkind to describe the family home as a morgue but Louise thought it so. She was even reluctant to tell her family about her new acting career, such as it was.

The worst news was that various people were coming to stay next week. Henry would bring his beloved Georgina, Sir Anthony Wilding would reside in Farnham but dine with the Wellesleys, Edmund would be back on deck and James "Pongo" Fingleton would be there for the weekend.

That was the final straw. 'Why on earth is Pongo coming?' asked Louise.

'Something to do with the bridal party,' replied Victoria. 'I gather James and Edmund will be best man and groomsman at Henry's wedding.'

Louise was depressed; Georgina the China Doll and Pongo the Lapdog together with Mummy's admirer, Prince Albert, were to be house guests. How long are the summer hols?

At least Louise had Nightie to visit. They talked theatre for hours until Louise saw the time.

'Oh my lord, Mother will not be pleased.'

Now if time flies when you're having fun, it positively dawdles when you're bored. Louise had the slowest summer of her life.

Sir Anthony was a relic of the Victorian era. Louise's mother was his Queen Victoria and he worshipped her. Surely they would never marry.

Henry and Georgina were to announce their engagement in the autumn and marry next summer and Georgina continued her muted doormat role to perfection. At least Pongo drew out some of Henry's old humour and Edmund managed to call Louise Plum. That caused Sir Anthony to awake from his slumber.

'I say, my hearing's not so good but I'm sure I heard you call your dear sister, Plum.'

'It's a family joke, Anthony,' said Victoria in such a way as to end the subject.

Doddery Sir Anthony would have none of that. 'A family joke? I say, do tell,' he replied.

Victoria rolled her eyes and Edmund began.

'When we were young, Sir Anthony, Father took his sons to watch Surrey play at The Oval.

'Cricket, hey. I could never understand the jolly game.'

'When a batsman was given out leg before wicket, Father and some of his cricketing chums would say, "That was plumb" and we boys took the expression to heart.'

Henry took over. 'It meant the ball was on a straight line as in a plumb bob and the batsman was definitely out.'

'I'm afraid I don't follow,' said Sir Anthony.

'They haven't finished, Sir Anthony,' said Louise.

'Might we talk about something else?' pleaded Victoria.

'Nearly finished, Mummy,' said Edmund.

'But as young boys,' continued Henry, 'we thought the cricketing experts said *plum* as in the fruit when in fact they said *plumb* as in plumb bob.'

Edmund set up the punchline. 'And when baby sister Louise was born, her christening gown was embroidered with her initials. Louise Beatrice Wellesley became L B W.'

Henry delivered the tag. 'And so we young cricket lovers saw those initials as Leg Before Wicket and called our baby sister, Plum.'

'Without the b,' added Louise.

'By jove,' said Sir Anthony and then lost all interest in the subject. Georgina was convinced insanity ran in the Wellesley family.

The next morning, the next day, the next week and month were all the same. Going to play-readings with Nightie and his group brought blessed relief but when the opportunity arose to return to Cambridge a few days before the new term, Louise took full advantage.

On the Cambridge platform, when looking for Elizabeth, Louise bumped into a young man. She knew his face. He knew hers and spoke.

'I know you. You're the girl we ran off the road.'

Louise remembered and said the first thing that came into her head. 'I was sorry to hear about your friend, Gareth.'

'I thought you were Welsh,' he said.

Louise gave an embarrassed smile. 'English, I'm afraid.'

'Gareth Llewelyn got what he deserved. He was a nasty piece of work.'

Louise was shocked. 'I know his former fiancée.'

'Well she's lucky. That Welshman had some pretty heavy enemies.'

'Do you know who murdered him?'

'Ha,' he scoffed. 'That's something you don't want to know, Miss, ever.'

He walked away. Louise was lost in the moment when she heard a familiar Cockney voice. 'Taxi, Miss?' Elizabeth Vestey's smile and banter were full of warmth and love.

The women embraced and Elizabeth sensed Louise's unease. 'Something wrong, Miss Wellesley?'

Louise looked at her then smiled. 'Only that I've missed you and your family something rotten.'

In her room at Girton Louise thought about the young man at the station and what he said.

That Welshman had some pretty heavy enemies.

Gareth's friend seemed deadly serious but why had the murder not been solved and who were these heavy enemies?

Emily arrived with bags and books. The women hugged, laughed and talked. It was late September 1938 and their second year was about to begin.

Louise had new lectures, possibly new acting opportunities and hopefully some new meetings with a certain Surrey doctor. Surely he must visit his aunt and uncle in Cambridge at some time.

With a free afternoon, Louise headed into town and the police station. She asked to see Inspector Williams and again he only wanted to talk about her acting career.

'So have you been a Frenchwoman or a Welsh lass this time?' he asked with a smile.

'Inspector, I feel I should tell you everything I know about Mister Llewelyn's murder.'

'Do you now? Don't tell me you've solved that as well?'

She told him about Gareth seducing and abandoning Carwen Hughes and about her vengeful family.

'Oh we know about the brothers Hughes and how they were all playing rugby in Cardiff on the night of the murder.'

This worried Louise but she described her meeting on the Cambridge station with Gareth's friend and his comments about heavy enemies.

'Yes we've interviewed Mister Llewelyn's friend and he told us about some colourful characters. But none of that should ever worry your pretty head, Miss Wellesley. You just concentrate on your brilliant acting career.'

And with that, Louise was politely ushered out of the police station by a young constable who was clearly smitten. He reminded Louise of Desmond Longbottom, the Shakespearean actor with the misbehaving tights.

'I'm Constable Harry, Miss. If you should ever need assistance from the police, I'd be very pleased to help.'

His smile was generous and Louise reciprocated. Her list of admirers was growing.

In heading to the bus stop she passed *The Eagle* public house in which she once performed as a limping Frenchwoman. Louise pushed open the door to the Ladies' Lounge. Two women were chatting with the barmaid. As she came over, Louise wondered if she should reveal her real identity.

'Hello, love, 'aven't seen you in 'ere before. What's y'poison?'

'Could I have a sweet sherry, please?'

'Course you can. Take a pew. I'll be right back.'

The barmaid brought the sherry and Louise reached for her purse.

'On the 'ouse, love,' said the barmaid. 'It's your first drink in 'ere, so 'ave this one on me.'

'Thank you, most kind,' said Louise and raised her glass in appreciation. The longer she remained silent about her previous visit, the harder it was to confess.

'Now I'm guessing you're a first-year student at the University,' said the barmaid.

'Actually I'm now in my second year.'

'Good for you. Jus' feel free to drop in any time.'

'Well actually, I do have a reason.' The barmaid was instantly interested and sat beside Louise.

'I'm Dorothy but everyone calls me Dot.'

'Hello. I'm Louise and I'm after some information, please.'

'Bet it's about a fella. Someone done you wrong, Louise?'

'Not me, it's my friend. And there is a gentleman involved but unfortunately he's dead.'

'Dead!'

'Yes and his name is Gareth Llewelyn.'

Dot snorted. 'Ha! Gareth Bloody Llewelyn is definitely no gentleman. That scoundrel ruined many a young girl's life. I even 'ad a French lass in 'ere a while back tryin' to track 'im down.'

Louise half smiled. 'My friend was once engaged to Mister Llewelyn.'

'Well she's lucky, 'im being dead like.'

'I want to help her understand the man she once agreed to marry. Can you help me?'

Dot shrugged. 'Where can I start? I 'eard 'e got some poor Welsh girl into trouble and she confronted 'im at the local hospital in front of the Mayor and a whole crowd of people.'

'I heard about that,' said an innocent-looking Louise.

'The latest is 'e got involved in drugs.'

'Drugs? That sounds terrible.'

'An' 'im trainin' to be a doctor. I 'eard 'e was blackmailin' some strange medical chap over drugs 'ere in Cambridge and the doctor decided enough was enough.'

'He was killed by a doctor?'

'So I 'eard. But anyway, you tell your friend she dodged a bullet when Gareth didn't, if you get my drift.'

Louise was most grateful, made her excuses and walked into the Cambridge sunshine. Her thoughts were many.

So Gareth was shot by a local doctor. But why would a doctor be subject to blackmail? And if what Dot said was true, why had the police not made an arrest?

Louise had returned to the pub so why not the hospital? She walked to the scene of her Welsh mother performance and stopped a nurse.

'Excuse me,' said Louise. 'I'm a student at Girton College. Could you recommend a local doctor?'

'Certainly,' said the nurse. 'Would you prefer a lady doctor?'

'No, thank you, in fact I'd really like a doctor with a strong reputation, someone who is aware of the latest drugs and methods.'

'I only know two. Doctor Carstairs is very good but semi-retired. Doctor Lovelock-Hall can be a little strange at times. I mean he's very good but is often rather abrupt. I have their addresses if you like.'

'That would be wonderful,' smiled Louise.

So one of the doctors was a little strange? Louise plumped for him.

Doctor Lovelock-Hall had a surgery as part of his home. Louise rang the doorbell. Expecting his wife or receptionist, Louise was surprised when a man answered the door.

'Yes?' The nurse was correct. The man was abrupt.

'I'm looking for Doctor Lovelock-Hall.'

'What do you want?'

'Oh. I wanted to arrange an appointment.'

'Are you ill?'

'Not exactly but ...'

'Telephone and make an appointment.' He began to close the door. As it was being closed, Louise spoke two words. There was a pause and then the door slowly opened. 'What did you say?'

'Gareth Llewelyn.'

Louise sat in a darkened sitting-room. The man stared at her then spoke.

'If you're a reporter you're wasting your time.'

'I'm not.'

'If you're some wretched lover of that bastard I have to tell you, the man was pure evil and I'm glad he's dead.'

'Did you kill him, Doctor?'

The question startled the man. He sensed she was not a threat but still regarded her as hostile.

'Who are you and why are you here?'

Louise decided to throw caution to the wind. 'I know he was blackmailing you.'

Lovelock-Hall froze then wilted. He collapsed on the sofa. 'How do you know? What do you know?' Then he shouted. 'Who are you?'

'My name is Louise Wellesley. I'm a student at Girton College and my girlfriend was once engaged to marry Mister Llewelyn.'

'But the blackmail? How do you know about that?'

'I heard that Mister Llewelyn was blackmailing a Cambridge doctor to obtain drugs but I didn't know who that doctor was until I came here.'

Lovelock-Hall sprang to his feet and shouted. 'You tricked me. You're as bad as he was. Now get out!'

Louise remained calm. Lovelock-Hall tried to stare her down but then lost heart. His fury faded. He sat and began to quietly cry.

Louise spoke softly. 'You have no reason to trust me but I've been involved with Gareth Llewelyn too.' Lovelock-Hall wiped his face and stared at her. 'I embarrassed him in public at the hospital. It was in all the papers.'

Lovelock-Hall was angry again. 'Stop lying! That was a young Welsh mother. Now get out you liar!'

Louise stood and prepared herself. The doctor was desperate and angry. Louise slipped into performance mode and spoke with her richest Welsh accent. 'Oh Gareth, how could you? The babi is crying and wants his Tad. Come home, Gareth, come home to Wales.'

The doctor's face was a picture. This woman wasn't threatening just utterly convincing. He sat then she sat. There was a pause before he finally spoke.

'What do you want?'

'To tell my friend who killed her fiancé.' She paused. 'Was it you, Doctor?'

He took a deep breath. 'I wanted to, we both did. But that London criminal got there first.'

'So why not tell the police? You're a victim, Doctor. Blackmail is as much a crime as murder.'

'Oh for pity's sake woman, Llewelyn was blackmailing me because I'm queer. What I do in private with another consenting male adult is a criminal offence.'

Louise fell silent. She could see the man was deeply upset. His life was a mess. Suddenly the doctor fell into a mini drama playing both parts. He stood and acted for Louise. Sarcasm dripped from his tongue.

DOCTOR Excuse me, officer; I'd like to report a crime. I'm being blackmailed.
POLICEMAN I see, sir, and what exactly have you done?
DOCTOR Nothing much, officer; just had sex with another man.
POLICEMAN Very good, sir. And is the other party a Grenadier Guardsman or employed in the Foreign Office?
DOCTOR Not quite; he's a barman in the local public house.
POLICEMAN Then, sir, I'm arresting you under *The Criminal Law Amendment Act 1885* on a charge of gross indecency. Empty your pockets please, sir.

Lovelock-Hall poured himself a drink but offered nothing to Louise. She spoke quietly.

'I'm sorry. I think I understand.'

He was angry. 'You understand nothing. I've escaped one maniac to be trapped by another. The criminal who murdered Llewelyn is my new blackmailer. He's some jumped-up London gangster who now deals directly with me.'

'Then you have to expose the murderer.'

Lovelock-Hall was never more shocked. Not only had he confessed everything to a complete stranger, and a woman to boot, she was now urging him to fight back. Until then, suicide was his only option. A pinprick of light appeared in a very dark tunnel.

Louise continued. 'When I asked if you killed Mister Llewelyn, you said, "I wanted to, we both did". What did you mean by *both*?'

Lovelock-Hall's thinking was muddled. This woman was polite, calm and seemingly honest and the only person who had treated him with respect and understanding. Without thinking he found himself revealing details he swore he'd never reveal. Lovelock-Hall was talking as if Louise was his doctor. He told all.

'Llewelyn promised he'd leave me alone if I gave him one last delivery. But he lied. He wanted more and on a regular basis. I was covering the drugs with prescriptions I couldn't justify. If I refused, Llewelyn would go to the police or the Medical Board or both. We agreed to meet the night he was killed. I had the drugs in liquid form in a syringe. It was dark and I hid. Then Llewelyn came walking towards me. I had a fake package in one hand and the syringe in the other. I stepped out of the shadows. He smiled and held out his hand for the drugs.' Lovelock-Hall was on a roll.

'Suddenly from behind Llewelyn a woman holding a large knife sprang from the shadows and raced towards him screaming. He spun around turning his back to me and I stepped forward to plunge the syringe into his neck. The woman and I were both about to kill him when thud; an arrow smashed into the side of Llewelyn's head. He dropped like a stone. I stood opposite this crazed woman, she with her knife and me with my syringe. We just stared at each other. We'd both come to kill Llewelyn and William Tell beat us to it. Then this London gangster Craddick appeared, crossbow on shoulder. "I'll be in touch, Doc", he said and strolled away.'

'And then you injected morphine into the dead body.'

Lovelock-Hall stared at Louise. She wasn't a reporter or a policewoman. Was she some type of spiritualist or a private detective?

'I only have one question, sir, if I may.' And she was so polite. 'Did the woman stab Mister Llewelyn before or after you injected him?'

Lovelock-Hall shook his head. What *didn't* she know? 'It was after. I admit I was ungentlemanly. It should definitely have been ladies first.'

Louise stood and examined a painting. Lovelock-Hall watched her intently. She was in total control. She spoke with her back to him.

'If the Cambridge Police were to engage Monsieur Hercule Poirot, the truth would come out as it did with the murder on the Orient Express. But having met the detective in charge of this case, I fear the truth may need a helping hand.'

Lovelock-Hall was hooked. This woman was hypnotic. Was there a chance he'd avoid a charge of murder or conspiracy to murder? He was a drug dealer and a practising homosexual. What chance did he have?

But if the doctor was shocked by the young woman's knowledge and questions, he was amazed when she suggested a plan of attack. It would involve her riskiest acting role—ever.

The *St Radegund* public house is a small Cambridge pub near the roundabout on Kings Road. An odd couple entered the pub that night. The man was a middle-aged chap who rather fancied himself as an actor. The woman was much younger and attractive albeit common with too much makeup and some eye-catching cleavage. The couple took their drinks to a corner table and started a lively discussion. The other drinkers ignored them until the couple raised their voices.

'You're weak, weak as water,' snapped the young woman.

'I told you to dump him,' fired back the man.

The volume and anger increased. The landlord called out to the argumentative couple. They ignored him and so a drinker sauntered over to the fiery pair.

'Spot of bovva 'ere, folks?'

'Get lost,' said the man.

'Now, now, manners, manners.' The drinker who joined the couple had a London accent, a ridiculous ego and a suit so cheap its tailor used a *nom de plume*. The drinker's name was Herbert Craddick who was a non-league drug dealer, novice blackmailer and of late, crossbow killer.

The young woman attacked her partner. 'I bet this gent could do the right thing. He's no coward. Not like you.'

The middle-aged man stood up and pushed his chair which tipped and crashed on its back.

'Well, let him. See if I care,' spat the man who strode out of the pub.

Herbert picked up the fallen chair and sat next to the young woman. The tension evaporated and the pub became quiet again. Herbert turned on his oily charm.

'Now wot's a pretty young fing like you doin' wiv a creep like 'im?'

'Ha,' she scoffed. 'That was my pathetic excuse for a big brother.'

'So not y'boyfriend then,' smiled Herbert. 'Allow me to 'elp.'

The woman went all shy. 'I don't know if I should be talking to you. You could be some horrible criminal, a wicked murderer.'

Herbert laughed. 'Well if you does need a real gent, I'm y'man.'

'I haven't got no money.'

'Who said anyfing about money?' Herbert placed his hand on her hand. 'Besides, there are lots of ways to pay for services rendered.' He squeezed her hand and maintained his gaze. 'So wot's the problem?'

The woman paused then told all. 'I have this boyfriend, *ex*-boyfriend, who just won't leave me alone. Tonight I've arranged to have him warned off but as you saw, my big brother squibbed it.'

'I can do that for you.'

'Can you, really?'

'No trouble.'

The young woman smiled and this time it was her hand on his. 'I'll be ever so grateful.' She looked deep into Herbert's eyes and he mentally cleared his diary for the remainder of the evening. They left the pub.

She took his arm as they walked through the town and headed to the river. 'Please don't do nothing nasty, Herbert,' she said. 'I just want him warned off.'

'Leave it to me, Matty,' said Herbert. They walked along the bank of the river. Suddenly a man stepped into view. It was the ex-boyfriend. He was surprised.

'Who's he? You said you'd come alone.'

'I'm a friend,' said Herbert, 'a friend wiv a message.'

Matty tried to calm things. 'I've brought Herbert to show you how serious I am. It's over between us.'

'Don't say that,' said the boyfriend and moved towards her. Instantly Herbert slapped the boyfriend. Matty screamed and the boyfriend fell back holding his face.

'You 'eard the lady,' sneered Herbert. 'She's finished wiv you, pal. Now walk away and don't never come back.'

The boyfriend was no coward. He took off his jacket and spoke quietly. 'She might be finished with me but I ain't finished with you.'

'No,' cried Matty.

'You silly little man,' laughed Herbert. 'I'll 'ave you for breakfast, Sunshine.'

Matty began to panic. 'I don't want this. Please Herbert, let him leave.'

'Last chance, pal,' said Herbert who was spoiling for a fight. Matty had no chance of stopping them.

The males circled one another. Herbert threw a jab and the boyfriend swayed back. Herbert smiled. This was going to be easy. He jabbed a few more times then launched a haymaker. The boyfriend's head was in mortal danger until the punch was expertly blocked leaving Herbert wide open. A solid fist smacked into his nose. He swore and felt his face. The shock was worse than the pain. His bloodied nose made him even more gangster-like. His anger became rage. He rushed at the boyfriend and they grappled. Matty was helpless. Herbert turned the boyfriend and got him in a headlock. They struggled.

'So you fink you can beat me?' spat Herbert. 'I've *killed* tougher men than you.'

'Killed!' exclaimed Matty.

'Liar,' yelled the boyfriend fighting back.

'Liar is it?' Herbert twisted his victim to face the river. 'Over there, I shot a bloke. Shot him dead.'

'Oh Herbert,' cried Matty. 'Please don't kill him, please.'

'Well where's your gun?' gasped the boyfriend.

'Guns are for losers,' oozed Herbert. 'I've got style. I use a crossbow. Now let's see 'ow you feel wiv a broken neck.'

Herbert suddenly gripped the boyfriend's throat and tensed his muscles to snap the victim's neck. A howl of pain exploded. Matty kicked Herbert's kneecap hard and he lost his grip. The boyfriend turned and gave Herbert an uppercut as approved by the Marquess of Queensberry.

Losing the fight was the least of Herbie's woes. The "boyfriend" was none other than the love-struck Constable Harry from Cambridge Police. Matty was the Surrey actress better known as Plum and her "brother" was an actor from the Arts Theatre. He was meant to tell the police the trap had been set but being an actor he had a problem following directions. The local police arrived just as Herbert was knocked out.

The London gangster attempted to murder a copper in front of a witness and confessed to murdering a man with a crossbow. Like most felons Craddick was his own worst enemy. He couldn't pour water out of a boot with the instructions on the heel and his criminal career collapsed. Miss Wellesley pulled off yet another real-life acting triumph.

Two hours later a police car pulled up outside Lovelock-Hall's home. Louise rang the bell. The front curtains twitched. Then a veranda light lit Louise in a warm, red glow. She thought it appropriate considering her racy appearance. The door opened and a nervous doctor spoke.

'Miss Wellesley? Is that you?'

Inside, when she finished her story, Dr. Lovelock-Hall began to silently weep. He couldn't believe the two men who'd blackmailed and bullied him were either dead or locked up. He spoke but the tears continued to flow. 'I don't know how to thank you. You've saved my life. And the man on the river bank; was he really a policeman?'

'I'm sorry, Doctor, but I couldn't possibly say.'

She smiled and through his tears he smiled. She stood to leave. He stood and moved to her. He took her hands and squeezed and kissed them, his tears mingling with his kisses.

The police car took Louise back to Girton. Both her onstage and offstage performances were winning excellent reviews.

Chapter 12

KURT WAS PRIMED. His troops, trucks and trains were primed. Germany's Polish Jews were to "quietly vacate the premises". They were offered a free, one-way trip to Hell.

Kurt's planning was impressive and he led from the front. His team entered an apartment block home to many Polish Jews with some being fourth and fifth generation Germans.

Kurt banged loudly on a door. Other banging sounds reverberated throughout the building. A terrified elderly woman opened her door. Kurt kicked it causing the woman to scream and fall. He stormed inside.

'Out, now, all of you,' roared Kurt. The woman's husband came into the room wearing his nightshirt. Kurt grabbed the old man's beard and dragged him towards the door. 'Out, now!'

The couple was thrust into the street wearing their night clothes. They clung to one another and were beaten as they hobbled towards a truck.

Kurt entered another apartment and bumped into a colleague. 'We're too late, he's killed himself.'

In a room Kurt saw an elderly Jew swinging from a rope tied to a light fitting. He'd climbed onto a table and stepped into eternity.

Outside in the street trucks were filling with Polish Jews. Some parents were desperate to find their children and vice versa. It was a Polish holiday where the brochures said nothing about reservations or the buffet car.

One confused Gestapo agent tackled Kurt. 'Some officers are taking children, others only adults. I thought you said ...'

Kurt was livid. His meticulous planning was being questioned. He smashed his baton against a passing Jew and stormed out to the street.

The wretched humans were pushed, kicked and bundled into trucks. The sight of a pregnant woman inflamed some Gestapo agents. They singled her out for particularly cruel treatment.

Once a truck was crammed with Jewish "passengers", the back board was lifted and the truck set off for the nearest railway station. Kurt's organizational skills were first class.

As the trucks trundled through the streets, locals appeared and hurled abuse. 'Get out you stinking Jews! Get back to Palestine!' The passengers were under no illusion. Thomas Cook had nothing to do with this trip.

Trains stood waiting. The locomotives were well watered and coaled even hissing anti-Semitic steam. The Polish Jews filled the carriages; everyone was in terror class. They lost their home, business, possessions and dignity. Some lost their family. It was a wretched, appalling situation; cruelty beyond belief. The Gestapo did a very nice line in evil.

Many Jews were not dressed for anything other than a warm bed. Some cried and wailed. Some upbraided the noisy ones. Many were silent.

In one carriage, an elderly Jewess felt strong pain in her chest. She was shivering but the cold was irrelevant. Her chest pain increased. She tried to cry out but couldn't. She slumped to the floor and died before the train got anywhere near the Polish border.

In that same carriage, husband and wife, Sendel and Riva Grynszpan clung to one another. They left Poland for Hanover in 1911. They made a modest living, paid their fair share of tax and raised their children.

Now, without warning, they were arrested, forced out of their home and travelling with only the clothes they were wearing. Their tailoring business was stolen along with all their possessions. It was theft, assault, cruelty and injustice all rolled into one.

But worse was to follow, if things could get worse. At the border, the Polish authorities refused to accept these expelled Polish Jews. Makeshift refugee camps were set up inside the Polish border. The Red Cross did all they could to help with food, shelter and clothing.

Riva Grynszpan wrote to her 17 year old son Herschel in Paris. It was a desperate plea to a desperate son. Herschel was unemployed, broke and an illegal immigrant. He read his mother's letter of despair. "If you can send any money, please do. We have nothing".

Kurt was happy. Thousands of Polish Jews were out of the Third Reich. Were they criminals? No, far worse; they were Jews.

But Kurt had no idea his mass deportation of Polish Jews would trigger an international incident.

In Paris, Herschel Grynszpan was incensed at his parents' treatment and vowed revenge. He borrowed money from his uncle, bought a handgun and entered the Germany Embassy. He was directed to the office of Herr Ernst vom Rath.

'What can I do for you?' asked the embassy official.

'I wish to protest at the horrendous treatment my parents and thousands of Polish Jews have received at the hands of the German government.'

'This is not the place for protest. Kindly leave.'

Herschel had been enraged for days. The refusal of vom Rath to even listen tipped Herschel over the edge. He pulled out the handgun and fired five times. His protesting was far greater than his ability to shoot straight.

While it was hard to miss from such close range, vom Rath was alive. He was rushed to hospital and given the best medical treatment possible. Hitler even sent his personal physician. Herschel made no attempt to escape and willingly confessed to his actions.

Despite expert medical care, vom Rath died. Cue the consequences. The Nazis took full advantage of vom Rath's murder.

Propaganda Minister Goebbels incited the people. 'If demonstrations erupt spontaneously, they are not to be hampered.' In other words, get out there and give those bloody Jews a right good kicking. Many did.

Synagogues and prayer houses were fire-bombed, Jewish businesses were ransacked and some 100 Jews were killed in random acts of violence.

In another example of German precision, any synagogue adjacent to a building owned by an Aryan had to be trashed but not burnt. "We cannot risk damaging the estates of the good people".

The destruction of Jewish property meant glass littered the streets giving rise to the event being called *Die Kristallnacht*, the Crystal Night. It was so widespread, spectacular and unjustified that the world took note. Foreign editorials railed against of this brutality. Hitler was furious; not at the treatment of the Jews but at being found out.

Kurt read reports of the mass rioting against the Jews and how it was triggered by a letter from a deported Polish Jewess. He couldn't have read it in a Jewish newspaper as the Nazis had banned them.

Kurt heard about Hitler's fury at the international condemnation. Would the Führer want a scapegoat? Kurt was worried.

Who was responsible for the riots? Who? Hartmann? Kurt Hartmann? From the Gestapo?

Kurt closed his boasting and self-promotion accounts and kept a low profile for several weeks. His star was yet to rise.

The last time Max and Kurt met was in a Berlin Gestapo cell with Max about to be shot. But they met again at Christmas 1938. Both believed this might be their last peaceful Christmas for some time. They enjoyed a glass of Schnapps in Max's father's study.

'You look better than when I last saw you,' said Kurt.

Max was sincere. 'You know I'm only alive because of you.' Kurt shrugged. 'You saved my life, Kurt and helped me win promotion.'

'Ah but you're not the only promoted Hartmann, Herr Oberst; although I was only commended by Himmler whereas you have shaken hands with the demi-God himself.'

Max was in a quandary. Kurt had saved him from a firing squad. Yet Max could not condone the work done by Kurt and his Gestapo colleagues. Max tried to steer a neutral course.

'So, cousin, what does the future hold for our great nation?'

'You should know that, Herr Oberst. The Wehrmacht makes war whereas we in the Gestapo simply tidy up the loose ends.'

Max shook his head. 'I am impressed with your use of language. "Tidy up loose ends" being code for *torture* and *murder*.'

'Somebody's got to do it.'

'No they don't.'

'What, you want the dregs of society roaming free destroying Germany and ruining the great work done by the Party?'

Max was stunned. 'My God! Kurt, will you listen to yourself. You actually sound sincere.'

Kurt's voice was louder. 'Listen cousin, I want this nation great again. I want the Third Reich to last a thousand years. And that will only happen when we remove the queers, communists and those blood-sucking Jews.'

Max said nothing. He finished his drink. Finally he spoke.

'What's your problem with language? You "remove" the so-called undesirables. What's wrong with *execute* or *murder*?'

Kurt sipped his drink. 'You remember the Crystal Night?'

'Remember it? The whole world saw the Fatherland apply naked savagery against innocent civilians.'

Kurt spoke calmly. 'I started it.'

Max was shocked. He knew Kurt was not prone to making false claims.

'You started it?'

Kurt explained his brilliant planning expelling Germany's Polish Jews, the resultant murder in the German Embassy in Paris and the consequent rioting in Germany. Max just shook his head.

'I'm not sure what's worse; the pogrom or your pride in creating it.'

Kurt moved close to Max. 'A word of advice, cousin; you got away with your last anti-Hitler adventure. The others involved in that scheme are dead. Don't push your luck.'

Sarcasm was rife. 'You mean you won't save me next time?'

Kurt was furious. 'You tell me to listen to myself. You should take your own advice. Hitler is leading our country to new levels of greatness. He'll make Germany the rulers of Europe and when that happens I'll be there with him in the bloody front row.'

Max shook his head. 'Oh cousin, be told, the man's a monster who's leading us all to hell in a handbasket.'

There was a pause. Both men stared at the other. Kurt was seething and Max was disgusted. Kurt put down his drink then suddenly lunged at his cousin's throat. The element of surprise and Kurt's strength meant Max was in trouble.

My God, he's trying to strangle me, thought Max. He felt dizzy. Kurt pressed harder. Max struggled to breathe. Then the study door opened and Kurt's three year-old nephew stood staring at the men. They froze. The child was curious.

'Are you playing a game, Uncle Kurt?'

Kurt slowly released his grip. Max turned away and struggled to regain his breath and balance.

'That's right, Richart,' said Uncle Kurt. He took his nephew's hand. 'Now come along young man and let's see what Saint Nicholas has brought for you this year.'

Chapter 13

LOUISE WROTE to Matty. It was a letter with plenty of home truths.

December 1938

Darling Matty,
I suspected you were involved in that business by the river when we met after Papa's funeral. It was the way you spoke about a certain person and your veiled reference to his demise. Unless you had seduced the Chief Constable, which I believe is quite possible, you could only have known important facts by being there.
Anyway, I have news. William Tell has been captured by the Sherriff of Cambridgeshire and the medico member of the duo of vengeful players is home and fancy free. I arranged a game of Let's Catch the Crim with the help of an actor and a constable, both of whom are madly in love with me. I could let you borrow either or both!
Remind me never to upset you and kindly leave the family silver behind when next we meet.
With things so dull at home, I plan to spend Christmas here in Cambridge.
All my love
Louise
xxx

Matty responded with a simple postcard.

Almost Christmas '38
Barcelona
Dearest Louise
Not only beautiful but clever too!
Love and kisses
Matty

Not going home for Christmas was a first for Louise. She plumped for Christmas in-house at Girton. Well, Girton was her base but the Vestey home was her HQ. She found it difficult explaining her decision to her brothers and almost impossible to her mother.

The St Peter's Players were staging a pantomime for their end of year show and as Louise had no offers of work at the Arts Theatre, she agreed to join the amateur company in their production of *Jack and the Beanstalk*.

Molly was overjoyed, Miss Finchley was still deaf and the cast and crew made Louise more than welcome. She was happy to play any minor role and have fun with some enthusiastic thespians.

One major worry in the health of the production was Amanda Crosthwaite-Dare or rather Amanda's mater, a stereotypical stage mother who had "encouraged" Miss Finchley to cast Amanda as Jack. Sadly the eponymous role soon had the poor girl in trouble.

She was far too large for a svelte Jack. She found it hard to project her voice, couldn't remember her lines and wouldn't look any of the other actors in the eye. Apart from that, she was brilliant.

Various company members were in Miss Finchley's ear—loudly of course—about how Amanda was simply not up to snuff. Miss Finchley was far too polite to sack anyone.

'Good heavens,' she said. 'We're not professionals. And besides, everyone must have a turn.'

As rehearsals proceeded and Amanda got worse, the tension edged higher. Amanda's mother was at every rehearsal adding her two bobs' worth. Something or someone had to crack.

Leading the cow across the stage, Amanda tripped and dragged the cow with her, er, him. There were three actors playing two characters with none of them upright. It was an udder mess.

Amanda burst into tears, claimed she couldn't go on only to have her mother storm onto the stage and tell her daughter to stop being a baby and to just get on with it. It was perhaps the most dramatic acting ever seen on that stage.

The cast became the audience waiting spellbound for the denouement. Would Amanda yield to her bullying mother or tell Mummy to hop it?

Amazingly she chose the latter. Amanda came of age that night. For the first time in her life, she stood up to her mother.

'It's no good, Mummy,' she cried. 'I'll never be a famous actress like you. I'd much rather make costumes and help with the makeup and hairstyles.'

And she did. Mummy was left to grumble, Amanda proved a wonderful seamstress and hair stylist and, of course, the White Knight from Girton reluctantly slipped into the main role—again.

Louise had never played a man. Now her lovely legs were covered with green tights and her jolly jacket made Jack a right champion.

His mother, the Dame, was played by a wonderful old gentleman, Fred Dawson, who fought in the war, walked with a limp and had a parched dry sense of humour. He was one of those natural actors sometimes found on the amateur stage who could step easily onto a professional set and be right at home. He and Louise became great pals.

Their affection for one another offstage was matched by their quarrelling onstage. The audiences loved them.

Louise enjoyed the genuine greetings from the cast and audience over the ubiquitous tea and cakes post panto. This was a bitter sweet experience because it was here she first met Tom. Tonight his aunt and uncle were again serving supper but their nephew was absent. His presence would have made Christmas special. But then it happened—again.

'Congratulations, Miss Wellesley,' said a beautifully-modulated male voice.

Louise looked at a tall, distinguished man old enough to be her father. He was proof that some men actually improve with age.

'Thank you, you're most kind.' Was he also a doctor bearing cakes or more likely a Don from an all-male college? He chatted.

'I understand you've been performing professionally at the Arts Theatre.'

'Oh only minor roles; my studies come first.'

'And after your studies; may one ask if you intend to follow a career in the theatre?'

Louise was non-plussed. *Who is this man and why the interest in my career?*

'Do forgive me,' he said. 'My name is Richard Graves. I run a theatrical agency in London and I'd be delighted to discuss representing you; that is if you're interested.'

'Goodness,' said Louise not knowing what to say. She took his card. 'Thank you, thank you so much.'

'When next you're up in London, do get in touch. And again, many congratulations.' He smiled and made an effortless exit leaving Louise to be hugged by the back half of the cow.

Louise thought she should perform more often with the St Peter's Players. So far she'd met Tom the possible husband and Dick the possible agent. Just who might Harry be?

So, thought Louise, *a theatrical agent wants to represent me. How does one celebrate such an offer?* She was bursting to share the news with the Vesteys.

That would be soon. Professor Vestey, Elizabeth and Molly had all developed their own reason for loving Louise and each was genuinely excited at the prospect of having her share their Christmas.

After lunch on Christmas Eve they were drinking coffee and keeping warm before a lively fireplace. A well-decorated tree stood in a corner. Alfred said what the others were thinking.

'My dear Miss Wellesley, you must not feel obliged to join in all of our little Christmas rituals. Just come and go as you please but do make yourself at home.'

'Oh but I want to join in,' replied Louise.

And so began a Christmas Louise would never forget beginning with everyone rugging up and walking to the chapel at Kings' College where the Christmas Eve service began at 3pm. There was light snow falling and a chill in the air but once she entered the chapel the grandeur of the building took away her breath. *The Festival of Nine Lessons and Carols* began and Louise was in awe. The singing was glorious and in that setting, ethereal.

They went to St Peter's for midnight mass. It was cold and the vicar may well have had more trouble with his drains as the rain beat heavily on the roof. Afterwards, the congregation gathered in the hall for a glass of mulled wine. Louise spied Miss Finchley and the Cambridge Queen of Cakes. They were sans Mr Bird.

'Good evening, ladies,' said Louise, 'and a very Merry Christmas to you both.'

The women fussed over their favourite leading lady and Louise was quietly bubbling with happiness in her new "home town".

'And how is your husband, Missus Bird; well I trust?'

'Oh George's arthritis doesn't like this winter weather.'

'Well please wish him the compliments of the season from me,' smiled Louise.

'Thank you, my dear. He's really looking forward to Christmas. Our nephew Tom arrives in the morning.'

Oh dear. A London agent wants to represent me and now the man who makes my heart race will be enjoying his turkey only three streets from the Vesteys. Could this be my best Christmas ever?

Elizabeth collected Louise from Girton on Christmas morning and in Cambridge, Alfred and Molly were eagerly waiting.

They discussed driving the 14 miles to Ely for the cathedral service but chose the parish church and hoped the vicar was not long-winded. Louise was delighted at their choice of venue.

The church was full and the vicar did the right thing by delivering a short, traditional sermon. After the service the congregation enjoyed a cup of tea sans biscuits. Most worshippers were leaving as much room as possible for what awaited at home.

Louise was happily chatting with the Vesteys when she spotted Dr Curzon. He was with the Birds and Miss Finchley. His eyes met Louise's. He smiled and she smiled. He began moving in her direction. Louise felt her heartbeat accelerate. Elizabeth saw Tom looming large.

'Isn't that the doctor who cared for your dear father?' Tom was almost there. Gathering her brother and niece, Elizabeth whispered, 'We'll find you later.'

Tom arrived just as the Vesteys left.

'Merry Christmas, Miss Wellesley.'

'And to you, kind sir,' smiled Louise.

'Was it something I said, your friends leaving just now?'

'No, they knew you cared for Papa and thought it polite to allow us some privacy.'

'This must be a really sad time for you with your father dying as he did last Christmas. But you're looking remarkably well and ... goodness, I nearly said as beautiful as ever.' Louise went quite warm. 'And your family; they are well I trust?'

'Thank you, they're all well and widespread, which is why I'm here in Cambridge.'

'I must congratulate you on your professional acting debut. I thought you were marvellous.'

Louise was shocked. 'You were there?'

'I was and popped round to the stage door to say hello but those friends of yours got in before me.'

'Well you should have come over. I mean, I would have liked to have seen you.'

They looked at one another. Both had things to say. Tom chose his words carefully.

'You probably don't remember but after your father's funeral, I wanted to say something to you.'

'I remember very well and also my friend's outrageous entrance.'

Tom smiled. 'Since then I've thought about contacting you a number of times.' He paused and despite the hubbub of the chattering worshippers, Louise heard or saw nothing other than the man standing in front of her. 'I'm not sure this is the right time or place. Is there a chance I might see you somewhere else?'

'Of course,' replied Louise and felt a growing sense of confidence.

'It's just that I'm leaving tomorrow. I'm off to Africa.'

Cue the dramatic music.

'Oh,' was all Louise managed to say. Tom continued.

'Could we meet this afternoon or perhaps this evening?' he asked.

Louise wanted to say "yes" to any and every suggestion but knew she couldn't. 'I'm very sorry, Doctor, but ...'

'Tom, please call me Tom.'

They paused and looked at one another. Louise smiled and nodded. 'Of course, Tom, but you see I'm staying with friends who have made all sorts of plans for me.'

Tom sighed. 'We seem destined to forever remain apart.'

'I hope not,' said Louise immediately. She was about to suggest a possible meeting when a small bell started ringing.

The room fell silent. The vicar made a short speech and wished all a Merry Christmas. The chatting resumed, people made their exits and the Birds and Vesteys arrived to collect their guests.

'It was lovely to see you again, Miss Wellesley,' said Tom as he was spirited away.

Louise was a buzzing mixture of hot and cold emotions.

The Christmas food and friendship in the Vestey home was overwhelming. But Louise kept thinking about Tom and wondering if she would ever see him again.

She didn't know Tom was once a medical missionary in Africa and that tragically the trip ended with the death of his wife. Moving to 1937 and his first meeting with Louise, Tom was seriously interested in this beautiful young woman who seemed to have the acting world on a string.

When he decided to tell her his feelings his explanation was sabotaged by Matilda and ever since Tom had lost his nerve and done a Francis Drake.

In early 1938 he decided to return to Africa and thought wooing Louise unfair so concentrated on his medical career. When by chance he saw her perform at the Arts Theatre in Cambridge he knew he still had strong feelings for her but again allowed his faint heart to not woo fair lady.

Now, at Christmas, here in Cambridge, he made one last effort to break the ice. But was he really trying? It seemed that fate would keep them apart. Tom decided to write from the ship.

Dear Louise,
I have always been impressed by your brilliant acting not to mention your wonderful smile. I'm sorry I haven't the skill or courage to explain how much I admire you. Hopefully this letter does the trick.
If ever our paths cross again, I promise I will not allow anyone or anything to interrupt our conversation! I look forward to reading about your continued success upon the stage.
With every good wish,
Tom

It was a letter Louise would read many times. She devoured every word looking for a new or alternative meaning.

But life, as her mother often said, goes on. Louise threw herself into the new term and put her acting ambitions on hold. She would complete her studies and then seek work as an actress.

Her mother wrote asking her to come home for a weekend. Louise was concerned. Her mother would never ask her home for a chat nor would she ever discuss important news in a letter. It had to be face to face.

Heading home to Surrey meant changing trains in London. She arrived in the capital and telephoned the theatrical agent, Mr Richard Graves. *He must consider hundreds of would-be performers. Would he even remember me?*

'Of course I remember you, Miss Wellesley, how lovely to hear from you.' Louise was taken aback. 'Where are you calling from?'

To Louise's surprise and delight, Richard Graves invited her to lunch. She was early so killed time drinking tea in different cafés, then wandered along Shaftesbury Avenue and read all the notices outside the theatres. Finally she arrived at the agent's office.

The reception area had many photos of well-known performers and there they stood smiling alongside Mr Graves. *He is obviously successful. So why is he interested in an untried, unknown actress?*

For their lunch date, Graves choose *The Ivy,* a restaurant, in the heart of London's theatre district.

Things became even more impressive when Louise found herself sitting but a short distance from Mr Noël Coward. When said gentleman nodded at her luncheon guest and said, 'Hello Dickie', Louise thought about the suppers in the hall with the St Peter's Players. Not quite the same thing.

But despite such exalted company and certainly feeling the junior partner, Louise decided to politely speak her mind.

'Mister Graves, please don't misunderstand me but I must confess to being a little perplexed.'

'Well that will never do, Miss Wellesley. How may I remove your discombobulation?' He smiled and she did likewise then continued.

'Your kindness is quite humbling but as I've had only the odd walk-on part at the Arts Theatre in Cambridge, I wonder why you would want to represent such an inexperienced actress?'

'Oh I do so want my clients to ask questions. Now what would you like to order? I can recommend everything.'

Louise was trying to think straight. She was mingling with famous theatricals and being given the chance to realise her dream of becoming a professional actress. Choosing between the fish and the lamb seemed almost irrelevant.

'Let me put it this way, Miss Wellesley,' said Graves. 'I have my spies and my success lies in my ability to find the best spies. If I were to mention the name, Beauford Nightingale, would that help?'

Louise smiled. She loved Nightie and found Richard Graves to be just as charming. *What was this thing with older men?* After a lovely lunch and more discussion Graves produced an envelope.

'Miss Wellesley, it's time, as the Americans say, to talk turkey. I'll be frank. I would like to represent you. I think you have a brilliant future and I know I can put your name forward for many interesting roles. If you choose to accept my offer, you will need to agree to this contract.'

Louise was stuck for words. Graves continued.

'I believe some members of your family are in the Law.' Louise spoke about her barrister brothers. 'Excellent. Now I insist on all my new clients seeking independent advice on their contract.'

Louise wanted to sign there and then. Instead she politely accepted the envelope. At home she too would have some news.

104

On the train down to Farnham she wondered what her father would have said about his daughter seeking a career upon the wicked stage. *What will Mummy say? If I ask my brothers for legal advice, I might have to do so in secret.*

Louise arrived in Surrey with a small Christmas gift for her mother and their greeting was long and strong. Life had changed for both women.

Victoria was never a person to rush her news but they got serious over the evening meal.

'My darling girl,' began Victoria. 'I'm sure you know there are things I need to tell you.'

'I hope it's not going to make me sad, Mummy.'

'Your Uncle Crispin is gravely ill and is not expected to live much longer.'

Louise said the first thing that came into her head. 'But who's caring for his cats?'

'I believe some kind people in the village have taken care of the cats and kittens. But with your Uncle's passing comes the matter of the title. Henry will become the eighteenth Viscount which should please his new in-laws.'

'And you, Mummy? Surely you must be pleased?'

'Perhaps, but I too have news. Henry and Georgina are to wed in June and so too will I.'

Louise stopped eating. She looked at her mother who was waiting for a response.

'I'm afraid, Mummy, that how to congratulate one's mother on her forthcoming nuptials was never discussed at finishing-school.'

Victoria smiled. 'Sir Anthony has proposed and I have accepted. It will be a very quiet registry office ceremony to which I hope you will come.'

'Of course, Mummy, how could you think otherwise?'

'Not as my daughter but as my attendant.' Louise was shocked again. 'Henry will be a witness and with Edmund present and Sir Anthony's sister, it will be strictly a family affair.'

Louise moved to her mother and kissed her. Victoria dabbed her eyes and the meal continued in an eerie silence until Victoria had more to say.

'The consequence of me marrying is that I shall move to Wiltshire to Sir Anthony's estate. That leaves our home empty. I have spoken with the boys. Apparently Georgina refuses to live here and Edmund is buying a flat in London. As you are away in Cambridge, I have a mind to sell it.'

Louise was shocked. She hadn't anticipated this and her shock doubled when her mother made her next announcement.

'Of course, my darling, if you were to marry and choose to live here, the house would be yours.'

Louise gasped. 'But what about the boys?'

'Their exact words were, "If Plum wants it, it's hers".' Louise couldn't speak. 'If you do choose to live here and later sell the house, you will need to share the proceeds with the boys. And if you don't want to live here, I will sell it and give you and the boys the money.'

This was staggering. Louise was being offered the family home or, alternatively, a significant sum of money. Usually the son or sons took precedence in the distribution of their father's estate. Daughters were cared for by their husband. Here Louise was being offered an equal share. Times were definitely changing.

Edmund arrived in the morning and he and Louise took Horatio for a long walk. They discussed their mother's forthcoming marriage and her suggestions about the house.

'But Eddie,' argued Louise, 'why don't you live here? You could marry and keep the Wellesley name going forever in deepest Surrey. Papa would be so proud. And you're just like him, the younger brother.'

Edmund laughed. 'Spare a thought for poor old Uncle Crispin.'

But *poor* was no longer a word associated with Louise Wellesley. Soon she would have significant wealth.

That night, after Victoria retired, Louise showed the theatrical contract to Edmund. He whistled. She was nervous.

'Is there something wrong?'

'No, no, it's perfectly plain and quite fair. I was simply expressing my admiration for the stunning success of my talented sister.'

'Thank you, Eddie. And please do think about coming to live here. It would be so nice for Mummy to have grandchildren running around the family home.'

Edmund put down his coffee and stood to stoke the fire. 'Listen, Plum, old girl, there's something I perhaps should tell you.' Before he could continue speaking, Louise moved to Edmund and hugged him speaking softly close to his face.

'You don't have to tell me anything, brother dear, but you must understand exactly what I'm about to say. I love you very, very much and always will.' She stood on tip-toe and kissed him then left the room speaking as she departed.

'Make sure the fire's out before you go to bed.' At the door, she turned. 'And I've put a mark on that expensive whisky bottle, so there.'

In the morning Louise signed the contract making Richard Graves her theatrical agent. She posted it enclosing a letter saying how grateful she was and how privileged she felt to be represented by such a prestigious agent.

Telling her mother caused barely a ripple. Victoria was preoccupied with two weddings and a funeral; the latter for her newly-deceased brother-in-law.

Back in Cambridge Louise was excited to receive a note from Richard Graves saying he would be passing through the city next week and could he take her to lunch.

They went to a quaint restaurant where Graves gave some advice. Louise should concentrate on her Cambridge studies but if any small roles at the Arts Theatre were offered, particularly during a university break, she could certainly accept that type of work.

Graves had a charming, avuncular style and soon had Louise talking about her life and family. She told him about the forthcoming weddings and how, since the death of her father, life had dramatically changed.

He asked about her father and what he would have thought about her becoming a professional actress. Louise noticed that she was the one doing all the talking. *Perhaps this is the way a good agent works.*

'Oh dear, Mister Graves, I seem to be doing all the talking.'

'And how do you feel about travel? If I could find you some acting work away from home, would you consider it?'

'If you recommend the part, I would be happy to take your advice.' Graves smiled. 'Have I said the wrong thing?' asked Louise.

'But what if it meant moving away from your family, your boyfriend or husband?'

Louise was thrown. This seemed a touch invasive. *Is he probing for details of my love life?*

'Goodness,' said Louise. 'I've never thought about that. Perhaps I should wait until I finish my studies and then decide. Is that the right answer?'

'It's a very good answer,' said Graves. 'And I should tell you I've heard a rumour about your ability to act whilst not exactly on stage. You even made the papers I believe.'

He smiled and Louise was a tad worried. *That would have to be Nightie.* She was surprised her guarded comments to Nightie had found their way into this conversation. Her agent certainly had done his homework but seemed able to keep a secret. She liked and trusted him. She could not have found a better agent.

They parted on the best of terms and Louise walked to the Vesteys to tell an excited Elizabeth and Molly about the meeting.

The term ended and Louise chose to stay in Cambridge over Easter. She threw herself into Chaucer and Shakespeare, went to church with the Vesteys and thought about Nightie, Tom and Dickie Graves, although not necessarily in that order.

She knew her social calendar had two important wedding dates. Victoria had insisted on being married after her son so as not to steal his and Georgina's thunder.

Louise found it hard to believe she was coming to the end of her second year at Cambridge. In that time a lot of the River Cam had passed under the Mathematical Bridge.

As the end of the academic year approached, a letter arrived from Richard Graves.

He mentioned a possible new acting job for her and wondered if they could meet to discuss it. He had another appointment in the area next week. Naturally she agreed and suggested her lecture-free day. He sent a telegram confirming the date and time.

Whatever could it be? And why did we have to meet in person? And why now when we agreed I would not launch my acting career until after I finished my studies at Cambridge?

She waited in the Girton lobby. Graves arrived by taxi and as it was a lovely day they strolled in the College grounds and sat on a garden bench.

'Miss Wellesley, I have become aware of a possible new role for you. It's unusual and I don't want you to make any sort of decision without first thinking about it.' Louise became increasingly curious.

'Forgive me, Mister Graves, but I thought your advice was that I should finish my studies before taking on any major roles.'

'I did and I apologise for giving confusing advice. But this role is rather special. I think it suits you beautifully.' Louise took a deep breath. The tension was killing her.

'I have a confession, Miss Wellesley. I have told you the truth but not the whole truth. I am indeed a theatrical agent but I do have a second job. It also involves actors and performing but not always on stage.'

As an agent, Dickie Graves made a damn fine actor. He knew the value of the pregnant pause. He looked intently at her. She said nothing and waited for him to speak.

'But before I spill the beans, Miss Wellesley, I'm afraid I must ask you to sign yet another contract.'

He withdrew a folded document from his pocket and handed it to her. Louise opened it and read the heading—*Official Secrets Act 1920*.

Henry's wedding was worse than Louise feared. She was completely ignored by the bride and bride's mother. However, Louise's mother's wedding was polite and stress free. The interior of the registry office in the old Marylebone Town Hall was the perfect setting for one of the quietest weddings on record.

Louise was a witness and as she signed the certificate, she thought about another document she'd recently signed. And, having signed it in secret, Louise was unable to tell anyone. But why?

What exactly is this new role? Apparently she was being offered the greatest part in her fledgling career and yet couldn't tell a soul. Anyone she loved would never know of what might be the start of her brilliant career.

Summer had come in and Edmund agreed to live in Surrey with Louise who was in no hurry to see the house sold. Edmund had a chum come to stay and Louise was left to her own devices. She had a reading list for her final year and was relieved when Richard Graves telephoned.

'I saw a photograph of your brother and his bride in *The Telegraph*. All jolly good fun I suppose.'

'If you must know, Mister Graves, it was ghastly and I can't wait to talk to you about ... well whatever it is you want to tell me.'

'Good show. So how are you placed for tomorrow morning at say, 10.30? Can you come up to London?'

'Yes, that's fine. I'll see you in the morning.'

In London, Richard Graves was his usual charming self. He grabbed his hat, escorted Louise into the street and hailed a taxi.

'I want you to meet a colleague who knows all about your possible new role.'

'Possible?' Louise was suddenly apprehensive.

'Oh the role is yours, Miss Wellesley, but only if you choose to accept it.'

They alighted in Baker Street.

'Good old Baker Street,' said the agent. 'Famous for you know who.'

'Did you know, Mister Graves, that until 1930, Baker Street was quite short and there was no such number as 221B?'

'You must stop showing off, Miss Wellesley.' She saw laughter in his eyes. 'Now come and meet Bunty. I think you'll like him.'

They entered a non-descript building, went upstairs and knocked on a door marked *Accountant*.

'Bunty,' said Graves and 'Dickie,' said Bunty. It was all hail-fellow-well-met stuff with genuine affection between the men.

Louise met Major Ralph Bunting. She thought he was rather dashing and moved well for a man with only one and a half legs. His manners and moustache were impeccable. He was up for a chat.

'Please, do sit down, Miss Wellesley. Dickie has told me so much about you. I feel as if I've missed something special not having seen you perform on stage.' Louise was stuck for words.

'Thank you,' was the best she could muster.

'Now please let me explain all this hush-hush palaver and then let you decide if you'd really like to accept the role. Dickie and I are part of a government department which is attached to the SIS, the Secret Intelligence Service. We're an independent arm and pretty much do as we please.'

Louise was fascinated, worried and excited. Bunting continued.

'My job is to find people to play a role in real life. They act a part, not on stage, although that could be included, in the good old real world. How does that sound so far?'

'Interesting,' said Louise and left the word hanging.

Bunting nodded and smiled. He was already agreeing with Graves' assessment of Louise. He explained further.

'The two things I need to remind you about are first, you are under no obligation to take the role but second, having signed the *Official Secrets*

Act you are under an obligation never to reveal any of the matters we discuss here. Is that clear?'

'Perfectly,' replied Louise sticking to her short answers.

'Dickie, how about you explain the political background.'

Graves spoke about the growing threat of war with Germany, its greatly expanded military forces and how Hitler had taken over various regions. While Britain wanted peace, we had to prepare in case of war.

Louise was aware of everything these men told her except for one thing. *What is the proposed role?* When they told her, she was stunned. Bunting spoke.

'We recruit people to play a role in a country which might go to war. In your case the country is France and the job is that of an actress. We provide you with a new identity, the necessary documentation and a life story. You live your life as this person and if a war begins and if we think you can help us, we make contact.'

'Do you want me to be a spy?' asked Louise.

Both men frowned and shook their heads. 'No, no, no; definitely not,' said Graves. 'We prefer to call our actors, sleepers. In theatrical terms, you are resting.'

Louise smiled. She liked the analogy. Bunting cut to the chase.

'We want you to move to Paris and live and work as an actress. Does that appeal?'

Louise's mind was spinning. 'I think so.'

'Think so, won't do, Miss Wellesley,' said a serious Graves. 'You must *need* to take this role. It has to be the role you would do anything to get.'

There was a pause. Both men looked at Louise. They waited.

Louise looked at one then the other. 'Gentlemen, more than anything else in the world, I *have* to play this role.' Bunting smiled and Graves nodded. 'But I do have some questions.'

Bunting jumped in. 'Well let me give you the details and then you can ask whatever you like. Your name is Mademoiselle Juliette Beauchamp. You were born in Marseilles in 1919. Your parents died in a car accident when you were five years old and you were raised by your maternal grandparents. The last of your grandparents has recently died and soon you will travel to Paris to try and fulfil your dream of becoming a professional actress.'

Louise was struggling to take it all in. Bunting continued.

'When you arrive in Paris you will have a room paid for at the Grand Hotel de Clement for one week. You will be supplied with a French passport, identification papers and 2,000 francs. In that first week, you must find accommodation and work, hopefully in the theatre. You will literally be on your own. You never contact us. If we need to contact you, there will be a code word for identification purposes.'

Louise's spinning mind spun faster. *This isn't a dream.* Bunting had even more to say.

'You will be paid a monthly salary of 24 pounds, 11 shillings and 6 pence, paid into a British bank account, which you will receive in full plus interest upon your return to England.'

Graves interrupted. 'If unfortunately you don't return to England, the person or persons you nominate will receive the funds in full.'

That was nice to know. But what about the "If unfortunately you don't return" bit? *Does that mean if I'm kidnapped, killed or just fancy living in a chateau for the rest of my days?* Louise paused. She was being watched. They waited for her response.

'When would this particular role become available?'

'Well we never like to rush our performers, Miss Wellesley,' said Bunting. 'Are you free next week?'

'Next week! To go to France?'

'Oh good heavens, no; to start training.' Louise was confused and her agent butted in.

'Not acting training, Miss Wellesley. We are more than happy with your ability to perform.'

'But you'll need to learn a few tricks,' said Bunting.

'You mean learn how to be a spy?' asked Louise again.

Bunting was upset. 'Please Miss Wellesley; you are not being asked to become a spy but a sleeper. You're far more likely to be exposed as a spy. As a sleeper you would be one of our contacts in a foreign country. Please forget all that cloak and dagger business. There are no spies on our books.' The atmosphere was tense. After a long pause Graves spoke.

'Do you have any questions, Miss Wellesley?'

Louise had questions aplenty but none related specifically to the proposed job. *What about my mother? What about my studies? And who can I ask?*

Well actually she couldn't ask anyone because she'd signed the *Official Secrets Act.* Whatever she decided, she couldn't tell a living soul. Talk about a career change.

Chapter 14

LOUISE AWOKE in a strange bed in a strange room in a strange building. She sat on a strange lavatory in a strange bathroom. It was the first day of her new life.

Yesterday she arrived at a deserted train station in Scotland. The only person in sight was a man leaning on a car. She walked towards him.

'First time, love?' he said flicking his cigarette.

'Oui,' said Louise. The man started the engine and Louise hurried to jump in with her case. They drove for a while, turned into a long drive then stopped in front of a large house.

Louise walked to the front door and knocked. Nothing. She knocked louder and hurt her knuckles. She turned the handle and pushed. The door opened and she entered. It was colder inside than out.

She stood in a tall hallway and heard a voice from upstairs. 'Hello. I'm up here.' Louise looked up and saw a young woman with acres of red hair.

Louise climbed the stairs which looked and felt bombproof. She heard sounds so walked along a corridor. The woman with red hair was plumping pillows on a bed. She spoke. 'You must be Louise.'

In perfect French, Louise replied. 'Pardon Madame, my name is Juliette.'

'Very good; start as you mean to go on. And it's Mademoiselle. Now this is your room. The loo's at the end of the passage. Make yourself at home and come down to the kitchen when you're ready. Oh I'm Kenna, by the way.' They shook hands and Kenna left.

Louise unpacked, looked out of the window at the forest behind the house then went down to the kitchen. Two men and Kenna were drinking tea. She poured a cup for Louise. 'Have a biscuit,' said Kenna.

Louise sat and looked at the others. Kenna didn't make any introductions. This was a training course not a meeting of the WI. The men spoke English.

'I'm Ruben,' said the first man.

'Fernando,' said the second.

'Juliette,' said Louise and all four drank their tea in silence.

Kenna finally spoke. 'Feel free to walk in the grounds or read in the sitting-room. We dine at seven.'

And that was Louise's introduction to sleeper training. Deep in the Scottish countryside, she spent a fortnight learning how to be accepted as a local in a foreign country.

She learnt how to maintain a new identity, become a part of a community, how to be aware of people who might be friendly and how to know the signs you were mistrusted.

The sleepers discussed under what circumstances they would return to England, and, if so, how and when. Their assignment was open-ended. A lot depended on whether war was declared.

They were reminded several times they were not spies. They were not to act as spies, consider themselves to be spies or even think like a spy. They would each be given a code word which, if delivered, would activate their sleeper status. Once activated, they were to wait for instructions.

They were given lessons in handling firearms and in self-defence and taught how to survive if on the run. Louise was a quick learner. Perhaps the fight instructor was a bit soft on the only female trainee because she put the strong man on his back—hard. 'Merci, Mademoiselle,' he ruefully muttered.

They created individual stories to keep their families ignorant and hopefully worry-free once their sudden and unexpected departure was revealed.

Louise chose playing a role in a travelling troupe of thespians performing Shakespearean excerpts in South Africa, Australia and New Zealand. She wrote letters and cards to her mother and addressed the envelopes. She wrote a letter of explanation to her brothers, Nightie and Matilda. The cards and letters to her mother would be posted by SIS agents in the respective countries at regular intervals.

Louise felt sick about the distress she might cause her family and her mother in particular. The only comforting thought was that if war did break out, her mother would be grateful her daughter was far, far away in sunny Australia.

On her final night of training, she thought of her father. What on Earth would he make of his daughter in this situation? He'd changed his conservative mind and allowed his daughter to study at Cambridge and then urged her to finish the course. Now she was dropping out—*I'm not being sent down, Papa*—and joining the Secret Intelligence Service as a sleeper. If war broke out, who knows what she'd be doing?

Is that okay, Papa? She smiled and wondered what Tom Curzon was doing just then. It would be wonderful if Paris had a need for medical missionaries. Dream on.

It was really difficult saying goodbye to people knowing the truth was hidden. Explaining to the Vesteys that she'd decided to postpone her studies and take the plunge into professional theatre overseas was terribly sad, particularly for Elizabeth and Molly who both genuinely loved Louise. But adieu it was and Girton College lost one of its more interesting residents.

Louise went to Wiltshire to say goodbye to her mother. Circumstances had clearly changed for both women. Victoria sensed her daughter was now a woman and very much her equal. If Victoria thought Louise was not telling the truth about this latest overseas venture, she asked no questions. The Wellesley home in Surrey was put on the market and Edmund was to handle its sale. Louise would soon become a wealthy young woman.

There was a final meeting in Baker Street with Major Bunting and Richard Graves.

'All set?' asked Bunting. Louise nodded. 'We heard you did rather well up in Scotland.' Louise smiled. 'Now there are a couple of things remaining. We do need your British passport, I'm afraid.' Louise handed it to Bunting. 'When you arrive back in Blighty, just ask the officer in charge to ring me or Mister Graves.'

Her French passport was safely tucked away.

'And the final and most important matter,' said Bunting, 'is your code word. It's *Albee*.'

'*Albee*,' repeated Louise.

'If ever we want to wake you from your sleeper status, someone will contact you and use the code word. If and when that happens, you simply wait for instructions. We have people in Paris who keep an eye on our sleepers.'

Louise was unsure. 'Does the code word have any significance?'

Bunting smiled. 'I believe it does, for you I mean. I'm told it's an Australian expression.'

'*Albee*? I've not heard it before.'

'I think it's short for Al*bee* Double U.'

Louise smiled, shook her head and then laughed. 'I thought Plum was strictly a family secret.'

'Not where the SIS is concerned,' said a smiling Graves.

So that was that. Tomorrow Louise or Plum or rather Juliette would pack her bag and leave Britain to do what and for how long, nobody knew. The men shook hands with Mademoiselle Beauchamp.

'Au revoir,' said Bunting.

'Break a leg,' said Graves.

Farewell England. Bonjour France.

In 1939 European leaders were talking about war. Britain and France rejected Stalin's request to be friends. Stalin courted Hitler and amazingly the two dictators agreed a partnership. Many said this was not a marriage made in heaven. They were right.

The British and French became nervous; the Poles very nervous. War was perhaps only weeks away.

And into this continent of festering fear, hatred and potential catastrophe, a young Englishwoman in disguise was about to try her luck in the French capital. Good luck, Mademoiselle.

Juliette Beauchamp arrived in Paris on July 14, 1939 exactly 150 years to the day since the storming of the Bastille. Was this an omen? She'd spent the previous night in a small hotel in Marseilles then caught the train to Paris.

She went to the Grand Hotel de Clement where her room was paid for as arranged. She sat on the bed with two French newspapers. She needed accommodation and work so job first and then a chateau. Well, maybe a garret or half a basement.

She scanned the newspapers for large Parisian theatres thinking they would be more likely to require many performers; even stagehands. Juliette wasn't fussy.

La Fête Nationale or Bastille Day was not a good day for job or flat hunting and with sidewalk cafes overflowing with celebratory Parisians, Juliette saw that war was not the prime topic of conversation. Was she a sleeper without cause?

She made her way to the Théâtre des Bouffes du Nord. It had many doors. One had a pinned sign stating *Rehearsal Today 10am*. Juliette opened the door and stepped into a long corridor. At the far end she heard voices. She started walking.

She was ten metres from the voices when she heard the blood curdling scream of a woman in distress. Juliette froze. Then she heard the sounds of a fierce fight and more screams. *Should I enter and assist?*

The fighting sounds accelerated. *Should I call a gendarme?* Suddenly the screams became very loud and more frantic. Someone was being murdered. That was it. Juliette decided she *was* her sister's keeper and ran to the door. She had up a full head of steam when she turned the handle.

The door opened easily inwards and Juliette fell into the room. She overbalanced and sprawled on the floor. The screaming stopped. She looked up and saw a group of surprised people. A man stepped forward and offered his hand.

'Welcome,' he said. 'That's what I call a spectacular entrance.'

Just as the sign said, this was a rehearsal. Juliette apologised for her unusual entrance and explained that she was an actress from Marseilles who had come to Paris to find work. The actors were friendly and invited her to stay and watch the rehearsal.

The play was new to Juliette. Its aim was confrontation. The performance was more important than the text hence the staged fighting. The genre was called *Theatre of Cruelty*. Let screaming be unconfined.

Juliette watched the intimidation, violence and crude movement. The sounds were brutal.

As Louise she wondered what Miss Finchley and the St Peter's Players would make of this "art"? Would any theatre in England perform such a play? If in Cambridge, at least the vicar would have something other than his drains to worry about.

When the actors broke for coffee, a man and a woman approached Juliette. The man spoke.

'I am Gustave, the director. This is Martine. You say you are an actress?'

'Yes.'

'What is your experience? Have you worked in this form of theatre?'

'No. I've mainly worked with the classics; Shakespeare and ...'

'Ha. That is holding up a mirror to life where the person is wearing rose-coloured glasses. Stay if you like and afterwards we can chat.'

The director left and Martine and Juliette sat.

'Ignore him,' said Martine. He thinks he's God's gift to the theatre. His last two plays have been monumental flops. So do not stay if this is not for you. I stay because I like new ideas in theatre but mainly because I am sleeping with the director.'

Juliette liked the honesty of the woman and spoke frankly. 'I'm just looking for work in the theatre. I've little money and nowhere to stay. Can you recommend anything?'

'I can do more than recommend. Later I will take you to meet Madame Mimi Baudin. She can help with work and accommodation.'

'Thank you, you're very kind.'

'Actually I'm quite selfish. You are beautiful and if you stay, Gustave will kick me out of his bed and appoint you as his new leading lady and mistress.'

Martine looked at Juliette. Their eyes spoke of understanding.

'Whatever your motives,' said Juliette, 'I'm still very grateful.'

After the rehearsal Martine took Juliette to meet Madame Baudin. She was remarkable and then some. Her make-up gave her bodyweight a serious boost. She looked "interesting", must have had shares in a leading French perfumery and ran a boarding house for women who had little money and a lot of woe.

Madame Baudin had once been a dancer in the glamorous music halls of Paris. Her figure then and now would be ideal as before and after images. Forty years over-indulging in gin, cigarettes and cream had created today's Madame Baudin.

'Bonjour Madame,' said Martine kissing the woman. 'This is my friend Juliette. She needs accommodation and employment. I told her you are the finest landlady and the best theatrical agent in Paris.'

Mimi laughed. She had a raspy laugh and a raspier voice. There was a groove on her lower lip which was the perfect shape for a cigarette. Once inserted the cigarette was never removed until replaced with another. She could talk effortlessly with a burning Gauloises affixed to her face.

Martine left and Madame Baudin ushered Juliette into her apartment. It was a cross between a Persian bazaar and a brothel trying too hard to be glamorous.

'I have a vacant room, Mademoiselle, but not until next week. The rent is twenty-five francs a month. Take it or leave it.'

'Thank you, Madame. I will take it.'

'That will be ten francs deposit. You can trust me.'

Juliette was living dangerously. She hadn't seen the room and was handing over money to a woman she barely knew. But Juliette decided to take risks. Her reason for being in Paris was a risk. She had accommodation and now needed a job.

'Pardon, Madame, but I am also looking for work. I have been an actress in different roles and would love to perform in Paris. If you can suggest any theatres or people I might contact, I will be extremely grateful.'

Juliette was hoping Martine was correct. If Mimi Baudin had contacts in the world of theatre, Juliette might find a home and a job in one fell swoop. But the young Englishwoman suddenly became alarmed when her landlady looked Juliette up and down and made a simple request.

'Please, Mademoiselle, show me your breasts.'

That afternoon Juliette did as Madame Baudin instructed. At the Folies Bergère Juliette was to ask for Monsieur Paul Derval and say, "Mimi sent me".

The landlady clearly had friends in high places. At the music hall her name caused the man in the front office to drop everything and escort Juliette upstairs. He knocked on an impressive door.

'Oui,' came from inside. Juliette entered a beautifully appointed office. 'Ah, you are from Madame Baudin. Entrez s'il vous plaît.'

Juliette met the director of the famous Folies Bergère and liked him immediately. He reminded Juliette of her father; beautifully dressed, fine head of hair, excellent manners and genuinely interested in people.

'So Mademoiselle, you wish to join the Folies. Allow me to explain the pay and conditions.'

Juliette was surprised. 'Oh, pardon Monsieur, but ...'

'There is some mistake? Madame Baudin has recommended you most highly. You are Mademoiselle Beauchamp?'

'Oui.'

'She described your figure as perfect. And I can see how your natural beauty will be a wonderful asset to our company.'

'You are most kind, Monsieur. It's just that I have a classical training in acting and wondered if you had any openings for an actress?'

'But every Folies Bergère showgirl *is* an actress. Are not stage movements, facial expressions and hand gestures all part of acting?'

'Well yes, they are.'

'Then you are offered a position as an actress. Do you accept?'

'But I haven't auditioned, Monsieur.'

Derval smiled. 'You obviously do not know the influence of your landlady and nobody knows the perfect Folies Bergère performer better than the wonderful Mimi.' Louise hesitated.

'Ah,' said the director. 'You have concerns about nudity; a jealous boyfriend or over-protective father, perhaps?'

117

'No, Monsieur,' replied Juliette, although she dared not think of what her family might say if they knew her present situation. 'It's just that my drama training encourages me to perform as a character.'

'Very noble, but do you know the difference in pay between an actress and a showgirl?'

Juliette found it hard to believe how much the showgirls were paid. She thought of Nightie's acting advice then smiled.

'If you will have me, Monsieur Derval, I would be delighted to accept your offer.'

The director was happy and Juliette gave the impression she was delighted although her smile hid a mountain of worry. She'd performed on many stages in many roles but always when clothed. Performing semi-naked was scary.

Still what a successful beginning to her new life in Paris. On only her first day in the City of Light, Louise had found both accommodation and employment.

She was lucky to have met such a charming gentleman as Monsieur Derval. His manners were impeccable with not even a hint of impropriety from the meticulous manager. Alas Juliette would not always find such gentlemanly behaviour elsewhere in Paris. A wolf in sheep's clothing was lying in wait.

Chapter 15

KURT ATTENDED a Gestapo meeting at which the all-powerful Reinhard Heydrich was speaking.

'Gentlemen, soon the Wehrmacht will lead a military response into Poland. Intelligence informs us we can expect an imminent attack from Polish troops and when that occurs, naturally German troops will respond with force. Our job is to locate all leading Polish intellectuals, priests and officials who may be a threat to the Reich.'

Locate thought Kurt. Was that a euphemism for *eliminate*? Cousin Max was right about the Gestapo's use of language.

But what was that business about Poland attacking Germany? Did the Reich have a crystal ball? And what on earth would cause the Poles to invade the Fatherland? Surely the far-weaker Poles would be committing military suicide.

Heydrich continued. 'Once the Wehrmacht repel the enemy, our job begins. We round up the VIPs and when the Poles see their leaders arrested, opposition will disappear.'

Kurt loved all this talk. He was now steeped in the beliefs and methods of the Gestapo. He was almost the perfect Gestapo poster boy.

He knew that the way wars were fought had changed and that a secret police force was never more useful. Today's wars were fought in towns and cities, in the streets and often against people who were not soldiers in uniform. The best army now needed expert help in finding these enemies in disguise. Kurt's task, the Gestapo's task was to locate underground fighters, prominent citizens, anyone who was a threat to the Reich.

'But why arrest them?' asked an agent behind Kurt. 'Why not just shoot them on the spot?'

Heydrich took a deep breath. The room was hushed. 'Use your head, man. Put these radicals to work in the concentration camps. Slave labour benefits the Reich. Besides, bullets cost money.'

The room echoed with laughter.

In August 1939, as Hitler made plans to stage a grand show in Paris, Juliette Beauchamp was doing just that.

She became a glamorous showgirl in the Folies Bergère wearing an over-the-top costume which didn't go over the top. On stage she was elegant, feminine and edible. Her style and looks had most men and many women feasting their eyes on her naked charms.

Max Hartmann was feasting his eyes on the theory of rapid warfare. His cousin, Kurt Hartmann, was feasting his eyes on the names of personnel in churches, universities and political institutions in Polish cities.

And while the Nazis planned and conspired, Juliette performed and went partying. Her room at Madame Baudin's was used only by day. By night she thrived at the Folies Bergère, followed by parties and visits to clubs. Juliette became very much a night person.

She knew little about jazz until Paris. Here it was intoxicating where Django Reinhardt and Stéphane Grappelli were part of the Quintette du Hot Club de France.

One night after toe-tapping their way into the wee small hours, Juliette and another showgirl found themselves at a party in a stylish Montmartre apartment. The host was a dashing Frenchman who enjoyed women and money. He ran through both with ease. Oscar Masson spotted Juliette and made his approach.

'Why haven't I had the pleasure?' he purred kissing her hand. 'Are you a movie star or, more likely, a princess?'

Juliette had been warned many times about the danger of certain males. Even the artistic director at the Folies gave the showgirls a reminder about men such as Oscar Masson.

He was charming, good-looking, wealthy and well-mannered but was only after one thing and it wasn't Juliette's stamp collection.

Even with warning bells ringing, Juliette found herself being charmed by Monsieur Masson. She was not to know his sexual CV could well have inspired Mozart to write Leporello a much longer aria.

One tried and tested way of seducing a young woman involves charm and alcohol. Oscar used both and with a little something extra in the drink to help the seducer seduce. Juliette knew about the dangers of alcohol. Her late Uncle Crispin had a liver with a life expectancy of two hundred and nineteen years.

But the music, the suave conversation and the superbly mixed beverage of gin, champagne, lemon and sugar tickled her throat and relaxed her senses, not to mention her elastic.

The party got louder. Juliette felt queasy and when the wolf in sheep's clothing offered to assist the damsel in distress, she gratefully accepted his offer.

They journeyed upstairs to a room with the most ornate bed in Montmartre. It was high off the floor and Juliette was politely placed on its covering.

She was drowsy and having her clothes removed seemed like a gallant exercise. The womanizer went to work. Juliette felt no pain. Too much alcohol induces sleep, but even drunks can be jolted from their stupor.

Suddenly the noise within the bedroom became very loud, close and frighteningly real. Juliette snapped out of her listless state. So too did half the neighbourhood. Repeated gunfire in Montmartre at 0336 hours has a way of being heard.

And if the sounds didn't grab Juliette's attention, the copious amounts of blood splattering on her face and chest certainly did the trick.

She struggled to push Oscar Masson off her undressed body. Then the door was flung open and light filled the room. Partygoers rushed in. Screams rang out and someone yelled.

'She's got a gun!'

It was only then Juliette noticed she was holding a revolver.

Chapter 16

EUROPE HAS TWO Eiffel Towers. Everyone knows the one in Paris but not its baby cousin, the Silesian Eiffel Tower. It's wooden, some 400 feet tall and access is via a ladder. It got its name because it has a similar shape to the famous Parisian structure.

On the night of Thursday, August 31, 1939 the two Eiffel Towers were linked by murder.

In France, Oscar Masson, who had been pumping women for years, was himself pumped with three bullets. The Parisian Eiffel Tower towered over the murder scene.

In Germany, Franciszek Honiok, who was allegedly too friendly with Poland, was also pumped with three bullets. The German Eiffel Tower towered over the murder scene.

Both murders had serious consequences. One threatened the life and covert career of a young English actress. The other started World War 2.

Hitler was a dictator and a cheat. He came up with a plan in which Poland attacked Germany—or so it seemed. Hitler was like the tough football coach. "Right then, lads, get your retaliation in first".

But why would Poland invade Germany? Poland was hopelessly outgunned. Germany had thousands of planes and tanks up against the Polish army with its sword-wielding soldiers on horseback. Attacking Germany would be suicide. But attack they did. Well, not quite. You see the Polish attacks were actually German attacks in disguise. It was a simple plan orchestrated by Adolf the sneak.

The Nazis killed prisoners from the Dachau concentration camp, dressed them in Polish uniforms and "arranged" them at various venues along the German/Polish border. The Nazis referred to these fake dead soldiers as "canned goods". Himmler boasted. 'We have plenty of canned goods.'

The fake attacks on German property included a railway station, customs office and a radio tower, Germany's Eiffel Tower.

Minor damage to German property occurred and the Nazis showed the press the dead Polish soldiers and the damage they caused.

Franciszek Honiok was allegedly a German collaborator working for the Poles. He was arrested, drugged, dressed in a Polish uniform and then shot. Arguably he was the first person killed in World War 2 even if the war didn't officially start until the next day.

Now this contrived invasion required lots of planning and preparation. You don't successfully go to war on a whim. German airmen, infantrymen, support staff and Gestapo agents rehearsed and rehearsed.

Oberst Max Hartmann played a part as did his cousin Kurt.

When the Germans invaded on the first of September 1939, Oberst Max Hartmann and his tank were in the first wave.

So powerful, so well organized and so quick was the German advance that within days vast areas of Poland were invaded and tens of thousands of Polish soldiers were captured. Within four weeks Poland surrendered. The Wehrmacht machine was helped by the Gestapo machine removing hundreds of Polish VIPs. Now you see them, now you don't. The cousins Hartmann were officially at war.

The Luftwaffe kick-started hostilities and crippled Poland. Airports, bridges and railway junctions were identified by aerial photography weeks before the invasion so pilots knew precisely what to target. The Poles were in a fist fight wearing a blindfold and with one arm tied behind their back.

Wehrmacht tanks moved swiftly into Poland. Max was leading and when he came to a wrecked bridge, instead of waiting for engineers, he found a fording spot, drove through the water and kept moving.

With the enemy scattered and supplies far behind, Max swung off the road and into a farm yard. There was a railway junction a hundred metres away and a poorly aimed bomb had landed near the farmhouse leaving a gaping hole in one wall. Chickens and pigs were not fussed about the invaders and went about their business.

The farm seemed deserted as Max and his two crew members wandered around eyeing their potential pork and chicken feast. Suddenly the backdoor of the farmhouse opened and the Germans grabbed their guns. But there was no threat.

The farmer's wife was a confused and frail octogenarian. Earlier that morning a Stuka missed the railway junction and dropped a bomb in her front garden. The blast killed her frail husband and coupled with her dementia, the woman was not exactly the greatest threat facing the Third Reich. Wearing only her nightdress she wandered about calling in Polish.

Max put away his weapon and approached the woman. 'Madam, do you speak German?' She ignored Max and the Panzer in her yard. Her ranting continued. Max turned to his men.

'Engel, you speak Polish. Talk to her.'

'I am not fluent, Herr Oberst but I'll try.'

Engel asked if she was all right. She gave rambling answers. Max ordered his loader to investigate inside the house.

Engel gave up. 'I can't make sense of what she's saying, Herr Oberst, but I think she's looking for a saucepan.'

'A saucepan? In the farmyard?'

'She does seem a bit soft in the head, Herr Oberst. She needs the saucepan to cook breakfast for her husband.'

The Germans watched the pathetic creature stumble. Max moved quickly to help. The crew member who went inside the house came out and explained that an old man was dead in the bedroom, covered in debris from the bomb blast. The Germans realised that the shock, perhaps coupled with some serious health condition, had left the old woman in an impossible position.

'What should we do, Herr Oberst?' asked Engel.

Max shook his head. 'Damn war! The kindest thing would be to shoot her now.' Max's men were horrified.

'Are you serious, Herr Oberst?' Max was furious.

'Of course I'm not bloody serious. But I didn't join the Wehrmacht to bomb old men and babysit feeble widows.'

Max looked at his men. They respected his bravery and plain speaking. They were glad they didn't have to make the decisions.

'Should we request the Red Cross to attend, Herr Oberst?'

'What and drive off leaving her to try and feed her dead husband? What happened to the good old-fashioned wars when soldiers fired at one another from trenches and civilians stayed home and wept when the telegram arrived?'

Max had never felt so frustrated. He sent his loader to search the outbuildings while he and Engel attempted to communicate with the wretched woman. They helped her sit on a bench. Max placed his jacket around her shoulders. Then more surprises when the loader returned with two young children.

They were Polish and extremely frightened. Engel spoke to them. Their story was horrific.

The children were siblings from the nearby town of Wieluń. It was the first town to be bombed when the German invasion began early that morning. Just why Wieluń was bombed is unknown. It had no soldiers and no important installations or military equipment. Its hospital had a huge red cross on its roof but that cross became the target for Stukas as they switched on their sirens, screamed out of the sky and dropped their lethal cargo on the hospital and town.

In their home in Wieluń the terrified children discovered the mangled and bloody bodies of their dead parents. The siblings fled Wieluń and found their way to this farm.

Max had Engel explain the situation to the children as delicately as possible. Their best chance was to stay put. He sent his men to remove the body of the dead farmer and discreetly bury him with a cross to mark the site. He hoped the children would care for the old woman and remain at least until some form of help arrived, if ever. God help them if murderous troops or fanatical Gestapo agents stopped here.

Max had his men butcher a pig and kill some chickens. They took a quarter for their supplies and left the rest for the Polish victims of war.

He ordered his men into their tank and drove back to the Warsaw road as fast as he could. He wondered if the Führer would personally congratulate him on this his latest triumph.

Kurt Hartmann was angry. The Wehrmacht invasion of Poland was supported by the Gestapo invasion of Poland. Kurt had enjoyed his trip to Vienna and was looking forward to a trip to Warsaw.

The Gestapo allocated tasks and Kurt missed out. His thoughts were private. *What? Why? Surely you aren't blaming the adverse publicity of the Crystal Night on me! I did a brilliant job removing those Polish Jews.*

And to make matters worse he was given another local job and a soft and simple one at that. He was appointed to oversee the new domestic slaves in the Fatherland. Women!

Kurt was furious but bit his tongue. His thinking was clear. *Do this job well, Hartmann and promotion will follow.*

Himmler's idea was to bring Polish women to Germany to perform domestic tasks for German households thus making life easier for the all-important German mothers. Himmler explained the plan to Kurt. At least Kurt was dealing with the most powerful of Nazi leaders.

'We saw your success deporting Polish Jews, Hartmann. Now we want your expertise importing Polish domestics.' Kurt was being damned with faint praise.

I'll show you bastards, he thought. And he did.

Thanks to Kurt, half a million Polish women were brought to skivvy in German homes. No pay of course and loyal Nazis got first pick of the slaves.

Kurt wanted to check his handiwork. He arranged to visit some Berlin homes and see for himself the effectiveness of his organizational skills. Frau Gottschalk was the wife of a prominent Nazi. Kurt was welcomed at the front door.

'Good morning Herr Hartmann. It is an honour to have you visit our home.'

It was a beautiful home inside and out. A small boy ran to his mother. Kurt bent down.

'Ah, Master Gottschalk I believe.'

'He is quite shy, Herr Hartmann, but one day will be a very proud German.'

'I'm sure,' nodded an almost-smiling Kurt who rarely smiled these days. 'Now, let us discuss your Polish domestic servant. Is she here?'

'In the kitchen, sir; please follow me.'

Carrying her toddler, the lady of the house led Kurt to a beautifully appointed kitchen. It was as large as some Jewish apartments. A Polish woman was kneeling and washing the spotless floor by hand. She kept working not daring to stop or look up.

Kurt enquired. 'And is everything in order, Frau Gottschalk?'

'We had some problems at first but now she understands what is required. I am free to look after my son and see that he grows into a true Aryan.'

Kurt looked at the mother, the house, the child and the slave. The world had certainly changed in the years since the Nazis took power. The Gottschalks were once good, decent people. Now, after years of Hitler and his policies of superiority, many such so-called "moral" Germans had no qualms about accepting some people as sub-human.

Frau Gottschalk put down her son. The three year-old ran across the kitchen to the Polish woman and yelled as he repeatedly struck her.

'Silly bitch! Silly bitch!' The woman flinched but kept working. The toddler kept slapping and shouting.

Frau Gottschalk was embarrassed. 'I do apologise Herr Hartmann. I can't think where my son learnt such language.' She politely spoke to the boy. 'Hans come back to Mummy.'

Kurt returned to his car. At least the next generation had learnt how a good Nazi should behave.

Give me the child for seven years and I will give you the man.

Chapter 17

JULIETTE SAT in a Paris police station. A blanket gave her blood-splattered body and clothes a semblance of modesty. She was being interviewed about the recently-deceased Oscar Masson. Murder was the charge as not many people commit suicide by shooting themselves three times in the chest.

The detective, Capitaine Émile Bonhomme, was polite making Juliette's misery a tad less awful. He was 64 and almost too nice to be a policeman. Few knew he once trained to be a priest. He spoke calmly.

'And you are sure you do not wish to have your lawyer present?' Juliette was still in shock. She shook her head. 'So tell me, Mademoiselle Beauchamp, how long had you known Monsieur Masson?'

Juliette spoke with difficulty. She wasn't acting. 'I only met him last night. I mean this morning.'

'Did you enter his bedroom of your own free will?'

Juliette hesitated. She really wasn't sure. Shock can linger for quite some time. Her suffering got worse. 'I think so.'

'Does that mean you cannot remember or you were too drunk to know?'

Her nightmare dragged on. She was the only suspect. Did she shoot Oscar Masson in self defence? Did he try to rape her? Did she grab the gun? Where was the gun? Did she fight for her honour?

'Would you like a glass of water, Mademoiselle?'

Juliette was glad of a break. She thought of the shame she would bring to her family and imagined the newspaper headlines.

In France it would be *Folies Bergère Dancer Murders Lover* while across the channel the press would have a field day with *Viscount's Sister in Naked Murder Romp*. Thank God her dear Papa would never know.

Juliette could never explain her lie about acting Down Under, let alone this scandal. She wasn't a Shakespearean actress in Sydney but a topless showgirl in Paris.

Then her confusion began to clear. Her shame may never reach Blighty. Her family believed she was touring the Antipodes. Juliette Beauchamp was the suspect. The young woman with the shapely breasts was the one with the gun. Who is she to Louise Wellesley? Perhaps all was not lost.

Juliette quickly shelved thoughts about contacting her brother Edmund and having him come to her aid. If he saved her from prison in France, her reward would be prison in England for breaking the *Official Secrets Act*. She made a decision. Stay in character, fight any charges and hope her family never finds out.

But family was not Juliette's only concern. Her SIS contacts in London may well learn of her scandal. How could she serve them now? She remembered Major Bunting's words back in Baker Street. "We have people in Paris who keep an eye on our sleepers". What a mess.

The detective spoke. 'You say you are from Marseille, Mademoiselle but I cannot place your accent. Where are you from, exactly?'

'Marseille, but I was educated by Italian nuns and their French was imperfect. I have inherited their accent.'

The detective looked at her. She couldn't guess his thinking. Then he switched topics and caused Juliette to feel physically sick.

'I do not wish to alarm you, Mademoiselle, but you probably know that three months ago a prisoner was publicly guillotined in Paris. Admittedly he killed six people and as it would appear you have killed only one, your punishment may not be as severe.'

Oh that's a relief, sarcastically thought Juliette. But the thought of being guillotined and in public was way beyond the pale.

'Mademoiselle, do you claim the killing as a *crime passionnelle*?'

Juliette stared at the detective. *What is he talking about?* She shook her head and covered her ignorance with more sobbing. He studied her response. Then he pushed a piece of paper across the table. 'If this list of your possessions is correct, please sign the document.'

Juliette read the list and signed her name.

A gendarme entered, spoke briefly with the detective and left. The detective smiled. 'You have a visitor. I will give you a few minutes.'

He left, the door opened and Madame Baudin entered. She was shocked at the sight of her tenant.

'Oh Madame,' wailed Juliette, 'I am so, so sorry.'

The women tried but failed to embrace. The blood on Juliette's clothes and body was distressing for both women.

'I can arrange a lawyer, Mademoiselle. He is fair and competent.'

Juliette was overcome with relief. 'Madame Baudin, I cannot find words to thank you. Your kindness is overwhelming.'

'But I fear ma chère you have broken the inviolable rule for dancers at the Folies Bergère.'

'Oh Madame, I did not kill that man.'

'That is not important, Mademoiselle.'

Juliette was almost breathless. 'Not important?'

'You must know the *crime passionnelle* is a way of life for us. Every Frenchwoman is entitled to behave as you did. But the unforgiveable sin as far as the Folies is concerned is that you were caught.'

Juliette burst into tears. The horror of the past few hours was too much. Madame Baudin squeezed Juliet's hand then moved to the door.

'I will contact the lawyer. He was once in love with me and probably still is. Until then, lift up your head and behave like the noble and beautiful Frenchwoman you are. Vive la France!'

She blew Juliette a kiss and left. The Englishwoman, pretending to be French, was never so alone. How could she act her way out of this?

Juliette couldn't sleep. After the interview she was photographed and finger-printed before being allowed to wash and change into prison clothes. She was locked in a cell. She drifted into fitful sleep and woke when the guard brought her breakfast. She longed for news.

'Good morning, officer. Has my lawyer arrived?' asked Juliette.

'He may be too shocked to be here, Mademoiselle. Hitler has just invaded Poland. France will be at war before the weekend is over.'

Juliette lost her appetite. As Britain and France were allies of Poland, if Germany declared war on that country, France and Britain would declare war on Germany.

Suddenly being a sleeper became dangerous. But how could the SIS contact her? And if she was found guilty of murder, what was the point?

Juliette thought about her code word. *What was is it again? Is anyone watching me? Do they know about my current predicament? And where on Earth is my lawyer?*

If anything good could be gleaned from the invasion news, at least tomorrow's newspapers would give little or no prominence to the gory Montmartre murder. War would dominate the headlines.

Juliette's lawyer arrived and Monsieur Grimhard lived up to his name. He was bald, bland and boring. He last laughed in 1926.

Juliette was grateful. 'Thank you for coming, Monsieur. Madame Baudin spoke very highly of you.'

He nodded. 'She is a wonderful woman. Now, Mademoiselle, I have read the police report and believe you should plead guilty.'

Juliette was speechless. He continued.

'Of course it was a crime of passion and that should go well for you.'

'Monsieur, why should I plead guilty? I am innocent.'

This was too difficult for the lawyer. Having read the police documents, the expression "open and shut" was his only thought. It was Friday morning, Hitler was being an enormous nuisance and the weekend beckoned. A guilty plea would see Grimhard heading for his country cottage with plans to remain there should war begin.

'But Mademoiselle, the gun, the blood, the absence of any other person in the room; everything points to you being guilty. If you fight the case and lose, the judge will sentence you to a much harsher punishment than if you tell the truth and plead guilty under provocation.'

Juliette couldn't remember handling a gun let alone firing one. She spoke sharply. 'But I don't know the truth!'

The lawyer stood. 'If you do not wish me to represent you, Mademoiselle, I will take my leave.'

Juliette panicked. 'No, please Monsieur. I apologise.' The pleading in her eyes caused the lawyer to wait. 'I will take your advice, Monsieur, but I would like to discuss the police report with you first … please.'

He paused then sat. 'Very well, but I do not see how it can help.'

'Thank you, Monsieur.'

He was blunt. 'Do you dispute anything in the police report?'

Juliette hesitated. 'Was the gun in my handbag?'

Grimhard was annoyed. 'How would I know? I wasn't there.'

'My handbag is quite small. Would the gun fit in my bag?'

The lawyer shrugged. 'If not then perhaps it was already in the room, on a bedside table, and when the victim tried to force himself upon you, you picked up the gun and shot him.'

Juliette was silent. That was possible. If only she could remember. 'Please Monsieur, could you explain the *crime passionnelle*?'

'Oui. But as a Frenchwoman, surely you already know such things.'

'Please, Monsieur, I am not a lawyer.'

Grimhard took a deep breath. 'In French law, a serious crime such as murder, can mean a custodial sentence of only two years if you plead guilty using the crime of passion as your defence. You did not plan to kill this man but your passion drove you to it.'

'But why would I be angry at a man I had only just met? Surely it would make sense for his wife or his lover to kill him. He was cheating on them, not me.'

Again the lawyer paused. Perhaps "open and shut" was the wrong expression. 'You could plead not guilty on the grounds of self-defence. The murdered man was forcing himself upon you and when he ignored your protests, you defended yourself. You discovered the pistol and shot him to save your honour.'

Juliette tried to think of any flaws in that argument. The lawyer's impatience was showing.

'I advise that you enter a plea of not guilty citing self-defence.'

Juliette's temper exploded. 'Monsieur, I am facing the guillotine!'

There was silence and neither looked at the other. Finally he spoke.

'I can only give advice, Mademoiselle. You must choose. You can plead guilty with a defence of the *crime passionnelle* or you can plead not guilty on the grounds of self-defence. Which do you choose?'

That did it. Juliette's temper broke free. Her sarcasm put on a silly hat. 'Begging your pardon, Monsieur, but I assumed a lawyer was meant to help the client explore every possibility. I assumed lawyers acted in the best interest of their clients and you, Monsieur, seem very keen to do as little as possible to help me escape this terrible situation. Well I happen to know two very successful lawyers who would patiently listen to my story and do all they could to have me found innocent!' Oh dear.

Grimhard looked at her, paused then called her bluff. He rose, motioned to the guard, moved to the door then turned to face Juliette.

'Then I suggest Mademoiselle you contact your two very successful lawyers and invite them to help you lose the case and possibly your head!'

The door opened and the lawyer departed leaving Juliette alone and miserable.

She had only one thought. *If only my brothers were here.*

On Sunday, September 3, 1939 Juliette was again interviewed by Capitaine Bonhomme.

'And how are you today, Mademoiselle?'

Juliette had cried herself to sleep. She despaired over the fact that she threw Madame Baudin's kindness back in the landlady's face.

'I understand you have dispensed with your lawyer, Mademoiselle.'

'I'm afraid, Monsieur I have made a bad situation worse.'

'Well, we're all in trouble now.' Juliette looked at the policeman. 'France has declared war on Germany.'

'And Britain?'

'Oui. France and Britain are at war with Germany.'

Juliette's dire situation got worse. The SIS might soon need her; pity about her current predicament. The policeman continued.

'Have you changed your explanation of the murder, Mademoiselle?'

She shook her head. Her confusion was real. 'I cannot explain or confess when I do not know what happened. I asked my lawyer some questions which he was unable to answer.'

'Such as?'

'I had a small handbag and do not believe the gun could have been hidden inside. If that's true, where did I find the gun?'

'And if you were so intoxicated, how were you able to operate it?'

Juliette froze. Why did the policeman ask that question? He was supposed to extract a confession from his only suspect. Was this a game he was playing; a trick to make her confess?

'Pardon Monsieur, but are you now the investigator or my lawyer?'

He did what any smart interrogator would do; he changed the subject. 'I am still fascinated by your accent, Mademoiselle. It is possible for someone to learn a language and speak it fluently, even adding the dialect of a region. But the accent always betrays a background.'

'I believe I've already explained about the Italian nuns, Monsieur.'

'Even the answers a person uses can betray their background. The fact that you, as a Frenchwoman, were unsure of the crime of passion, suggests you are not French at all.'

Juliette remembered the technique of breathing slowly and deeply. This was a game. She knew he was testing and he knew she knew.

She spoke sincerely. 'Will the fact that we are at war have any impact on my case, Monsieur?'

'And by "we", Miss, do you mean France?'

Bonhomme had chosen to use the English word *Miss* in a French sentence. Was it a slip of the tongue? Did he know Juliette's true identity? Was he guessing, probing? On the outside she remained calm.

'As I have said, Monsieur, if I knew how I came to be holding the gun I would tell you. But I was intoxicated or drugged or both and cannot remember. I respectfully request I be returned to my cell.'

Bonhomme paused then nodded. He moved to the door. 'My advice is that you ask your lawyer to return.' He left and Juliette was taken back to her cell. The guard spoke as he opened the door.

'Soon you will be transported to a prison outside Paris, Mademoiselle. But that is not such bad news. If Paris is bombed, you will be safe.'

The cell door clanged shut. Juliette's thinking was clear.

Safe? I don't want to be safe. I want to be free.

Chapter 18

CAPITAINE Émile Bonhomme was good at his job. In the Oscar Masson murder case, Bonhomme had doubts about the guilt of Juliette Beauchamp. He was unsure if she was who she claimed to be and unsure if she fired the murder weapon. She signed the paper listing her possessions with her right hand yet the gun was in her left hand. Was she guilty? If not, who was?

The case became far more difficult when war was declared on the weekend of the murder. Gas masks, taped windows and sandbags appeared in a Paris expecting Hitler's bombs any day.

Bonhomme investigated the murdered man and met several women who'd been seduced by Oscar Masson as well as some cuckolded husbands. All were delighted the womaniser was dead. Bonhomme arrived at the home of Masson's long-time business associate, Brian "the Maggot" Lachance, so named because he robbed the dead.

Masson used Lachance as muscle but always looked down on the hired help. Masson was far too grand to become involved in violence and kept his hands clean for unbuttoning brassieres.

Lachance protected Masson and threatened angry husbands. But Lachance had long been exploited by the playboy. Masson treated his associate as a third-class criminal and the angry Maggot knew he was at least second-class. And when Masson cheated Lachance out of his share of a major blackmail sting, the Maggot flipped; enough was enough. It was payback time.

Bonhomme arrived at Lachance's apartment. His wife was alone. Just as her husband hated Masson, she hated her husband. Normally Candice would never help the police but being so annoyed with the Maggot, she invited the detective inside.

'I am investigating Monsieur Oscar Masson's murder and want to ask about your husband's whereabouts last Friday night.'

Candice was curt. 'He was out.'

'With you, Madame?'

She scoffed. 'Ha. I can't remember the last time he took me out.'

'Do you know where he was?'

The Maggot's missus was thinking. She wanted shot of her old man.

'No, but in the morning he told me some tart had shot the lovely Oscar three times.'

'Three times; he used those exact words?'

'Those exact words. He sounded like he knew exactly what happened.'

'And where is your husband now, Madame?'

'Probably with his tart, Charlot. I call her C. Harlot. She plies her trade in the Quartier Pigalle from an apartment next to the Cabaret Beau.' The detective started to leave but stopped when Candice spoke. 'Oh and you might find something interesting in that second drawer.' She indicated with her eyes.

Bonhomme looked at the woman and saw anger and revenge. Using his handkerchief, he opened the drawer and removed a box of bullets. Madame Lachance's face was expressionless.

'Merci beaucoup, Madame. You have been most helpful.'

The detective returned to police headquarters and spoke with the technical department. They found no fingerprints on the trigger of the gun used to kill Oscar Masson. Mademoiselle Beauchamp was not wearing gloves. So where were her prints? There were many fingerprints in the room but none belonging to the arrested woman. It was as if she'd been carried into the room and placed on the bed.

Bonhomme gave the bullets to the technician and asked for a report.

With two gendarmes, Bonhomme went looking for the Maggot. His wife was an ideal grass. Lachance was with his mistress and the arrest could not have been worse. The suspect was in the bath. Three fully-clothed policemen added indignity to the Maggot's anger. Being arrested was bad enough; being arrested when naked was bloody annoying. Charlot too was peeved as she now required a new pimp.

Back at the police station Bonhomme received damning evidence regarding the bullets found in the Maggot's apartment; they were the same bullets retrieved from the body of Masson and the Maggot's fingerprints were on the box and the bullets. Faced with such evidence, the Maggot tried to bargain. The only card he could play was to tell all. He did.

Lachance broke into Masson's home on the night of the murder planning to take what Masson owed him; his share of the blackmail money. When Lachance heard footsteps, he dived under the bed and listened as Oscar began his well-rehearsed seduction routine. The fact that the woman was intoxicated was typical of Masson. The Maggot saw his chance. He could get rid of his partner and pin the murder on the latest lover.

'Now Goldilocks,' purred Oscar as he unbuttoned Juliette's blouse. 'Let Daddy Bear put some honey on your porridge.'

Lachance slid quietly out from under the very high bed. With head bowed, he moved into a kneeling position.

'Oh my,' said Oscar, 'what beautiful dumplings you have. All the better to ...'

'Suck on this, Oscar!' spat the Maggot as Lachance bobbed up and fired three shots at his astonished and instantly dead associate.

Oscar slumped forward and bled profusely over his would-be conquest. She was rudely woken and in panic mode as blood spurted over her face and chest. The Maggot quickly wiped the gun, shoved it into

Juliette's left hand and was out the window and halfway down the balconies before the partygoers stumbled in.

The Maggot only escaped the guillotine by naming names and telling tales. Bonhomme solved several crimes from a single arrest and was pleased to deliver the good news to the beautiful showgirl from the Folies Bergère.

Juliette was shocked. From a cell without any help or hope she was suddenly a free citizen in Paris. She looked terrible but felt fantastic. People stared at her. She hadn't gone a hundred metres when a siren sounded and Parisians panicked. She was knocked over in the rush and no-one stopped to help.

Juliette remembered. France was at war. She followed others down into the Metro. The trains were running but most people simply gathered on the platforms. Then another siren sounded and people returned to the streets.

Juliette reached her apartment building and knocked on Madame Baudin's door. The landlady was shocked. She helped her young tenant inside, gave her a large cognac and ran the bath.

'Strip,' said Madame Baudin and Juliette smiled. Undressing here was becoming routine. The bath was luxurious, full of scented oils. Madame Baudin scrubbed Juliette's back and washed her hair. The landlady could cook too and wearing one of Mimi's silk dressing-gowns, Juliette devoured scrambled eggs which would have won praise from Monsieur Escoffier.

Juliette explained her tale and Mimi cried with happiness.

But despite her newfound freedom, Juliette was worried. 'I suppose, Madame my career is over at the Folies Bergère?'

'Oui, ma chère, but there are other clubs in Paris and a job is a job, especially now we are at war.'

'I could try to find work as an actress, Madame. That is my training and experience.'

'But Juliette, you have exquisite beauty. Women would kill for your body and men will pay a great deal to look upon your charms and far more to touch.'

'Oh no. I've had enough of men, Madame; looking *and* touching.'

The former dancer looked at her young tenant. 'You are a fine woman, Mademoiselle. You make me proud to be French.'

Juliette embraced her landlady, again thanked her profusely, then climbed the stairs to her room, fell on her bed and slept a long and delicious sleep.

When she woke it took a few seconds to remember where she was. She was free but out of work. Then it hit her. Of course! She had an idea to make money. She laughed and gave thanks to Uncle Crispin.

Juliette was full of beans, ate some for breakfast and was buzzing with her latest idea. She woke her landlady who was definitely not an early riser.

'Oh Madame, I have a new performing idea but need an outfit. Please may I borrow one of your enchanting costumes?'

Mimi was delighted to help her now favourite showgirl. Juliette went to the drawers of clothes Madame Baudin had faithfully kept since her retirement and chose a gorgeous satin outfit with the shortest of short skirts. Juliette's breasts would be hidden but her glorious legs would be out on show.

'Madame, this is perfect.'

Juliette needed stockings and heels but the outfit looked fabulous. Mimi took hold of the material.

'It needs taking in. You are even slimmer than I was, Mademoiselle. I will fix it.'

'God bless you, Madame!' Juliette had trouble kissing the older woman and removing her new outfit at the same time. Both women were smiling. What a difference a day makes.

An hour later, wearing her new outfit under her coat, Juliette set off for the clubs of Paris. Her new act was simple but clever. If only the dim-witted managers agreed. She had a list of venues. Some were seedy, some pretentious and a few seemed promising. But there was a war on. "We're not taking any new workers" and "Come back after Christmas" were the usual responses. One lecherous manager asked to see her breasts. This was the real world and Juliette's idea was a flop.

She had one club left on her list and was despairing but determined to keep going. Tomorrow she would try even more clubs. She had to find work. The Club Paradiso was small. Inside a man was emptying ashtrays.

'Bonjour, Monsieur.'

'Bonjour.' He stopped working. Most men stopped when Juliette approached.

'Is the manager here? I am an artiste and wish to audition.'

'I am the manager. What can you do?'

Juliette was thrown. After a day of knock-backs, finally she was given the chance to audition. She seized the opportunity.

'Monsieur, please may I have a spotlight?' Juliette removed her coat and stepped onto the stage and into the light. She looked divine.

She performed a very old routine in a new and exotic way. Juliette performed the song she sang for Uncle Crispin all those years ago; a nursery rhyme but now performed with a cheeky style and innuendo. She translated the words into French although a cock-crow was a universal refrain. She finished with a flourish. Silence reigned. *What did he think? Please don't ask me to disrobe.* He was blunt.

'Can you start this evening?'

Hallelujah! Juliette proved the value of perseverance. Now she was working, even writing her own material. The pay was poor. She took hats and coats from the patrons and sold cigarettes. She fended off lecherous males and she got to perform.

She recited nursery rhymes with all the innocent allure of a child but dressed as a sensual woman added double entendres and suggestive expressions. She was a hit. Then, as emcee, she introduced the singer. France was at war and Juliette was surviving in Paris. Air-raid sirens came and went but central Paris was bomb free. The Germans were coming but nobody knew when. It really was a phoney war.

With Christmas approaching, Juliette hoped the cards she wrote months ago would find their way safely from Wellington to Wiltshire and from Canberra to Cambridge.

A week before Christmas and before her second performance that night, she was re-doing her make-up in the broom cupboard labelled *Dressing-room* when someone knocked on the door.

'Come in,' said Juliette and dropped her lipstick when a man appeared. It was Capitaine Émile Bonhomme.

'Bonsoir, Mademoiselle. Do you remember me?'

'Of course, Capitaine. But please don't tell me I'm under arrest.'

'On the contrary, Mademoiselle; I would like to take you to supper.'

Juliette's second performance that night was not her best. She was distracted. *Why was this police officer inviting me to supper?*

Capitaine Bonhomme was in a jovial mood as they strolled along the Champs Elysées. It was bitterly cold and the policeman offered his arm. It was in some ways like walking with her dear Papa. Juliette felt safe and alive and despite France being at war, the shopfronts did their best to celebrate the festive occasion.

They came to a club. Bonhomme was a regular and he and Juliette were warmly welcomed and shown to a table. Bonhomme held up a bottle. 'Champagne, Mademoiselle? After all, it is Christmas.'

Juliette looked at him. 'You will forgive me, Capitaine, but you did promise to explain the reason why you are being so generous to someone you once suspected of murder.'

Bonhomme smiled. 'Never seriously, Mademoiselle; now, let us have some champagne.'

Juliette sipped her drink and was about to press for an explanation when the emcee began.

'Mesdames et Messieurs, please give a warm Parisian welcome to the Little Sparrow.'

There was enthusiastic applause as the club became dark and a spotlight shone on a tiny woman in a simple black dress. The room became deathly quiet. A piano was heard then the woman sang. Juliette was transfixed. She wasn't alone.

When the singer finished, the audience erupted with delight. She sang two more numbers to rapturous applause. Soft lighting returned and the club was buzzing.

Juliette was thrilled. 'Oh Capitaine, she is wonderful; her voice, her emotion and acting, magnifique.'

'I agree but why not tell her yourself?'

Juliette was momentarily thrown then saw Bonhomme's eyes looking over her shoulder. She turned to see the singer approaching her table. Bonhomme stood and kissed the woman's hand. She was indignant.

'Émile, you are so naughty. Why did you not tell me you would be here tonight?'

'My darling, may I present a friend, Mademoiselle Juliette Beauchamp.'

Juliette stood then had to bend to kiss the tiny Edith Piaf. All three sat and Edith consumed her champagne with relish. Bonhomme was enjoying being with two remarkable women. He described Juliette.

'Mademoiselle Beauchamp is like you, ma chère, an artiste.'

Edith was impressed. 'A singer? I should like to hear you sing, Mademoiselle. Where can I hear you sing?'

'Alas no, Mademoiselle; I am an actress who can sing and dance a little.'

Bonhomme interrupted. 'She is being very modest. This young lady has graced the stage of the Folies Bergère.'

'Of course,' said Edith. 'Some of us have the voice and others the body. And I suppose Émile has recruited you as well.'

'I am working on it,' added an embarrassed Bonhomme.

Edith stood and kissed Bonhomme then smiled at Juliette. 'It was wonderful to meet you, Mademoiselle. Make sure the Capitaine brings you to my Christmas party. Au revoir.'

She moved amongst patrons. Juliette looked at Bonhomme. 'So, Capitaine, what is this recruitment you are working on?'

He smiled. He liked the young woman. Apart from her dazzling beauty and enchanting personality, there was something mysterious about her which he found fascinating.

'My dear young lady, in another life I served in the French army and then after the war I became a policeman. But now France is at war again and I am too old to fight. But I will help wherever I can. My task is to find artistes who will entertain our troops when they come home from the fighting. I would be honoured, Mademoiselle, if you would join my humble concert party and help your fellow countrymen.'

Juliette was speechless. She was English, pretending to be French, a sleeper in a foreign country, waiting to begin work for the SIS, and was now being asked to work for the French supporting their war effort. What would her London masters say?

'You are hesitating, Mademoiselle. You are not patriotic perhaps?'

'Oh I am patriotic, Capitaine. But I fear my humble acting skills will not be of much use. Alongside Edith Piaf, I am a very modest performer.'

'Au contraire, Mademoiselle. I am a very good judge of a French soldier and can say with confidence your cheeky rendition of nursery rhymes together with your stunning beauty and exquisite legs will guarantee you amazing success.'

He smiled, she smiled and they toasted their new partnership. The lights dimmed and the Little Sparrow stepped onto the stage. She sang and the patrons stood as one to acknowledge her virtuoso performance. Juliette tried to imagine performing with Edith Piaf.

Christmas 1939 was like no other. Accompanied by Capitaine Bonhomme, Juliette stood in Edith Piaf's crowded living-room. Wine and cheese were in good supply and to hell with the war and those appalling Nazis. Besides, Parisians knew how to celebrate.

Juliette was never alone. Men and women wanted to meet this young beauty. The party was humming when somebody called for quiet.

Downstairs, the brothel was humming. Upstairs the party was hushed as the Little Sparrow sang *Silent Night* as she once did years ago as a street entertainer collecting coins from passers-by. Now she was famous and had money to spare.

Juliette could not believe her luck. She was in a Parisian apartment with fascinating people and being serenaded by one of France's most adored singers. There were toasts and Christmas greetings. Then Bonhomme made an announcement.

'I want to thank our dear hostess, Edith, for her generous hospitality and all of you for your loyalty to our beloved France. We live in dangerous times but have triumphed before and will again.' There were murmurs of agreement. Bonhomme raised his glass. 'Vive la France!'

Everyone joined the toast. Juliette felt quite emotional. And then the Little Sparrow began to sing *La Marseillaise*. She led and everyone followed. Juliette had studied the anthem when training in Scotland. The singing was strong. You could sense the passion as every Frenchman and woman and one Englishwoman sang with gusto, made all the more emotional because of the war.

Just as the final note ended there was a loud banging on the apartment's door. Suddenly silence. Everyone froze. Fear replaced festivity. Had the Germans arrived during the night? Bonhomme took charge. Defiantly he strode to and opened the door only to reveal the madam from the brothel downstairs.

'Do you mind,' she snapped, 'you're frightnin' me punters.' Uproarious and relieved laughter filled the room.

Despite the war, it was Christmas and these Parisians would continue their unique way of life. Bugger the Bosch.

A new guest arrived. He was a distinguished, middle-aged man with piercing brown eyes. He wore a Saville Row suit and the finest shirt, socks and underpants. Juliette saw and heard him being warmly greeted by Bonhomme. The new arrival's French was good but it was obvious he wasn't French. He actually sounded terribly English and when he told

Bonhomme he was glad to be out of London, Juliette felt both alarmed and excited. Thoughts raced around inside her head.

An Englishman here in Paris, standing but a few feet from another person from that same green and pleasant land. Gosh, I say, how are things in dear old Blighty?

Bonhomme introduced the Englishman. 'Mademoiselle, may I present a dear friend from England, Monsieur Godfrey Silsbury. Godfrey, this is the brilliant French actress, Mademoiselle Juliette Beauchamp.'

Silsbury kissed her hand never once breaking eye contact. 'Bonsoir, Mademoiselle. Joyeux Noël.' He held her hand and Juliette smiled.

'Merci, Monsieur,' said Juliette sure he was mentally undressing her. Perhaps he thought Juliette had slipped upstairs from her day job below. Perhaps he considered the word *actress* to be a synonym for *prostitute*.

Bonhomme continued. 'Mademoiselle Beauchamp is one of the entertainers who will inspire our wonderful French soldiers.'

'Well Mademoiselle,' said the English gent, 'if your acting matches your beauty, you will be a sensation.'

A woman stepped in and claimed the actress. Juliette was relieved. The woman had heard about Juliette's brush with the law and was keen to get the inside story. Many French women wanted the intimate details of any crime of passion. Tips on successfully disposing of an unwanted husband or lover were always welcome and Juliette was glad to depart the presence of the dishonourable Englishman.

Eventually Bonhomme arranged for a car to take Juliette home. She kissed the hostess who was delighted with Juliette. 'I look forward to seeing you perform for our troops, Mademoiselle. Joyeux Noël.'

Downstairs in the street, Juliette thanked Bonhomme for his kindness. He opened the car door.

'I will be in touch, Mademoiselle, to discuss your work for the Army. You have done your country proud. Joyeux Noël.'

He closed the car door then saluted. As Juliette was driven through the deserted streets of Paris, a soft rain gave the roads a sheen. It was surreal, the eerie calm before the tempestuous storm.

Christmas decorations were everywhere. The Luftwaffe was only hours away. Thousands of German tanks, troops and armoured vehicles were only days away. French and British troops were just up the road and all hell could break loose at any moment. Her family believed she was in sunny Australia. If only they knew.

Chapter 19

KURT HARTMANN was impatient. The war began and he was stuck in Berlin running a domestic cleaning service. He became a Gestapo joke. Want a nanny? See Hartmann.

1940 saw the Phoney War in full flight. The Blitzkrieg or Lightning War became the Sitzkrieg or Sitting War. Hitler postponed invading the Low Countries some sixteen times. Meet Adolf the Great Procrastinator.

And while Oberst Max Hartmann checked his Panzer tank making sure it was ready for action, Cousin Kurt was summoned to 8 Prinz-Albrecht-Strasse and a meeting with Reichführer Himmler.

'Congratulations, Hartmann, on the success of the Polish domestics. You have the gratitude of countless German mothers.'

'Thank you, Reichsführer.'

'We are sending you to Spain.' Kurt was thrilled but remained motionless. 'You will go to Madrid and see how General Franco handles communists and other renegades. Time you waged war against grown-ups.' Kurt battled to hide his delight. 'Once we conquer France, the Resistance groups will become seriously active. I'm sure your talents can be put to good use in Paris. You leave for Madrid tomorrow. Heil Hitler.'

It was freezing everywhere but Kurt had a spring in his step as he strode along the foot-stampingly cold Berlin streets.

In rural France, the snow lay deep and crisp and uneven where Juliette Beauchamp was preparing to entertain French officers in a magnificent chateau.

The dressing-room was chilly. Wearing a skimpy outfit in the middle of winter was a challenge. Her legs and arms were awash with goosebumps. Her chattering teeth were not a part of her act.

But those things didn't dampen the ardour of the audience. The room was cold but the girl was hot. The applause was generous and Juliette was an undoubted hit. Spring was weeks away and with it the Germans would be in Paris.

Enough waiting already. The weather's warm, the shells are loaded and the tanks are set. For Oberst Max Hartmann and his crew it was time to roll. Everyone waited on the word of the Führer. Come on, Adolf.

In the Battle of France, the Germans would attack in three waves; through former and predictable routes but surprisingly, through a new and unexpected route, the magnificent Ardennes Forest.

What a setting; huge trees, rugged mountains, spectacular gorges and mighty rivers. No army would or could travel through such a forest. Ah, but that was the genius of the Nazi plan.

The French and British never suspected the Germans would come through the Ardennes. Surely no heavy artillery or armoured vehicles could penetrate such terrain so let's put our tanks and fighting forces elsewhere. And they did.

Max was thrilled to be part of the push through the forest. All those training drills back in Germany would stand him in good stead. It was a typical German attack reeking of precision.

Elsewhere paratroopers dropped onto a pfennig in Holland, engineers landed gliders on top of a Belgian fort and Max, his tank and other Panzers crashed through a forest.

The massive canopy overhead meant enemy planes had no idea the Germans were moving quickly to France. The convoy stretched for miles.

Max set a cracking pace. Startled animals fled. Max loved the surprise element. They would cross the River Meuse before the French could defend let alone destroy the bridges.

Then, suddenly, Max was stopped. Was it the impregnable forest, enemy troops or anti-tank guns? No. It was good behaviour. Max was stopped because he was too damn good at his job.

He got the message. "Slow down. The supplies are miles behind. If you're attacked, you'll have no cover". Max was furious and frustrated. After Poland they waited for months. Now, finally, when the war was back on, they were part of a daring manoeuvre which was suddenly ordered to stop.

'Why are we stopping, Herr Oberst?' asked his driver.

'Because our masters in Germany don't like to take risks.'

'But if we press on we can cross into France and trap the French and British in a perfect pincer movement.'

Max shouted so fiercely he was frightening. 'Don't tell me what I already know!' He took a deep breath. 'Make camp.'

The next day Max moved forward. They were low on fuel. The forest was thinning; the oldest river in the world was close. Cross the Meuse and hello France.

Suddenly bullets bounced off Max's Panzer. 'Enemy fire,' he shouted and pulled in behind some trees.

'I see them,' called his driver. All of the Panzers were under fire but not one was seriously damaged.

'There are no anti-tank guns,' yelled Max. 'Let's go!'

He fired up his tank and headed straight towards the unseen enemy. The other tanks followed. The enemy fire became sporadic then stopped. Max cleared the tree line and saw the River Meuse.

It looked majestic in its forest setting. A major bridge was a hundred metres ahead and Max drove straight at it. Enemy soldiers ran back along the bridge. One turned and aimed his rifle at the Panzers. He was dead before his body dropped onto the bridge.

Max reached French soil. Enemy fire was non-existent. Then his driver cried out.

'White flag, Herr Oberst, they've surrendered.'

'Cease firing,' yelled Max and passed the message to the other tanks.

All was still. The birds had long since flown. The only sound was the rumble of the Panzers. A French soldier appeared with a white flag.

'We'll secure the bridge,' said Max. 'Engel, you're with me. Fiedler, cover us.'

Max and Engel moved towards the man. In his good French, Max addressed the soldier.

'Do you surrender?'

'We do, sir.'

Max looked at the Frenchman's white hair and wrinkled face. 'Are you in charge?'

'Second Lieutenant Leroux,' he said saluting.

Max returned the salute. 'Oberst Max Hartmann. At the risk of being impertinent, Lieutenant, you appear to be quite senior for the life of a soldier.'

'I am seventy-four, Herr Oberst and some of my men are older.' Max was shocked. 'We are reservists. We have one machine-gun and our own collection of rifles, most of which were probably fired against your father's generation in the last war.'

Max shook his head. 'Tell your men to lay down their arms and come forward.'

The proud but bedraggled Frenchmen did just that. They were not so much Dad's Army as Grandad's Army. Their machine gun had stopped firing because the ancient weapon had jammed. Two of the elderly French soldiers were wounded. Max called for first aid.

He waited for fuel. It took several hours but then the Panzers and armoured vehicles left the French pensioners and set off along the Gallic side of the Meuse.

They met with light resistance from other reservists and were making good time heading west until the fighting became serious. These were not elderly, former soldiers but regulars with anti-tank guns. Shells were exchanged and the Panzers had a real fight on their hands. That was until the German cavalry rode over the hill.

Actually they flew over the hill and the Luftwaffe made a mess of the French. This allowed Max and the other tanks, armoured vehicles and mobile infantry to speed towards the French and British forces who were fighting bravely but vainly against the Germans sweeping down through Belgium.

The Allies were in trouble. Two speedy and well-armed German forces were driving them back to the sea. The Allied air cover was missing in action.

Dunkirk became hectic, a jam-packed, frantic seaside town. The Allies were trapped. And then it happened—again.

143

Hitler baulked. With hundreds of thousands of French and British troops there for the taking, the Führer cried "Halt!" The man who took ages to start the race stopped it in the bell lap. Max was ropeable.

He and his comrades pulled off a great military manoeuvres, and just as they were about to claim their prize, they were told to mark time. *'Halt? But why? The enemy are sitting ducks!'*

Perhaps Hitler was convinced the Luftwaffe could do the Dunkirk job with fewer casualties. Whatever the reason, one of the worst potential defeats for the Allies turned into a moral victory as some 340,000 French and British troops climbed aboard a motley collection of hundreds of fishing boats, paddle steamers and pleasure boats—plus the odd warship—and sailed back to Blighty to fight another day.

France was on its knees. Thousands of its troops were dead. Those left behind at Dunkirk were captured and the Battle of France was over.

Max and his fellow tank commanders pointed their Panzers south. Bonjour Paris.

To prevent Paris being bombed and to hopefully prevent an unconditional surrender, the French declared it an open city. Millions of Parisians fled. Jews who remained were terrified. France joined the growing list of countries conquered by Germany.

After the Battle of France, Juliette's job of entertaining French troops was no more. Her audience had been captured or killed. She continued at the Paradiso club but nobody knew for how long. Already there were shortages of food and fuel. Who could afford black market prices? *Joie de vive* became an endangered species.

Friday, June the 14th, 1940 dawned fine when Juliette knocked on her landlady's door. Madame Baudin looked worried. The German success was soul-destroying for everyone but particularly for those old enough to remember the last war.

Juliette spoke to her landlady. 'I am going into the city, Madame, to buy whatever food I can. I hear that the Germans may arrive today. Is there something I can get for you?'

Mimi had aged overnight. 'Damn Germans. I lost two brothers in the last war and the man I was to marry was so damaged he spent the rest of his life in an asylum.'

'Forgive me, Madame. That was so thoughtless of me.'

'Go, Mademoiselle. But be careful. These are dangerous times. Go.'

Juliette found the heart of Paris strangely quiet. On a sunny Parisian morning, the City of Light seemed dark. Many shops were shut. People wandered aimlessly.

In a street off the Champs-Élysées Louise heard a commotion. A woman yelled and pointed. Others looked. People moved to the boulevard. Juliette joined them. The crowd surged forward. People stared. Juliette heard softly spoken swearing. A man had tears running down his cheeks. It was a sight to crush every citizen of France. The enemy was within.

From the Arc de Triomphe they came. Line after line of German troops marched past. It was matter-of-fact not pompous; no goose-stepping just precise, orderly steps. Soldiers on horseback and gun carriages pulled by horses moved along the grand boulevard. A German military band played. German officers saluted. The Nazi flag flew from the Eiffel Tower.

Juliette's father had fought in France. Was she now poised to do the same? She drifted away and came to the Place de la Concorde where she joined many silent, grieving Parisians.

Then new sounds were heard and people turned to look as Panzers rumbled into view. It was incredible. There were German tanks in the heart of Paris. They drove into the centre of the Place de la Concorde. Max Hartmann was atop his Panzer surveying the city. From a distance Juliette stared at him.

She'd seen enough. She walked to her club needing to know if she still had a job. There was a note pinned to the door.

Due to a family bereavement the Paradiso Club has ceased operations

Juliette had no job and no prospects. She was owed wages. She was living in a foreign city conquered by a foreign power. She went home without any food and even less hope. She was climbing the stairs when her landlady called.

'Mademoiselle, you have a letter.'

'Thank you,' said Juliette taking the envelope. It was addressed to her but bore no stamp.

'It was pushed under the front door, Mademoiselle. I only found it after you went out. I hope it is not bad news.'

Juliette smiled grimly and went upstairs. She didn't recognize the handwriting and her curiosity was tingling. Who knew she lived here? Her SIS training in Scotland kicked in. The envelope was sealed. She studied it, sniffed it and felt the contents. It seemed harmless. Carefully she slit the envelope. Inside was a single card. She withdrew it, turned it over and read the one word. *Albee.*

Sleepers awake.

Once the initial excitement faded Juliette became despondent. London had contacted her but left no instructions. With her income gone, how could she exist?

If really desperate, Capitaine Bonhomme and Madame Baudin might help but Juliette's last hope was Edith Piaf. They worked on the same bill when entertaining French army officers. Juliette set off for the Little Sparrow's nest and was greeted warmly.

'Bonjour, Juliette, entrer.' The sat for a chat and Juliette began.

'Edith, I am in desperate trouble. I've lost my job at the Folies and the club I work in has closed. I have no family or friends and unless I find work soon, I'll be turned out into the street.'

'We are all in the same boat, chéri. Damn the Bosch to hell.'

'So can you suggest something? I'll do anything to make money.'

'Anything, Mademoiselle?' Edith smiled and left the question hanging. Juliette twigged.

'No, no, no. I'm a good Catholic girl. Capitaine Bonhomme will vouch for me. But acting, emceeing, showgirl, reception work, cigarette girl, anything like that, I'll jump at it.'

Edith looked at Juliette. They were about the same age but as different as chalk and cheese. Edith was tiny and had endured a tough childhood. She grew up in a brothel, was a teenage mother, had been pressured to become a prostitute and made money singing on the streets of Paris. It was only a few years ago that her singing was discovered and she'd won fame and francs.

'Juliette, we both love performing, hate the Germans and both were suspected of murder.'

'You too?'

'Oui. And as Capitaine Bonhomme will tell you, we both were innocent.'

Juliette was fond of the French song bird. Edith reciprocated.

'I like you, Juliette. I am jealous of your magnificent legs but you are not like any Frenchwoman I have ever met.' Juliette smiled. 'And I know I can find you work, well-paid performing work, but there is a catch.'

Louise groaned. 'I have to sleep with the manager.'

'Far worse, chéri; you have to entertain Nazis.'

Juliette hadn't expected that. *But I'm not a collaborator. And surely the British Secret Intelligence Service would want me to have contact with the enemy. I could earn my living and possibly kill two German birds with the one stone.*

'Edith, I'm not a collaborator. Like you, I hate the Germans, but what else can I do?'

'That depends on how much you want to stay alive.'

'But if the Germans will pay, why not? Surely they won't harm me.'

'Forget the Nazis, chéri; it's the Resistance you should fear. They have their spies in the clubs, bars and brothels and if they catch you entertaining the Bosch, you'll wish the Gestapo had arrested you.'

'But you are entertaining the Bosch?'

Edith was silent. She nodded. 'Only with my voice; I refuse to collaborate horizontally.'

'So aren't you afraid of the Resistance?'

'They won't touch me. They know I can use my fame to help French prisoners of war and any Jews I know. But you are not famous and must be very, very careful.'

'Are you singing in a club or a theatre?'

'In a brothel.' Louise was stunned. 'Chéri, the best brothels in Paris offer fine food and wine. They have women as guests. Famous painters and poets have lived in our brothels. The English Prince of Wales once had his coat of arms above the bed in his own suite. And now that the Bosch are here, the best brothels are full of high-ranking Nazis who want sophisticated entertainment.'

'I had no idea.'

'You really *are* a convent girl.'

'Who desperately wants to perform.'

'Then just for you, chéri, I will ask the manager of the *One Two Two Club* to squeeze you in.'

'On stage or in his office?'

They laughed and Juliette felt excited with some of those about-to-go-on-stage nerves.

Chapter 20

WHEN FRANCE fell Kurt Hartmann was excited. He was to leave Spain and head to Paris. This was brilliant.

His train arrived at Gare de Lyon and he chose to walk to Gestapo HQ in the 8th arrondissement. It was a beautiful city and a beautiful day.

The locals watched him without watching him. He sensed this and felt good. They knew him to be a stranger danger. He even smelt like trouble. Jewish Parisians melted into the crowd.

Kurt headed for the Seine, past Cathédrale Notre Dame de Paris and Musée du Louvre, swing right and which way to number 11, Rue de Saussaies? He arrived at the Gestapo building and entered the office of his supervisor. His file was produced and his record discussed.

'Now Hartmann I see you are to be congratulated on your achievements with the Polish Jews and domestics. Splendid work.'

'Thank you, Herr Direktor.'

'I need a man with your efficiency, Hartmann.' Kurt died inside. *More mundane jobs, more crap dealing with the detritus of French society.* 'I have men working on the Jewish situation but not the Resistance.' Kurt felt a pang of excitement.

'I would be honoured to serve in any way you see fit, Herr Direktor.'

'You can lose the obsequiousness; I hate sycophants. Now go and study the Paris Resistance. I want to know who's involved, what they're doing and planning to do and how you'll capture or kill them. Report in a week. Heil Hitler.' Kurt saluted. 'Oh and you would do well to remember that elderly Jews and Polish lavatory cleaners are not quite as dangerous as members of the French Resistance who have real guns with real bullets.'

Kurt saluted and left thinking happy thoughts. *Gott im Himmel. At last, a real Gestapo job.*

Oberst Max Hartmann was in Paris and frustrated. That told you a lot about the man. It was summer in a beautiful and cultured city and Max was bored. After months of fighting in both real and phoney battles, he was on duty doing nothing. Rommel had spoken to him about North Africa and Max was keen to get involved. But when?

In the meantime, he "endured" superb accommodation in the luxurious Hôtel Meurice on the Rue de Rivoli. *What the hell was a Wehrmacht officer doing in such opulent surrounds?* The Louvre was a few minutes' walk away and Max considered wandering its corridors. He thought about his lot. *For God's sake, we are at war. Britain is dropping bombs on France and Germany while here I am swanning around gay Paree living the life of Riley.*

Max knew Parisians were doing it tough. He saw long queues outside butchers, bakers, dairies and tobacconists.

A third of all animals brought into Paris for slaughter were reserved for the all-conquering Germans. Millions of Parisians went hungry. Every Parisian hotel, except the Ritz, had been taken over by the Nazis. Commercial buildings were occupied by the German police, Gestapo, agencies and countless administrators.

Almost everything was affected although the arts managed to keep their "Business as usual" signs out front. The Paris Opera and Ballet entertained the masses. Cinemas, theatres, cafes and bars were open. So too brothels and many did a roaring trade with all ranks of German soldiers enjoying the rampant debauchery.

Edith Piaf was correct about some of the swanky Parisian brothels under the Nazis. They had quality entertainment and vertical dancing in the public rooms with more primitive entertainment and horizontal dancing in the private rooms.

Sex was serious business from the war point of view. All "horizontal collaborators" required thrice-weekly health checks and VD was considered an act of sabotage. You got more than the strap for the clap.

At the insistence of a fellow tank commander, Max went to the upmarket brothel Le Chabanais. Inside he watched the antics with growing disgust. Outside in the street, Jews were being rounded up, tortured and sent to work and die in concentration camps. A few suburbs away, British bombs were being dropped on French factories. And here was the cream of the Wehrmacht, swigging fine French champagne and groping fine French breasts.

Max stormed out. His fellow tank commander ran after him.

'Hartmann, what's wrong? Are you sick?'

'I'm sick of depravity. Hitler raves about the moral fibre of the so-called master race, as the Wehrmacht's finest go boozing and whoring.'

'I agree. Come on, I know just the place.'

They set off along the Rue Auber heading for the famous *One Two Two Club*. Yes it was a brothel but one with a difference. They found a table and saw Germans mingling with compliant French locals.

A drum roll and lighting change brought silence. A spotlight picked out a solo performer. Max was hooked. A slim, gorgeous woman with legs flown in from heaven and wearing a small jacket, shorts and top hat smiled. Men and women sighed. Max felt alive.

Juliette Beauchamp performed one of her nursery rhymes with verve and the tag line brought an instant, strong laugh. Then she slipped effortlessly into an emcee role and introduced the Parisian songbird, Edith Piaf. What an act *she* was. The French loved her. Here the Germans and French had something in common. Everyone loved Edith.

Max felt great. If he had to remain in Paris, finding some culture with beauty and style certainly made his night.

Half an hour later he was searching for the *Gents* when he heard a scream. He moved along the corridor and stopped. Inside a room he heard what sounded like a slap and a cry then someone calling, "No, no".

It was a woman's voice. She was kneeling before a Wehrmacht officer with an unbuttoned jacket, abundant body hair and surplus sweat. In his left hand he controlled the woman by yanking on a large amount of her hair. She was in agony as he jerked her head. With his right hand he struggled to unbutton his trousers. The woman's arms were flailing causing the man to jerk her head more ferociously and to interrupt his fly unbuttoning by slapping her face with his free hand. The woman's blouse was torn and her nakedness added to her misery.

Max opened the door. The fellow-German saw him and yelled.

'Fuck off, she's mine!'

Max moved quickly, half turned the man then smashed a clenched fist into the would-be rapist's face. The punch produced a broken nose and free-flowing blood sending the brute crashing to the floor. The shock and pain left him dazed and helpless.

The young woman was hysterical. Max knelt beside her and was shocked to recognize the gorgeous performer he'd seen on stage. 'It's all right, Mademoiselle. You are safe now.'

Juliette sobbed and tried to cover her body. Max removed his jacket and placed it on her shoulders. She nodded but was still terrified and her terror increased when she saw her attacker pick up a chair and loom large behind Max.

Juliette screamed and Max turned as the chair crashed on his head and shoulder. He dropped like a stone and sprawled on the floor partly on top of Juliette. Her attacker did the gentlemanly thing and helped remove his military colleague but only because he wished to resume his encounter with the tart from the show.

The attacker was overweight, ugly and drunk. With a bloodied face for good measure he was not a girl's first choice for a nice night out. And there was nothing nice about what he intended to do.

He grasped her hair again. 'Come here, bitch.'

That was the last thing he said. Juliette acted instinctively. A few years ago in a French town not far from Paris, Matilda Gonzales-Jones had once whispered to Juliette, a.k.a. Louise, "You kick his shins, I'll kick his balls and we'll run in different directions".

Juliette found it hard to kick but her arms were still free and punching was an option. She exercised that option and punched as hard as she could. She wasn't aiming for his shins.

Her blow landed with seemingly little impact. Nothing happened. Then the grip on her hair was slowly released. Tears welled in her attacker's eyes. He gave a sort of weird laugh then swayed sideways, lost his balance and crashed to the floor. He gingerly touched his crotch then screamed in agony.

Juliette was on her feet. She picked up a leg of the smashed chair and moved to her attacker. She stood straddling him. He looked up blinking away blood and tears. His face pleaded for mercy. She raised the chair leg high. His skull was in perfect position. Plum had a plumb bob line of attack. She took a deep breath then decided to smash the bastard's head.

'No!' cried Max. Juliette froze. Max had rolled onto his side and watched the last few seconds. He raised a hand. 'Don't! They'll kill you.'

Juliette looked at Max and then at the evil man beneath her. She decided. Max screamed, 'No!' as Juliette smashed the table leg into the floor right beside the attacker's head. He endured terrifying fear in the instant when the weapon whipped down from above. He was not to know Juliette had chosen to let him live.

She tossed the chair leg aside, knelt beside Max and spoke. 'How badly are you hurt?'

'I think it's only bruising but my head hurts like hell.'

'Let me help you.' Juliet dragged a chair close to Max and helped him sit. He slumped in the chair, his head in his hands.

'Thank you, Mademoiselle. You are most kind.'

'Let me call you a doctor.'

'No, no doctor. I need to get back to my hotel. This incident could ruin my career.'

'But you saved my life. And that madman tried to kill you.'

'The truth, Mademoiselle, is not always relevant in the Wehrmacht.'

'Well let me get you a taxi.'

'Please, I'll be fine.'

Juliette would have none of it. 'Wait here. I'll be back.'

She went to the dressing room and put on her jacket and coat covering her torn blouse. She avoided mirrors to miss seeing her hair and make-up. She returned to find Max on all fours. He'd tried to walk but collapsed.

'Monsieur, you're not well. I'll fetch a doctor.'

No!' Max was almost angry.

'Well please allow me to find you a taxi.'

She put his jacket over his shoulders and he winced. She helped him stand and they moved slowly. He leant on the wall. Juliette walked behind him to open the door. As she passed the still groaning thug, she stamped hard where his pain was greatest.

The thug gasped at this new level of agony. With mock concern, Juliette apologised. 'Pardon, Monsieur, do please forgive me.'

She opened the door and walked Max along the corridor. A customer came out of the *Gents*, saw the situation and moved to help. Together they got Max into the street and found a taxi. The man opened the door and Juliette helped the Panzer commander. He slumped on the seat.

Without thinking, Juliette climbed in to help. The man in the street closed the door and the taxi took off.

Max managed to say, 'Hôtel Meurice' before he passed out.

Max was still groggy when the taxi reached the hotel. Juliette paid then helped him get out but in so doing his cap fell off. Juliette picked it up just as two Wehrmacht soldiers were passing.

'Herr Oberst?' The men saw Max struggling and went to his aid. 'Herr Oberst, it's Dieter Friedel from the Warsaw campaign. You remember?'

Max looked at the corporal and nodded. Friedel and his comrade helped Max into the hotel. Juliette followed. The concierge stepped forward but stopped when Juliette indicated Max's cap.

'Bonsoir Monsieur. Herr Oberst's cap. Oh, and I have forgotten his room number.' Without hesitation the concierge informed Juliette. 'Merci,' she smiled so warmly, the concierge glowed.

Max was helped into the lift. Juliette addressed the young soldiers. 'Thank you, gentlemen, I can manage Herr Oberst from here.'

The soldiers got the message. They saluted Max, nodded to Juliette and left. She pressed the button and stood beside Max as they ascended.

The lift stopped. Max was struggling and accepted Juliette's assistance. They moved along the corridor. She looked at room numbers and stopped outside his door. They looked at one another.

'I'm hoping you have the key, Herr Oberst.'

He produced it and Juliette opened the door. Oh my. What are the poor people doing tonight? She guided Max towards a settee. From the liquor cabinet she poured a brandy. Max nodded and drank.

She explored the suite. In the sumptuous bathroom she ran the bath. In the bedroom she turned down the very large bed then returned to Max and sat beside him.

'You saved my life tonight, Herr Oberst.'

'And you mine. And please, my name is Max.'

'I've run you a bath. Is there anything else I can do?'

He looked at her. Through his pain he remembered her stage performance. He remembered her legs, her waist and her smile. From afar he thought she was beautiful. Up close, she was stunningly beautiful. Despite her ordeal, her femininity was dazzling. He managed to stand.

'If you'll excuse me, Mademoiselle, I would like to change.' He started towards the bedroom but stopped and turned. 'I think you are a magnificent actress.'

'Merci,' said Juliette and watched him disappear.

Minutes ticked by. Juliette went into the bathroom and turned off the taps. She crept towards the bedroom and listened. She tapped softly on the door. No sound was heard. Slowly she opened the door and entered. 'Herr Oberst?'

Max was lying on the bed sound asleep. His boots, trousers and jacket lay crumpled on the floor. Juliette gently turned him so his head lay on the pillow. Carefully she drew up the bedcoverings. He stirred briefly, muttered *Danke sehr* then drifted back to sleep.

Juliette left the bedroom and closed the door. She sat on the settee. What now? The blackout and curfew were in place and she could ill afford a second taxi. She walked to a mirror and looked. Ouch. Her head ached and her face was painful to touch.

She walked to the bathroom and saw the bath full of hot, steamy water. What a waste. She dropped her clothes and slipped into the most seductive bath in Paris. She luxuriated in the soapy liquid and thought of the misery millions of French people were enduring right now.

She wondered what certain people would say if they knew where she was. She imagined the response from her mother, brothers, Elizabeth Vestey, Matilda, Richard Graves and Beauford Nightingale. Thank goodness her dear Papa would never know. But then again, perhaps he would be extremely proud. She wondered what Dr Tom Curzon would think of her current situation.

It was a crime to get out of the bath. She dried herself, borrowed a Wehrmacht officer's shirt and using Herr Oberst's dressing gown as a blanket, curled up on the settee and slept. More bliss.

She heard a gentle knocking and was instantly awake. Her watch showed almost 6am. She carefully opened the door to a hotel waiter holding a tray. He was more than surprised.

'Merci,' said Juliette and took the tray. She looked at the food and the aromas set her gastric juices flowing. She went to the bathroom, made herself as respectable as possible then carried the tray to the bedroom door, knocked and waited. After a pause, Juliette heard, 'Come in.'

Max was waking up. He felt sore but better. What was happening? Who was in his suite? He stared as Juliette entered wearing one of his shirts and carrying his breakfast.

'Bonjour Herr Oberst. I trust you slept well.'

Max was in awe. 'Have I died and gone to heaven?' Juliette smiled and Max's pain and tiredness evaporated.

'Today we have a superb French breakfast with coffee, croissants and a baguette with what looks like real French butter.' She placed the tray on the bed. 'Bon appetit.'

Max sat up his mind spinning. 'Please,' he indicated, 'do join me.' Juliette sat on the bed.

They shared the breakfast in silence. Anyone with scissors could have cut the atmosphere. Finally Max spoke.

'If I may make a personal comment, Mademoiselle, you look far better in that shirt than any goose-stepping member of the Wehrmacht.'

Juliette smiled and Max had never been more awake in his life.

'Forgive me, Mademoiselle, if I don't stand.' Juliette laughed. 'My name is Max Hartmann.'

They shook hands. 'Juliette Beauchamp.'

'Well Mademoiselle Beauchamp, as much as I am enjoying your enchanting company and the sight of your exquisite legs, I have an appointment with my commanding officer in an hour and ...'

'Of course,' said Juliette standing and collecting the tray. 'If I may have the bathroom for two minutes I'll get dressed and be on my way.'

She took the tray and departed. Max gazed in wonder. She looked as gorgeous from the rear as from the front.

He dressed and came from the bedroom. She dressed and came from the bathroom, her hair and make-up looking natural and almost perfect.

'Thank you again, Mademoiselle.'

'Juliette, please.'

Max smiled. 'Merci beaucoup, Beauchamp.' They laughed. Max took Juliette's hand and kissed it. She felt his stubble brush her skin. It tingled. 'Will you be performing at your club tonight?' Juliette winced remembering her ordeal. 'Please, do not be afraid. I'll report the man responsible and ensure he never goes there again.'

Juliette was thrilled and relieved. She leant forward and kissed Max's cheek. They froze and stared at each other. Both wanted to kiss the other. Just as Max began to move towards her, a loud voice was clearly heard. Max moved to the door, opened it slightly and looked. He closed the door and turned to Juliette.

'That is Lieutenant General Schaumburg, the commander of all Paris operations. His suite is next door. He cannot abide misbehavior and is a stickler for the honour of the Fatherland. Some Germans prefer the Kaiser to the Dictator.'

Juliette understood. 'And he would not take kindly to an officer entertaining an actress in his room.'

Max hesitated. 'Forgive me. I can show you the private exit.' He opened the door, saw the coast was clear then escorted Juliette to a door marked *Private*. He opened it and Juliette saw a flight of stairs. She turned to thank him but he spoke first.

'I will be at your Club tonight. I look forward to seeing you then.' He kissed her hand then closed the door.

Juliette took a deep breath. *Well that wasn't rehearsed,* she thought. *Home James and don't spare the horses.*

She came out into the sunshine in a laneway behind the hotel. It was a fair walk to her bedsit but she had a spring in her step. She knew the short cuts in central Paris and bounced along a narrow street thinking all happy thoughts when a woman bumped into her. Juliette stopped, turned to face the woman and suddenly everything went black.

Chapter 21

KURT WAS FURIOUS. In Paris word had spread amongst Gestapo officers that "Nanny" Hartmann was in town. "If you want your lavatory cleaned, see Hartmann".

These jibes only made Kurt more determined. *I'll show you bastards,* he thought. He devised a plan but kept it secret. From the Gestapo files he located a Resistance publication and popped it in his briefcase. Then he went looking for Parisian printers. He entered different premises demanding to see their latest work. The first three drew a blank. In the fourth, the printer was nervous.

'Bonjour Monsieur. How may I help you?'

'Show me samples of your printing work for the last month.'

'Is there something in particular ...'

'Do as I say or I'll arrest you now.'

The worried printer returned with documents. Naturally there was nothing subversive but Kurt found the document he wanted. He produced the Resistance screed. The printer blanched.

Kurt was hostile. 'Did you print this?'

'Oh course not, Monsieur; that is illegal.'

Kurt held up the printer's document. 'But you did print this?'

The nervous printer nodded. Kurt held up both screeds.

'Well as these have identical typefaces, paper and ink, you must have printed them both. So I'll ask you again. Did you print this Resistance document?'

The printer put his hands to his face and whispered, 'Oui'.

Kurt exploded. 'And who paid for this work or did you print it for free because you're in the Resistance?'

The printer was desperate. 'No, no, no! Please Monsieur, I have a family. I have nothing to do with politics or the Resistance.'

Kurt's voice was full of menace. 'So who paid you?' The printer could not speak. 'If you want to see your family again you'll tell me the name of the person who ordered this material—now!'

The printer told the truth. 'I do not know his name, Monsieur.'

Without warning Kurt punched the man hard in the face. He crashed against a glass cabinet then slumped to the floor. Kurt was behind the counter in a flash and raised a clenched fist.

'But I know where he works,' blurted the terrified printer. Kurt drew back his fist to strike again. The printer spoke frantically. 'He works in a bookshop on the Rue de Memoire; number twenty-three.'

Kurt pointed at the printer. 'Breathe a word of this and you're in a concentration camp.' The printer felt a sharp pain in his chest.

Kurt found the bookshop and saw a notice in the window. There was a meeting of a literary society there that evening at 7pm.

Back at headquarters he recruited two junior Gestapo officers. They arrived at the bookshop at 7.10pm and stormed inside. A group of men and women reacted with fear. Kurt was in full flight.

'Who is in charge?'

A man protested. 'Please Monsieur, we are a literary society.'

Kurt withdrew his pistol and grabbed a young woman. 'Tell me who is in charge or I'll shoot this woman here and now.'

She screamed. Kurt pushed his pistol against her head. The atmosphere was electric. Even the Gestapo officers were stunned by Kurt's venom.

Quickly the man spoke. 'Wait. Please Monsieur; my name is Laroche. I run this literary society. I am in charge. Please.'

Kurt pushed the frantic woman aside and took the Resistance screed from his pocket. 'So, a literary society with politics?'

Laroche was shocked. Kurt snapped at him. 'You are under arrest. Take him.'

The Gestapo officers dragged the man away. The woman was petrified. Kurt grabbed her hair. 'You too,' he said ignoring her screams.

Half an hour later the man and woman were in separate cells. Kurt interrogated the man who refused to speak. Kurt ordered torture. Laroche was punched and kicked. He spat blood and teeth and when unconsciousness, a bucket of cold water drenched him.

Kurt moved in close. 'Sooner or later you'll tell me the names of your Resistance colleagues.'

Despite his fear and pain and with great difficulty the prisoner spoke. 'How do you sleep at night?'

Kurt was shocked. He wasn't expecting the man to speak at all and certainly not to defy him. Kurt sneered.

'Listen Laroche, if you think that's bad wait'll you taste the razor blades and salt. You dare not imagine the pain. So give me your Resistance colleagues or I'll send you to Hell.'

'Typical,' said the Frenchman, 'incapable of answering a simple question.'

Kurt was seething. He desperately wanted success. He was being watched. The other agents would spread the word that Hartmann couldn't crack a suspect. Kurt dare not fail. He was struggling. And not only was his first suspect defying him under brutal torture, the man was taunting him, exposing him as a murderous bully. Kurt tried a new tactic. He stopped. That gave him the edge. The Frenchman was expecting more violence. Silence was disconcerting. Do what your enemy least expects.

Kurt left the room. This was a powerful Gestapo tactic. It was the unknown, the waiting which caused the victim to imagine horror.

Then the woman from the bookshop was pushed into the cell. Kurt followed, grabbed her hair and dragged her close to Laroche. They were both on the floor. Their faces spoke volumes. Kurt calmly lit a cigarette. The woman was traumatized. Kurt leant forward and ripped the woman's blouse. He allowed the tension to build. He moved the glowing cigarette close to the woman's body. You could touch the fear.

The man spoke. 'She knows nothing.'

Kurt brushed the burning cigarette across the woman's naked shoulder. She whimpered. Kurt spoke softly. 'But you do.'

Suddenly he rammed the burning cigarette into the woman's neck and she screamed in agony.

Her comrade roared. 'Stop it! Stop it! I'll tell you! I'll tell you!'

His cries were louder than her screams. Kurt indicated to his colleagues and the shattered woman was removed.

Kurt withdrew a notebook. 'Congratulations, Laroche. You saved her from a very nasty rape. Now forget the foot soldiers, I want generals. Names!'

Laroche paused. Stronger men than him would yield to Gestapo maniacs. He could not resist when his comrades, and especially a woman, were tortured. He had only one name to give. He spoke softly.

'Silsbury, Godfrey Silsbury.'

Chapter 22

JULIETTE STRUGGLED to breathe. She was tied to a chair with a hood over her head. She could hear voices. Then a door opened and she heard footsteps. The hood was ripped off. She was in a darkened room with six people. They were French and angry; very angry. The leader spoke.

'So, who have we here; the whore, the filthy French collaborator?' Juliette held firm.

'My name is Juliette Beauchamp.'

'Shut up, bitch.' A man slapped Juliette's face hard. 'You speak only with permission.'

The woman who bumped into her in the street put her face very close to Juliette's. 'You are a disgrace to your sex, your family and your country. The Bosch treat us like pigs and you spread your legs for these murderous bastards. You make me sick.' She spat hard at Juliette and the spittle lingered then slid slowly down her face.

The leader, Gerard Blanc, was a communist and hater of Germans. He wanted two things; the defeat of the Nazis and the establishment of communist France. His face was very close to Juliette's.

'The others want to kill you but I prefer something more exotic. You're going to become less attractive to your Nazi lovers. We'll start with a bald head and then scratch a little swastika on your face.'

'A *big* swastika,' sneered the woman and the others laughed.

Blanc continued. 'You'll be a walking advertisement for any French women who fancy fucking the Bosch.' He looked at a comrade. 'Do it.'

A man stepped forward with a large pair of tailor's scissors. They could easily slice through serge. He clicked the scissors and grabbed a chunk of Juliette's hair. 'I hope you like it short, bitch.'

It was hopeless to struggle and Juliette didn't want to cry or beg for mercy. Her only hope was to say something unusual. Just as the barber was about to cut her hair, she spoke calmly.

'I can give you a top Nazi.'

The barber wasn't impressed but Blanc grabbed his arm.

'Cut her,' snarled the woman.

'Wait!' snapped Blanc. He bent very close to Juliette. 'If this is some stunt, I'll leave you to my insane comrades. So think very carefully about your next sentence. Your life depends on it.'

He stood back. The six Resistance fighters glared at Juliette. She thought about breath control, diction, sincerity and above all, eye contact. Beauford Nightingale would have been so proud. Fixing her gaze on Blanc, she took control.

'I know the room number in the Hôtel Meurice of the top Nazi in Paris. I know the staff entrance and exit. I know what the room waiters wear. I have the Wehrmacht colonel who resides in the adjacent suite wrapped around my little finger so if you want to capture one of Hitler's favourite pals, I can make it happen.'

What a pitch; script beautifully crafted and a perfect delivery. Juliette dared them to ignore her.

'She's lying,' said the woman.

Blanc threatened. 'Nobody touches her. If it's true, we think again. If she's lying, she'll beg us to kill her.'

Juliette looked at them. They stared back. She attacked. 'I can't believe you're all so stupid.'

Now for someone who was helpless, whose captors hated her and were hell bent on inflicting grievous bodily harm, Juliette's remark was either a death wish or a brilliant tactic. Her captors were stunned. Juliette milked it.

'No wonder the Bosch have conquered half of Europe. With imbeciles like you in the Resistance, we'll never win the war.'

It was so audacious the underground fighters were speechless. And Juliette became even more aggressive.

'You reckon the Nazis are immoral morons, yet here you are, kidnapping a loyal Frenchwoman and playing judge and jury without a shred of evidence. Your moral bankruptcy goes well with your gross incompetence. If you're the best we've got against the Krauts then God help France because as sure as hell you lot can't.'

This was a double whammy. The dialogue was credible and the delivery utterly convincing. If this woman was acting, she was damn good.

Blanc beckoned to the others. They spoke in the other room. There was anger aplenty. They returned. Blanc spoke softly to Juliette.

'They want to kill you. I want to listen. So talk.'

'Untie me first.'

The others complained.

'Untie her,' said Blanc. The barber stepped forward. 'Not you. Her.'

The woman who spat on Juliette shook her head. 'She's a whore, a traitor!'

'Do it,' yelled Blanc.

The woman paused then angrily untied Juliette.

She rubbed her wrists. 'I need water.'

'Oh Jesus!' screamed the woman.

'Get it,' spat Blanc and the woman stormed out. They waited and Juliette said nothing. She had the audience in the palm of her hand. The water was brought and Juliette raised the cup then stopped and handed it to the woman.

'You drink it,' said Juliette. The woman refused.

Blanc was furious and yelled at his comrade. 'Drink it!'

'I'm not thirsty,' snapped the woman.

There was a stalemate. Blanc insisted. The woman snatched at the cup and the water spilt on the floor. Blanc stared at his comrade.

'Try that again and *you'll* get the haircut. Now get her a clean drink.'

The woman did. Juliette drained the cup then described her plan.

'I let the Resistance team in. Disguised as a waiter, one of you knocks on the Kommandant's door. The waiter produces a gun, pushes into the suite and the others rush in. The Nazi is abducted via the staff exit and spirited away. And the Bosch will panic. They dare not kill anyone in reprisals for fear their beloved Kommandant will be tortured or executed. And the whole of Paris, the whole of France will know that the Resistance can outsmart the Bosch. Hitler's master race can't even protect their own. And you, you are the ones who can do it. It's risky but oh so possible.'

Silence. Who was this woman? Blanc and three others bought Juliette's pitch. The woman and the barber were non-believers.

'Who *are* you?' asked Blanc.

'Why do you ask? You know all about me. You've obviously been watching me. You know my name, where I live and work. But here's the truth, this plan won't work without me so if you want to kidnap Lieutenant General Schaumburg, let me go and butter up my colonel.'

The listeners were shocked. Could this woman do what she offered? If truthful, it was too good an opportunity to miss.

Ten minutes later Juliette was released with threats aplenty. Into the Paris sunshine she went, looking and feeling terrible. What would the SIS want her to do? She needed help. There was only one person she trusted.

Capitaine Émile Bonhomme was distressed. 'Mademoiselle, forgive me for saying this but you do not look like a beautiful actress.'

She told him about the nightclub fight, Max Hartmann's hotel suite, the Resistance abduction and her offer to help kidnap a prominent Nazi.

Bonhomme shook his head. 'For a convent girl you certainly know how to find adventure.'

'Capitaine, if I don't help the Resistance, they will kill me. If I do, the Nazis will kill me. I am desperate. Please, what do you advise?'

'Mademoiselle I am not the person to give advice. There is only one man in Paris who can help you now. You must speak to a man you met at Edith's apartment; Godfrey Silsbury.'

Juliette froze. 'But he's English and appalling.'

The policeman smiled. 'Silsbury appears to be a disreputable civil servant from the Foreign Office in London but he's really a brilliant English spy and the best link between Britain and the Resistance here in Paris. He is your only hope. I have his address although you will not have fond memories of this area. He lives in Montmartre.' Juliette winced. Her involvement in the murder of Oscar Masson was still fresh in her mind. 'And please, Mademoiselle, be careful. The Germans are watching me. You must not come here again. You must act like a member of the Resistance or even like a spy.'

Juliette remembered Major Bunting's words back in Baker Street. "Please Miss Wellesley; you are not a spy but a sleeper. You're far more likely to be exposed as a spy than a sleeper".

Juliette thanked Bonhomme and left. Silsbury's address was indeed a location she dreaded.

She found the Montmartre building and climbed the stairs to the third floor. Everything was quiet. Going alone into the apartment of a man she disliked and distrusted was worrying. Was Bonhomme's description of Silsbury correct? She knocked.

Nothing. She knocked again. Still nothing. She descended when a man came around the bend in the stairs. They stared at one another.

'Monsieur Silsbury, you won't remember me.'

'Remember you?' Silsbury moved quickly. 'How could I forget such dazzling beauty?' He took Juliette's hand and kissed it with enthusiasm. Her skin began to crawl.

'Capitaine Bonhomme suggested I seek your advice.'

'Well God bless the Capitaine. And please, do come in.'

He unlocked the door. This wasn't the Hôtel Meurice. The bolt-hole was spartan. It was cold and Juliette was nervous.

'Let me get you a drink.'

'No, thank you.'

'Nonsense; a beautiful Frenchwoman and a glass of French wine are perfection.' He poured two glasses.

Juliette's fear increased. She had a flashback of another suave gent and his alcoholic "kindness".

She spoke. 'I really have to tell you something, Monsieur. It's a matter of life and death.'

'I say; how fascinating.'

Juliette's heart was racing. She decided to tell all.

'I'm helping the Resistance kidnap a Nazi.'

She stopped. He stopped.

'But why tell a humble Englishman struggling in a foreign land?'

Juliette's spirits sank. 'I was told you know people in the Resistance.'

'Me?' Silsbury brought the wine and sat beside her. He smiled and Juliette felt despair. 'Santé,' toasted Silsbury. Their glasses clinked. Juliette had a sinking feeling as Silsbury moved closer and turned on what he considered to be his irresistible charm.

'So tell me, Mademoiselle, what does a Frenchwoman know about cricket?' Juliette froze. 'I was thinking of the leg-before-wicket law.'

Juliette's brain struggled. Silsbury switched to impeccable English.

'I would have thought *Albee* was right up your street, Plum, old girl.'

Juliette went from despair to delight. He was smiling. Juliette caught the grin and instinctively hugged Silsbury then immediately regretted it. Silsbury's eyes were dancing. He continued in English.

'Jolly nice to come clean, Miss Wellesley. And please, I'm Godfrey.'

Juliette began to regain her composure. Silsbury insisted they return to speaking French then explained how he delivered the envelope to Juliette's apartment and was waiting for orders from London before making contact with her again.

He was mightily impressed with her news about the kidnap plot and listened as Juliette explained every detail. Silsbury's advice was simple. She was to go ahead with the kidnap tonight after her final performance at the *One Two Two Club*—sometime after midnight. Silsbury would get additional Resistance forces to ensure it was successful.

They drank the wine. Everything was perfect. Juliette's SIS life was off and running. She now had an ally, an English gentleman in Paris. Well, the English and Paris bits were right.

Silsbury's gentlemanly instincts vanished as he took her glass and placed both to one side. Looking "lovingly" into her eyes he took her hand. He kissed it then his eyes blinked switching to the default setting of *lascivious*. The actress was in strife.

Pleading a full bladder, Juliette fled. She peed and pondered. She adjusted her dress and grabbed the lavatory chain when a heavy door-knocking began. She aborted the flush as a loud voice called.

'This is the Gestapo. Open the door now!'

She peered out and saw Silsbury in panic mode. 'Just a moment,' he called. He saw Juliette and pointed to the bedroom. The banging and calling increased.

'I'm coming,' yelled Silsbury then slowly unlocked the door. Kurt Hartmann burst in brandishing a Walther PPK. Silsbury fell on the floor as Juliette dived into the bedroom.

'Get up, Silsbury. You're under arrest,' said Kurt.

Two Gestapo officers grabbed the confused Englishman. Kurt looked in the kitchen and bathroom then entered the bedroom. Juliette had opened the narrow French windows and stepped onto the tiny balcony. She closed the windows and stepped up onto the railing. There was no time to think as she stepped from the railing onto a ledge barely six inches wide. She dug her fingertips into the crack between the bricks. Looking down was not an option. She flattened herself against the building as her thumping heart began pushing her backwards into space.

Kurt walked to the French windows, opened them and checked the empty balcony. Juliette stopped breathing. All the man had to do was look up and to his left. He didn't. Kurt closed the windows and returned to Silsbury. The protesting Englishman was dragged downstairs.

Juliette heard the door close. She was petrified. Which was worse; death following Gestapo torture or plummeting to the street below?

She looked to her left then, never once looking down, inched slowly back towards the balcony. Ants took bigger steps. Clinging to the space between the bricks, she lifted her left foot and felt for the railing. She missed it and tasted her heart.

She edged even further left. Slowly she again felt with her foot until it touched the railing. She applied a little pressure; it was solid. But she dared not twist her body. She moved her fingers along the brickwork. Pressing herself hard into the building, she took longer breaths.

Then it was time. With fear you could touch, she pushed off from the ledge crashing onto the balcony. She cried with relief and only then felt a shooting pain from landing on the rock-hard surface. But she was alive.

Bonhomme warned her never to contact him again. It was too dangerous for both of them. Her only hope, her SIS contact in France, had just been arrested by the Gestapo.

So what next, Plum?

Chapter 23

KURT WAS SMUG as he faced the captured Resistance leader.

'So, Monsieur Silsbury, you know the drill. I ask the questions, you give the answers and we all go home happy, n'est-ce pas?'

Silsbury wasn't worried. He leant forward, looked hard into Kurt's eyes and spoke slowly in German. 'Du bist ein Dummkopf.'

Kurt was shocked but quickly recovered. He was holding all the aces.

'I like your approach, Silsbury. But let's see how you respond to our persuasive techniques.'

Silsbury didn't flinch. 'If you lay a finger on me, you'll regret ever being born.'

Kurt was incensed. Who was this prick? 'You piece of shit!' thundered Kurt and lunged at Silsbury. He grabbed the prisoner's hair and drew back a clenched fist to smash his face. It worked. Silsbury was terrified.

Then the cell door flew open and a voice roared, 'Hartmann!'

Everyone froze. Kurt was shocked to see his commanding officer. Standartenführer Helmet Lischka was not a man to be trifled with. Kurt let go of Silsbury, stood upright and addressed his superior.

'You wish to interview the prisoner, Herr Direktor?'

'I wish to interview *you!*' Kurt paused. His brain was struggling. 'My office, Hartmann; now!'

Kurt's embarrassment hit new heights. He glared at Silsbury then left. He waited outside Lischka's office and stood to attention when the officer finally arrived. 'In,' snapped Lischka and Kurt followed.

Lischka sat and stared at the confused and uncomfortable Kurt. There was anger in Lischka's voice. 'I know about your nickname "Nanny" Hartmann. I confess I thought it harsh.'

'Thank you Herr ...'

'Do not speak.' Kurt became mute. 'But your latest blunder puts "Nanny" Hartmann in the shade. "Moron" Hartmann or "Shit-for-Brains" Hartmann are much closer to the truth.' Kurt was not tap-dancing.

Lischka continued. 'You go off half-cocked trying to impress everyone with your so-called superior abilities and end up creating a disaster.' A disaster? Kurt was struggling. His commanding officer's voice began a long crescendo. 'Your brilliant sleuthing has only gone and netted one of Germany's best double-agents!'

Double-agent! It would not have been manly but Kurt wanted to cry.

Lischka gave Kurt both barrels. 'Had you followed basic protocol and consulted your superiors you would know that the British spy, Godfrey Silsbury, is not only the Allies' top contact for the Resistance and Free

French Army, but also Berlin's best source of allied intelligence.' Kurt went numb. Lischka exploded. 'He's working for us, you fucking idiot!'

Lischka stood up and turned his back on Kurt who thought about leaping from a nearby window. Kurt's name was mud, his agony seemed endless and his career was in ruins. Finally Lischka turned.

'The only thing saving you from latrine duty in Siberia is your damn family.' Kurt was even more confused. 'Your cousin, Oberst Max Hartmann, is here in Paris.'

Kurt was afraid to respond.

'He's unwittingly involved in some Resistance plot to kidnap Kommandant Schaumburg from the Hôtel Meurice late tonight.'

This was too much for Kurt's confused brain. *Max in Paris, a kidnap plot, the Resistance—how do those words fit in the same sentence?*

'You have one chance to survive. Stop the kidnap plot and capture or kill the Resistance members. Their ringleader is an English actress claiming to be French and using the name Juliette Beauchamp. She must be taken, dead or alive. If she escapes, you're dead. If the plot succeeds, you're dead. Now, about your appetite.'

Kurt paused then with trepidation finally spoke. 'Herr Direktor?'

'On the menu tonight we have humble pie and you will eat all three courses while your English guest dines on the finest French cuisine. Silsbury has the kidnap details. Any questions?'

Kurt was outstandingly obsequious. 'No, Herr Direktor.'

Dining with Silsbury was galling for Kurt. It wasn't that he'd arrested, abused and assaulted the English double-agent, which was bad enough, but rather that Kurt had made a colossal and avoidable blunder. His new nickname of "Cock-up" Hartmann was well deserved.

Over the meal Silsbury made Kurt grovel and their hatred was mutual. But co-operation was essential. Both men needed the other.

Everything Juliette told Silsbury was told to Kurt. The fact that Max was involved meant nothing to the Gestapo agent. Here blood was thinner than water. Kurt's reputation, career and even his life were all on the line. He would do whatever it took to save his own skin.

He drew up a plan and took it to his superiors. Kurt dared not do anything now without prior approval. They looked over his plan. Kurt sweated. He had no religious beliefs but at that very moment was inclined to consider prayer.

Kurt's plan would see Kommandant Schaumburg quietly escorted to safety. Gestapo officers would be in the Kommandant's rooms and elsewhere throughout the hotel. Kurt would take personal charge of invading his cousin's suite. If that Englishwoman posing as a French actress was there, nothing would stop Kurt from killing or capturing her.

Silsbury gave Kurt a final warning. 'Juliette Beauchamp is the key. If she discovers my link to Berlin, my cover is blown. If that happens, I'll be off to Germany and you'll be off to Eternity. Get that woman.'

Kurt secretly admired Silsbury. He was a thorough-going bastard and it took one to know one.

The Gestapo heavyweights approved Kurt's plan. They weren't exactly sure if or when the attempted kidnapping would occur but if it did they'd be ready. For the Resistance kidnappers and the English rose, the hotel would soon become a death trap.

Chapter 24

JULIETTE ZIG-ZAGGED to avoid followers. She reached her address, entered her room and collapsed on the bed. Only then did the tears flow. Every thought brought misery. Her shoulder and elbow ached. Her mind was a mess. She shunned every mirror.

Then horror struck. Silsbury knew where she lived. Under torture he might tell the Gestapo. She changed quickly, washed, then packed a small case and left via the back door.

As she walked away, Kurt and two Gestapo officers ran up the stairs and burst into her room. They missed her by minutes. In the foyer, Madame Baudin opened her door then closed it when she saw the Gestapo trio. Kurt called out.

'Hey, old woman; open your door.'

He banged ferociously and slowly the door opened.

'Monsieur?'

'The woman upstairs, Juliette Beauchamp, where is she?'

'I have no idea, Monsieur. I am old and cannot see very well.'

'Where does she work?'

'At the flea market opposite the Eiffel Tower.' Kurt began to leave and Madame Baudin yelled. 'Tell her she owes me rent.' She smiled imagining the Bosch combing the market in vain.

Juliette went to the *One Two Two Club*, the only safe place she knew. In her dressing-room she made a bed from old curtains and fell asleep.

An hour later, Edith arrived. 'Hello, what have we here?' Juliette was awake and worried. Edith teased her. 'Don't tell me. You're hiding from a jealous wife because of your affair with a married man.' Edith looked closer at Juliette. 'And it looks like the wife has caught you in the act.'

Juliette didn't laugh. They put on their make-up.

'Edith, I have a big favour to ask.'

'I never share my music or lovers.'

'If I get into trouble tonight, please, may I drop in on you?'

Edith looked serious. 'Of course but only if you tell me every juicy detail.' They laughed although Juliette's laughter was contrived.

The show went on but it was hard to wear a happy face. Juliette worried about the beast from last night, about the Gestapo probably hunting for her right now, about Silsbury's arrest and the crazy kidnap scheme she suggested. Her thoughts were buzzing. *Would the Resistance turn up? Would Max come here to the club? If so, would he invite her back to his hotel? What if he did? If he didn't appear, where would she spend the night?* There was no script for this play.

After their final show the performers were changing when someone knocked on the dressing-room door. The women fell silent. Any such sound in Paris in 1940 was intimidating. Edith opened the door.

She saw a magnificent bunch of roses. 'Oh là là,' said Edith, 'c'est magnifique!' She wasn't so effusive when she saw the man holding the blooms. It was tank commander, Oberst Maximilian Hartmann. Juliette was excited. She gratefully took the roses and introduced.

Max was genuinely humble. 'I am privileged, ladies, to enjoy your brilliant performances. You are an honour to your country and craft.'

Juliette was impressed and Edith saw how this German was so unlike most of his murderous compatriots. He spoke with sincerity and charm.

'I would like to invite you beautiful ladies to supper. I know a perfect restaurant nearby which still manages to do justice to your glorious French cuisine. Please, will you do me the honour of being my guests?'

Max had a way with words. Edith offered her apologies but Juliette graciously accepted. She looked at Edith and the women's eyes engaged.

The restaurant Max chose thrived because it obtained quality ingredients from the black market.

Max spoke about last night. 'I cannot thank you enough, Juliette. Last night you saved my life and reputation.' He kissed her hand. This was nothing like the Silsbury kiss. This was soft and warm. Juliette tingled. He squeezed her hand and that same tingle quickly changed location.

They finished their meal. Max paid and Juliette was worried he would find a taxi, even after curfew, and have her safely delivered home. She couldn't accept that. Her home was probably being watched and the Resistance fighters were probably hiding right now near the Meurice Hotel, depending on her being inside Max's room. He spoke.

'Please don't misunderstand me, Juliette. But I have obtained a bottle of your finest French champagne. At this very moment, it is being chilled in my suite and before I arrange to have you taken home, perhaps you would like to share a glass.'

Juliette's heart beat faster. 'Herr Oberst, I would be delighted.'

They walked to the hotel. Juliette took Max's arm and his body felt strong and masculine. She had no idea what would happen with the planned kidnap. But equally worrying, no idea what would happen once she entered Max's hotel. Despite the war, despite her status as a sleeper for the Secret Intelligence Service, and despite Max being a sworn enemy of her beloved homeland, Juliette was drawn to him. His nationality, training and job screamed danger. But as a man, he was attractive, interesting and desirable.

They approached the Hôtel Meurice and Juliette considered her options. If she was in Max's suite, how could she rendezvous with the Resistance fighters? Wait till Max fell asleep? But if he fell asleep, surely it would be after they made love.

Right now Juliette was inventing her lines and had no idea how this "play" would end. They entered the hotel foyer. A few guests were chatting before retiring. A group of women was to one side enjoying one another's company. Juliette took Max's arm in both her hands.

'Oh Max, over there is one of my fellow dancers from the Folies Bergère. I must say hello.'

He was impressed. 'You were in the Folies Bergère?'

'Once upon a time.' She held up her case. 'I even have my little costume in my little case.'

Max's eyes lit up. His imagination ran wild. 'Ah yes, you go. I'll wait for you upstairs.'

He kissed her cheek. Another tingle for Juliette. She walked towards the women. She thought about Beauford Nightingale's advice, about eye contact and conviction.

As Max headed to the lifts he saw a woman warmly embrace Juliette. He stepped into the lift and felt like a kid on his first date. What he didn't see were two Gestapo agents watching in a darkened corner of the foyer.

Juliette's ploy worked. It was a sisterhood thing. "Please pretend you know me and look excited. Otherwise I'm in big trouble".

Thanking her "sisters", Juliette headed to the rear of the foyer. Only one door seemed a possibility. It led to an unfamiliar corridor. She chastised herself. *Great. The kidnappers are waiting and I'm lost.*

Suddenly a cleaning woman came out of a storeroom. The two women stared at each other.

'Can you help me?' asked Juliette. 'My over-protective parents think I'm in moral danger and want to take me back home to the country. Please, where is the rear exit?'

The cleaner smiled and pointed. 'Go to the end and turn left. The door is straight ahead.'

'Merci,' said Juliette. She found the door, took a deep breath, and turned the lock.

The door jerked open and a masked man confronted her. He spoke.

'So, you were not lying.'

Juliette recognized Gerard Blanc's voice. Then a hotel waiter appeared carrying a tray with a bottle of wine.

The woman who spat at Juliette pushed her way inside. She carried a pistol and spoke rudely. 'This had better not be a trap.'

Juliette answered. 'If I wanted to betray you, the Gestapo would have opened the door.'

'Shut up,' said Blanc.

'I'll need ten minutes,' said Juliette. 'The stairs are over there. If anything's suspicious, I'll leave this handkerchief on the stairwell. Otherwise you're on your own. And for God's sake get the right room number.'

She climbed the stairs. At the door marked *Private* she stopped. She could hear muffled voices. They faded.

Slowly she opened the door a fraction. She waited. Silence. She spoke to herself. 'It's now or never my girl.'

With a look of complete indifference, she opened the door and set sail along the corridor. She was doing fine until just ahead of her a door opened and a German officer came out of his room. He'd been told by the Gestapo to remain inside his room; no reason, just stay indoors. He stared at Juliette.

Without missing a stride, she smiled and as she walked past the man she spoke in German. 'Something has to be done about those damn lifts.'

She knocked on Max's door. The officer she spoke to had not moved. He was thinking. *Who the hell is this gorgeous Fräulein and why isn't she knocking on my door?*

Max's door opened. He stepped out and kissed Juliette. Max saw his fellow officer staring. He ushered Juliette inside and called to his colleague.

'Good evening, Schabel. You haven't met my cousin.' Max grinned, stepped into his suite and closed the door.

Chapter 25

MAX WAS RIGHT. The champagne was superb as were his manners. But Juliette was worried and her heartbeat began jogging.

She knew they were attracted to one another but love and war made for a dangerous mix. They toasted each other. Did her SIS training cover being romanced in a 5 star Parisian hotel by a Wehrmacht tank commander from the elite 7th Panzer Division?

Did she want this man to be her first lover? Her mind was racing. *How does one make love knowing a daring raid by the French Resistance is about to happen in the corridor outside one's boudoir?* Being seduced by a German officer was one thing. Surviving a possible gun battle was another. Which came first; the sex or the slaughter?

Juliette was listening for even the slightest sound from the French Resistance. Max was thinking about another type of French resistance, the type he might get from this gorgeous Frenchwoman. He worked on his timing.

'I can't believe you were a dancer at the Folies Bergère.' Juliette looked miffed. He immediately saw his faux pas. 'No, no, no. Of course you are more than beautiful to be a star but ...'

He looked sheepish. Juliette smiled. He really was a charming man.

'Max, I don't quite know how to say this.'

'Say nothing,' said Max taking her glass and placing both to one side. 'Let's forget we're at war and just enjoy the moment.'

He stared at her, waiting, hoping for a response. She said nothing and that seemed to speak volumes. He leant closer and paused. Their faces were very close. They could feel each other's breath. Louise's eyes were inviting yet scared.

Max leant in and kissed her lips with the lightest of touches. She felt a strong tingle and wanted him to repeat the routine. He paused then kissed her again and just as their lips touched those metaphorical fireworks exploded.

But the metaphorical became the literal as the fireworks became the firearms. The gunfire was very loud. Obviously that killed the budding romance and with ferocious screaming thrown in for good measure the lovers' tryst was trashed. Part of World War 2 was being waged in a corridor of the Hôtel Meurice.

Max grabbed his pistol and Juliette saw her life flash before her eyes.

'Don't move,' said Max. He opened the door a fraction then immediately closed and locked it. 'Gestapo. God help us.'

The gunfire stopped but the shouting continued. Juliette spoke. 'Max, I need to explain. The Gestapo may be looking for me.'

He was stunned. 'You?'

'Some of my friends hate the Germans. It's possible the Gestapo believe in guilt by association.'

Max was desperate. 'Are you in the Resistance? Tell me, Juliette; please tell me the truth.'

'No, Herr Oberst, I have never been a member of the French Resistance.' So much for the whole truth.

Someone knocked loudly on Max's door and called. 'Herr Oberst! Open this door!'

Max looked at Juliette. He was starting to sweat and she to shake. He gave her one champagne glass. 'Take this, your coat and case and hide on the balcony.' More door banging. Max snapped at her. 'Do it now; go!'

Juliette fled. *Not another balcony.* But this one was large with furniture and plants. She closed the French windows and hid.

Max opened the door and got a real surprise.

'Mein Gott, Kurt.'

Brandishing his pistol Kurt Hartmann pushed past his cousin and into the suite. 'Where is she?'

'And it's lovely to see you too,' said Max.

'I don't know whether you're part of this but she is.' His voice got louder. 'Now where's the woman?'

Max was furious and sarcastic. 'Listen, *officer*, I know your Gestapo creed advocates torture and murder but since when has politeness to a fellow German become verboten? Can you at least not offer a half decent *Guten Abend* to your own cousin?' Both men were furious. 'Pardon my French, Mein Herr, but whatever happened to fucking manners?'

Kurt was suddenly aware of his behaviour. His zeal to wreck the Resistance plot and capture the British spy dominated. Now a pinprick of conscience awoke inside his head. He holstered his gun. He almost smiled. He changed.

'So, the life of a Wehrmacht colonel really *is* all beer and skittles.' He picked up the bottle of champagne. 'Expensive. Too expensive to drink alone, surely? May I join you?'

Max looked at his cousin.

'I'm expecting a friend,' said Max.

'I know. You were seen arriving. So where is she?'

Max remained calm. 'What do you want, Kurt?'

'You are supping with the Devil, Herr Oberst. Just now, in your corridor, I foiled a kidnap plot against Kommandant Schaumburg. The Resistance thugs are dead or soon will be. Only one remains unaccounted for. Your lady friend is not who she claims to be. And I will find her and kill her and if necessary, you too.'

The cousins stared at one another. Max said nothing. Kurt got the message and so explored the suite. He looked in the bedroom and bathroom. He walked to the French windows. In the darkness Juliette crouched behind a plant. Kurt opened a French window and peered into

172

the gloom. Max felt for his pistol. Kurt saw only plants and chairs, closed the window and came back to his cousin. He stopped at the main door and spoke.

'This is the only way in or out. I'll get her, cousin, that I can promise and if necessary, you too.' Kurt opened the door then stared at his cousin. 'Guten Abend ... Herr Oberst.' Kurt left.

Max locked the door. So much for an evening of unbridled passion with the divine Mademoiselle Beauchamp. Scheisse!

Kurt had wanted to make a detailed search of Max's suite but couldn't bear the humiliation of not finding the woman. He took no chances and placed an agent in the corridor. He sent men to search the hotel and others to again search Juliette's bedsit and her real place of work. The hunt for the pretend Frenchwoman was on in earnest.

Juliette came back into the suite. She and Max looked at one another. Their magical romantic moment was over.

'Herr Oberst, I am truly sorry for involving you in my troubles. I never wanted to hurt you.'

Now she was calling him "Herr Oberst". The Resistance gang members were captured or shot and so was Max and Juliette's budding affair. But Max's feelings were still strong. He wanted to help her not just because he hated the Gestapo but because he knew he liked her. He wasn't sure if that was like, love or lust.

'Right then, Mademoiselle Beauchamp, we need a plan. As much as I'd delight in having you as my house guest, I fear you need to get as far away from here as possible.'

Juliette spoke. 'But if I explain to the Gestapo, they ...'

'Are you mad?' Max was angry. 'Those men are animals. No civilized country would ever countenance the Gestapo's barbarity. I don't care if you're the head of the French Resistance, I will not allow you to be captured by that scum. And particularly not by the man who came in here looking for you—my cousin.'

'I heard,' said Juliette. She was clearly frightened yet at the same time glad she'd met a man who cared about others and hated war as much as she did. The fact that he was German and her country's sworn enemy only made her feelings even stronger. Max was thinking aloud.

'They'll be watching all hotel exits. Unless we're mountain goats, our best hope will be to walk out under their noses.'

Juliette thought the idea insane. 'But they're looking for me.'

'For a woman, yes, but not for a man.' Max opened the door a fraction then closed it. 'There's a Gestapo agent in the corridor. We need him in here and unconscious.'

Juliette had an idea. 'I have a sleeping draught in my case.' Max looked at her. She explained. 'A while ago I was drugged and nearly raped. The man who drugged me was murdered and I was charged with his death.'

Max was hooked. 'You murdered him?'

'No, no I was framed. And the policeman who found the real murderer is a World War 1 hero who then arranged for me to entertain some French troops.'

'Before the Battle of France?'

Juliette nodded. 'And that could be why the Gestapo think I'm in the Resistance. But as you saw last night, there are men who attack women and this sleeping draught is one of my weapons.'

'Brilliant,' said Max. 'Here's the plan.'

Twenty minutes later Juliette was getting dressed. The Gestapo agent from the corridor was sound asleep on Max's bed. He'd stepped inside for a glass of champagne with his "prisoner" and was now in the land of Nod. His outer garments had been removed and Max was helping Juliette to dress. This was not his original plan.

He'd hoped she'd be removing garments rather than adding new ones. The Gestapo agent was of medium height and build and because Juliette was wearing her normal clothes underneath, the new uniform was a reasonable fit.

'Are you sure this will work?' asked Juliette.

'Of course not but what's the alternative?'

'And we're going out the front door?'

'Exactly. The more brazen the better. But I suggest you remain silent throughout. A Gestapo agent speaking fluent French is not a good look.'

Juliette replied in German. 'But I could speak German if you wish.' Max was stunned. Juliette dropped her voice. 'And in a deeper voice as well.'

Max laughed. 'Not just a brilliant and beautiful performer but a linguist as well. I suppose you also speak English.'

Juliet nodded and spoke in English with a French accent. 'Oui but only za little.' Max shook his head in wonder.

The tension was rising. Their sexual chemistry mingled with the danger and threat of capture. As Max helped Juliette to dress, he touched her arms and shoulders and when he knelt to hide her dress underneath the Gestapo coat he touched her thighs. Both of them knew they were dicing with death but bursts of electricity zapped between them.

When she was finally "dressed", Max repeated the plan. Juliette felt her busy heart get busier. If she made it into the city, she would stick to her original plan and seek refuge in Edith's apartment.

Time to go.

Max checked the corridor. It was empty. The sleeping agent had a moustache and Juliet used lipstick to decorate her upper lip. Her hair was scrunched under her Gestapo hat and the tie pulled tight.

It was well after midnight and despite the earlier bloody battle, the hotel was now asleep. Max led the way to the lifts. There were blood stains on the carpet where Resistance fighters had died in the botched kidnap.

It took a while for the lift to arrive. They were seriously worried. What if Kommandant Schaumburg was being escorted back to his suite? What if Kurt appeared? What if he was parked in the foyer? This game of chance meant the loser would surely die.

They watched the indicator showing the lift rising to their floor. Higher and higher it came. Juliette was sure her heart beats were audible. The lift stopped. There was nothing they could do. If Kurt or his cronies were inside Max and Juliette were as good as dead.

The lift stopped. There was a pause then the doors opened. The lift was empty. Max was calm on the outside but even his military training and wartime experience didn't help in this situation. Worse he was aiding an enemy of the Reich. If they were caught, they would both be tortured and shot. It was that simple.

They entered the lift and Max pushed the foyer button. The doors closed. They looked at one another. Juliette wanted to kiss her co-conspirator. He gave Juliette a final once over and pulled her hat a tad tighter. His face was close to hers when he spoke.

'Driving a Panzer into battle can be bloody frightening but this is something else.' He leaned in and kissed her cheek. 'Be brave, Mademoiselle. Vive la France.' She turned her face towards him. The lift began to slow. He gently kissed her lips.

The lift stopped and the doors opened.

Godfrey Silsbury was worried his cover was blown. The British trusted him implicitly. He was one of them; Harrow, Oxford and the Foreign Office. He had a brilliant mind making him ideal for wartime duties and the SIS.

But Silsbury had been turned well before the outbreak of war. He hated the Establishment. Not a Russian lover but definitely an anti-Semite and racial supremacist. In the early 30s he was posted to Berlin and saw first-hand the rise of the National Socialists. Why couldn't Britain do away with its indolent riff raff? Silsbury was convinced Jewish bankers were holding hard-working Englishmen to ransom. A bloodless revolution would do quite nicely.

With war looming his German contacts came a-calling. They promised a new Britain once it sued for peace. In the meantime Godfrey's Geneva bank account kept growing thanks to Nazi donations. Once war was declared, Godfrey's value soared.

Now, due to a fanatical Gestapo agent and a meddling English actress, his double life was in danger of being exposed.

Silsbury met with Kurt after the kidnap plot was foiled. Silsbury sat in on the torture sessions when those who survived were grilled. The Resistance fighters were told that Juliette Beauchamp betrayed them. Would their anger encourage them to tell the Gestapo anything about her? If they knew anything about the French actress they said nothing. As it happened they had nothing to tell.

And where was that bloody actress? She was the key. If she discovered that Silsbury was a double-agent, she'd tell London their top European spy was a secret Nazi, his life in Britain would be over and the Nazis would lose an invaluable ally. Come on, find that English bitch.

Max and Juliette walked out of the lift into the dimly lit foyer. A token hotel employee was behind the reception desk. Four Wehrmacht officers were smoking and chatting about the failed kidnap plot. A cleaning woman was emptying ashtrays and in a very dim corner a Gestapo agent was pretending to read a newspaper.

Max saw the Gestapo agent and effortlessly crossed in front of Juliette allowing Max to partly screen his companion. He spoke to the officers but kept walking.

'Good evening, gentleman. Please note my security companion as I take a short constitutional.' The officers laughed.

The Gestapo agent stood up. Max wished him a good evening and indicated Juliette. 'He's checked my room—nothing.'

Juliette tapped her watch and spoke softly. 'Twenty minutes.'

The Gestapo agent made to intercept the couple but the comments and laughter from Max's Wehrmacht colleagues caused the agent to pause. They were relaxed. It must be okay. Juliette's heart was thumping. The unlikely couple kept on walking.

Suddenly a man sprang from the shadows and Max felt for his gun. It was a hotel doorkeeper who refused to travel home in the blackout. 'Gentlemen,' he said and opened the door. Max and his "Gestapo minder" kept on walking out into the cold Parisian night.

It was seriously dark. The city had long since turned off its lights. The couple walked away from the hotel. Juliette wanted to run. Max slowed. 'Relax. We're taking a stroll.'

Max dropped his comb, bent to pick it up and at the same time glanced back. He saw the Gestapo officer running back into the hotel.

'Our Gestapo chum is off to ring my dear cousin. Time to move.'

It wasn't long before Kurt received a phone call at Gestapo HQ. The English actress was not in Oberst Hartmann's suite and there was no sign of her in the hotel. But there is a drugged Gestapo agent on Oberst Hartmann's bed and the tank commander has just left the hotel with an unknown Gestapo agent.

It was accurate to describe Kurt as apoplectic. Silsbury observed Kurt's reaction.

Max led Juliette across the road into the Tuileries Gardens. They walked into the darkened acres of lawns, trees, statues, paths, ponds and more, not that you could see much. They headed towards the Seine. They'd gone about a hundred metres when Max stopped and spoke. Their whispers were the only sounds.

'How far to your safe place?'

'About four kilometres. It will take me an hour or more.'

'There'll be patrols. You must be careful.'

Juliette looked at Max. In the crisp blackness of the early morning, she struggled to find words to express her feelings.

'You saved my life, Herr Oberst, and put your own at risk. And yet we are fighting on different sides. What does that tell us?'

Max was emotional. 'Perhaps that even in time of war love will always survive.' He paused. 'I am going to find it very hard to forget you.'

They looked at each other. Juliette was frightened with a real feeling of sadness. She started to disrobe but spoke in a calm voice.

'I want you to go back now. You can use the hotel's rear entrance. Take these clothes and dress the man in your room. He'll be too embarrassed to admit anything. We will both survive.'

Max laughed quietly and accepted the Gestapo clothes. He too was struggling for words.

'I wish we could have met under different circumstances.' She gave a restrained smile. They stared at one another. Everything was still and deathly quiet. Paris was on hold. Their lives were on hold.

Suddenly Max tossed the clothing aside, grabbed Juliette's shoulders and pulled her close. His kiss was tender but passionate. She responded in kind and for a few seconds they forgot about the war and their deadly predicament. They hugged and kissed one another as never before; their passion overcame their fear. But that changed instantly when a strong torch light shone from the darkness.

'Nobody move.'

Max and Juliette froze like rabbits caught in some headlights.

Kurt Hartmann walked slowly towards them. 'I'm very disappointed in you, cousin. You ignored my warning. The Chancellor will not be pleased.'

Max stepped in front of Juliette. Kurt was unimpressed.

'Oh come now, Herr Oberst, you're aiding a spy.'

Max was defiant. 'She's not a spy, Kurt. She's a French actress and has nothing to do with the Resistance.'

'Not true. The lady is English.' Max was stunned but said nothing. 'She is Miss Louise Wellesley, Cambridge undergraduate and recently awakened operative for the British Secret Intelligence Service.' He paused and edged closer. 'It's true. Go on, ask her.'

Juliette spoke quickly and quietly. 'Keep him talking. I'll make a dash for it.'

Max tried to reason with his cousin. 'Oh for pity's sake, Kurt. It's time you stopped torturing and murdering and left the real war to professional soldiers.'

Juliette whispered. 'I'll count to three then run. I'll go left. You go right.'

Kurt inched closer. 'Now this is what you're going to do.'

'One,' whispered Juliette.

'Both of you; get on your knees.'

'Two.'

'Think of your father, Kurt,' said Max.

Kurt screamed. 'Get on your knees!'

'Three,' spat Juliette and ran like mad in a zig-zag way. Max took off to his right.

Kurt was thrown. He roared his frustration and waved his torch trying to catch the woman. Max's running caused confusion. Kurt ran after Juliette. He thought he could hear her. He fired twice, three times. Bullets whizzed past the running woman. Max stopped. He turned and ran back after Juliette, determined to help her escape.

The inky blackness was superb cover. Kurt ran waving his torch, trying to hear the woman, dodge the plants and shoot when he thought he saw or heard her. Juliette didn't stop. She was terrified but simply ploughed ahead. She knew the River Seine was close.

Suddenly she tripped and fell. This gave her a chance to hear her attacker. But it sounded like two people running. She saw a torch bobbing and ran away from that. More shots. Then a scream.

She crouched and listened. Nothing. She heard groaning and crept towards the sounds. She stumbled over something. No, it was someone and the groaning increased. She knelt and peered in the darkness. She saw Max. He was lying face down. She touched his back and felt blood. Gently she rolled him over, his unfired gun in his hand. He groaned again.

'Herr Oberst,' she whispered in despair. He coughed blood.

'Go,' he croaked. 'Go now.'

Suddenly Kurt's light lit the scene and Juliette was blinded.

She screamed at the light. 'You've shot your cousin, your own flesh and blood, you evil bastard.'

Kurt was stunned. 'Shut up! Shut up you bitch!'

Juliette cradled Max's head. Shock gripped his body. Kurt lost control. He almost screamed.

'It's your fault, you did this, you fucking English whore.'

He walked slowly towards Juliette his gun and torch aimed straight at her. She didn't care about herself. She only wanted Max to survive.

Kurt edged closer. Through all his hatred, racism and ambition he suddenly felt pain. He had shot his cousin. His thoughts were a mess. *Yes, my cousin was helping an English spy but blood can be thicker than water and I've shot the man I've long considered to be my brother.* Kurt despaired. He was an entire chapter in a psychology text-book.

Juliette screamed. 'Go away! Just go away!'

This screaming from Juliette jolted Kurt. He shut down his emotions. He was striding quickly now only a few metres away with his torch and gun pointing at Juliette. He stared at her and tightened his trigger finger. He was going to watch her face as he shot her. Closer and closer he came. Her face was pure hatred. He started to squeeze the trigger.

Then he tripped, stumbled and fell and his torch jerked away. He was lying close to his cousin's feet. Kurt was demonic with rage. He stood and as he swung his torch back to illuminate Juliette, he aimed his pistol, started to squeeze the trigger and a single shot rang out. There was an eerie silence and time seemed to stand still.

Kurt dropped his torch which blazed wildly into the night. In the darkness he stood like a statue. He stared at Juliette then crumpled. Juliette had fired Max's gun aiming at the torch. She dropped the gun.

Kurt was dead. In the silent darkness, Juliette gently supported Oberst Hartmann's head, and kissed him as he died.

Someone was calling. 'Juliette! Where are you? Juliette!' She knew that voice. Another torch approached Juliette. She struggled to find Max's gun. This new torch shone on her. The person spoke English.

'It's me, Godfrey. Thank God you're all right.' He saw the bodies. 'Jesus, what happened?'

Juliette too spoke English. 'The Gestapo thug shot Oberst Hartmann and I shot the thug.'

'Well good for you. But come on, young lady. We can't stay here.'

Silsbury put Max's gun in Max's hand and Kurt's torch and gun in Kurt's hands.

Silsbury explained 'There'll be fewer reprisals if they think it was two Germans killing one another.'

They heard voices and saw torches waving in the darkness. Silsbury grabbed Juliette's hand and dragged her away. They stumbled through the gardens. She was exhausted, in shock and struggled to keep up. They crossed into the city and kept close to buildings.

Juliette wanted to stop. 'Where are we going?'

'My place.'

'But the Gestapo know where you live.'

'My *other* place.'

They kept moving along dark and deserted side streets until Silsbury stopped, pushed open a door and guided Juliette inside.

They climbed some stairs and Silsbury unlocked a door. Inside he turned on a weak light. It was a single room with a bed and a chair—the glamorous digs of a top secret agent. No window, no bathroom and damn cold.

'The loo's down the corridor,' he said. 'Do you need it?'

Juliette shook her head.

'Right, have a seat. I've got some Scotch.'

Juliette examined herself. She had scratches on her hands, grazes on her knees, her hair was a mess and her clothes were dirty with many twigs and leaves. Silsbury handed her a glass.'

'Drink this. You've earned it.'

They drank in silence. Juliette had a million questions. Silsbury took over.

'You've been bloody marvellous. I'm going to recommend you for a medal. But look old girl, you're my last hope. You have to get back to England and tell the SIS I'm alive and well. Can you do that?'

Juliet was struggling to make sense of the last two hours. 'I think so. But how did you escape the Gestapo?'

'A bloody mistake; would you believe that idiot you shot mistook me for Bonhomme.'

'Capitaine Bonhomme?'

'Yes. Then I overheard the Germans. The Resistance gang was captured at the hotel and under torture gave up Bonhomme and you. They even told the Gestapo the whole kidnap plot was your idea.'

'But it *was* my idea. I told you.'

Silsbury appeared stunned. 'What? Oh God, of course you did.' He seemed confused. 'But London hasn't sent any new orders. I was instructed to tell you to be ready, not to go on some lunatic scheme which saw me arrested and half a dozen resistance fighters killed.'

Juliette felt terrible. 'But you know I had no choice. I told you the Resistance kidnapped me as a collaborator. They only let me go when I promised a kidnapping.'

Silsbury shook his head. He seemed surprised then depressed. 'Of course, I'm sorry. I don't know where I am. Bloody Bosch!'

Juliette paused. 'I didn't know Capitaine Bonhomme was in the Resistance. I feel terrible knowing my kidnap plot got him arrested.'

'He's a good man. He won't talk.'

'So what do we do now?'

'Stay here for a day or two. I'll have you moved south then flown home. Remember, you're the only person who can assure London I'm still operational. It's vital they know the truth.'

'Can't you radio that news?'

'With what? They raided my apartment, captured Bonhomme and now I have to start again. Only a firsthand report from you will work. Can you do that?'

Juliette nodded. Her plot had failed and she'd killed another human. Two men she really cared about had been arrested or shot. There was nothing to celebrate.

'I say, you're bleeding.' Silsbury touched Juliette's face. She flinched.

She removed his hand. 'No, it's lipstick. I painted a moustache to ... never mind.'

She began to softly cry. Silsbury embraced her and whispered in her ear. He spoke in their native English.

'There, there, you're safe now, my lovely Plum.'

She didn't feel safe. And if only she knew.

The light was out with Juliette asleep on the bed. Silsbury checked his gun and pondered his options. If he shot her now or handed her over to the Gestapo, would that be the best way to keep his secret life secret?

Certainly the ideal result would be if she believed he was the real deal and went home to deliver that message. They'd believe a believer. It was the perfect way to preserve his double-agent status.

He was half dozing when someone knocked softly on the door. Juliette was instantly awake. Silsbury checked his gun and moved to the door.

'Shhhh', whispered Silsbury. Juliette slipped off the bed. Silsbury pointed his gun and slowly unlocked the door.

Suddenly he jerked it open and prepared to fire. In the dim light Capitaine Émile Bonhomme stood with a raised hand preparing to knock. The two men froze. Bonhomme was all smiles.

'Godfrey, dear chap; aren't you going to invite me in?'

Juliette's heart leapt with joy and she moved to Bonhomme.

'Mademoiselle!' he exclaimed and they embraced.

Silsbury closed the door, switched on the light and spoke French. 'Keep quiet.'

Juliette was emotional. 'We thought you were caught by the Germans.'

Bonhomme explained. 'Almost. I turned into my street just as the Gestapo came out of my house. I was lucky. It pays to be late.'

Silsbury was calm. 'How did you know we'd be here?'

'I didn't. But your other apartment is being watched so I took the chance. I fear, my friend, something is rotten in the state of Denmark.'

Juliette became nervous. 'Capitaine, do you know about the disaster at the Hôtel Meurice?'

'Every police officer in Paris knows.'

Silence. After a pause, Bonhomme spoke.

'I'm surprised you escaped Mademoiselle. You seem to have a knack of getting in and out of very tight corners.'

'I was lucky. First Oberst Hartmann saved me from the Gestapo and then Monsieur Silsbury did the same. Without them I'd be dead.'

'Unlike your comrades,' said Bonhomme.

The temperature dropped.

'But Capitaine, you know I am not a part of the Resistance.'

'I know that you planned the kidnapping and that you are the only one to escape.'

Juliette was devastated. Her ally, the one man she respected and admired doubted her.

Silsbury butted in. 'Émile, I was there. This woman is brave. She killed a Gestapo agent.'

'Which is why, as a Frenchwoman, she should make her report directly to the Resistance. I'll take her to my people in Paris.'

'No!' Godfrey spoke too quickly.

Juliette was never more afraid.

Bonhomme was insistent. 'I can get her across town before dawn.' He took Juliette's arm and turned her towards the door.

'Stop!' snapped Silsbury. He raised his gun.

'Oh Godfrey, don't be so bloody melodramatic. We French deal with our own people. Now kindly put down your gun.'

'I have my orders, Émile. She must return to England.'

Juliette froze as the men argued.

Bonhomme was determined. 'Return to England? She comes from Marseilles.'

Bonhomme eased Juliette closer to the door.

Silsbury moved to stop them. 'Don't make me do this.' His gun was pointed at the Frenchman.

Bonhomme let go of Juliette and turned to face Silsbury. The policeman was relaxed. 'You know, dear Godfrey, apart from those taking part in the raid, only three people knew about the kidnap plot and we're all in this room.'

'Meaning?' asked Silsbury.

'The Gestapo knew everything about the kidnap and then they came to my home. Someone, as you English would say, has blabbed. And if it was the lovely Mademoiselle, then the Resistance would like her to explain.'

'She's going to London,' snapped Silsbury.

'Please Godfrey; we're all on the same side.' He paused. 'We *are* all on the same side?'

Silsbury hesitated. 'This is vitally important. I need her.'

'I think we all do.'

Stalemate as neither man moved. Juliette's fear edged higher. Bonhomme moved between Silsbury and Juliette and spoke calmly.

'And is this so she can tell your English colleagues what a loyal chap you are, the perfect British spy, and thus allow you to safely continue working as a double-agent?'

Juliette went into shock. Silsbury was seething but calm.

'Big mistake, Émile. Now both of you; move.'

Silsbury waved his gun to indicate where the others should stand. They were slow to move. 'Move,' snapped the jumpy double-agent. The "prisoners" shuffled a little. Silsbury watched them but in moving bumped against a chair. In the split-second he took his eyes off the couple to negotiate the chair, Bonhomme hit the light switch and shoved Juliette hard. The room was pitch black. Salisbury fired in the darkness.

'Run, Juliette!' screamed Bonhomme.

Juliette found the door handle. Silsbury fired again. There was a sharp cry of pain. Louise opened the door and fled. She leapt down the stairs. Bonhomme followed her. Silsbury fired again and Bonhomme collapsed. Stepping over him, Silsbury fired at the fleeing woman. She felt a bullet brush her hair as she dived into the dark street.

She had no idea where she was. She ran using lamp posts and horse troughs for protection. A gun fired and glass shattered ahead of her.

After what had happened in the Tuileries Gardens, Juliette was sore and exhausted but wanting to survive made it easy to dismiss pain.

She swung into another street, a little wider with businesses at street level and apartments above. Thank God for the blackout. In the pre-dawn silence she heard someone running.

Silsbury had only one goal; kill the woman. He'd done for the bloody Frog. With the woman dead, Silsbury's secret was safe.

He saw her. He stopped to shoot. She turned a corner. Shit! Juliette was in a small courtyard. The road swung around but straight ahead was a long flight of steps. If she got to the top ahead of Silsbury he wouldn't see which way she went. Her body pleaded for rest.

In the darkness, she saw him about fifty yards behind. If she didn't get to the top of the steps in time, he could shoot her from below. Then she heard voices. Four German soldiers, a little worse for wear, came out of a restaurant. Juliette ran towards them and called in fluent German.

'Gentlemen, help me. I am Kommandant Schaumburg's niece.' The soldiers were immediately interested. 'There was a kidnap plot against my uncle tonight.'

'We know Fräulein, but how can we help?'

'One of the Resistance fighters involved in the plot is trying to kill me.' The soldiers drew their guns. 'He's coming around that corner right now with a gun.'

On cue, Silsbury, struggling for breath, ran around the corner and saw four Germans with guns pointed straight at him. In French, one soldier called to him.

'Do not move, Monsieur. We have you covered. Drop your gun or we shoot.' The Englishman was desperate.

'Don't shoot, don't shoot.' Silsbury raised his hands but still held the gun. He spoke in flawless German. 'I am Herr Godfrey Silsbury, a German agent working directly for Reichsführer Himmler.' He pointed at Juliette. 'She is an English spy.'

That stopped the soldiers.

Juliette returned fire. 'This man has just shot and killed Capitaine Émile Bonhomme of the Paris Police. I can take you to his body right now. Look, he even has the murder weapon in his hand.'

A soldier moved to Silsbury. 'Put down your weapon, Monsieur and we can talk.'

Silsbury was angry and frantic. 'Listen to me you morons. That woman is an English spy and if you allow her to escape you will answer to the Gestapo.'

The soldier was unmoved. 'Put down the gun ... please.' Silsbury paused then slowly placed his weapon on the cobblestones.

'You bloody fools,' growled Silsbury.

'Now kindly step back,' requested the German.

Silsbury shook his head but stepped back and the other soldiers rushed to collect the gun. One began to search Silsbury and he reacted. 'Idiots, I'm a German agent!'

A scuffle began and Juliette slipped away.

Silsbury yelled. 'Look! She's getting away! Stop her!'

The soldiers saw the disappearing woman, looked at one another and shrugged. The enraged Silsbury was led to their vehicle.

Juliette ran constantly changing direction. She collapsed in a doorway. She was a physical and mental wreck. She took deep breaths. Her mind was spinning.

She got her London message from Silsbury. He was her handler and everyone trusted him; literally everyone because Silsbury was also working for the Nazis.

My God, I was being sent home to say Silsbury was a star. I would have been responsible for him betraying even more French Resistance fighters.

And Capitaine Bonhomme, the decent man, the brave, kind and wise man who saved me from jail and possibly the guillotine, and who was a true friend to the Resistance, died saving my life. He was murdered by Britain's top man in Paris.

Juliette had to tell London. Her Paris contact was a double-agent. He tried to murder her. But how could she tell anyone let alone London? The Resistance believed she betrayed them. The Gestapo and her British contact wanted her dead. The French police would want to interview her about Capitaine Bonhomme's death. She had no friends. She was absolutely alone—except for the Little Sparrow.

She had to find her way to Edith's apartment. She started walking and then she saw it. The Eiffel Tower was unlit but visible in the pre-dawn light. Juliette knew if she stayed on this side of the Seine and kept the Tower to her left, she would eventually reach the 16th arrondissement.

There was only an hour or two of darkness left. She had to find refuge. Being on the streets during curfew was insane. Being English in Nazi-controlled Paris was worse.

And word would have spread that the woman who ran the kidnap plot, who murdered two Germans in the gardens and who escaped with the secret of Berlin's best double-agent, was on the loose. She definitely needed shelter.

Then the thought struck her. Once Silsbury was rescued by the Gestapo, he would give them a list of possible hiding places. Edith's apartment would be one. But Juliette had nowhere else.

She arrived at the Little Sparrow's nest. The brothel on the ground floor was quietly humming. Juliette climbed the stairs. The foyer was quiet. She listened at Edith's door. Nothing. She tapped softly. Still nothing. She knocked louder fearful she would wake the wrong citizens.

184

Her spirits had never been so low. Her one last haven was shut. Edith was out carousing, sound asleep or afraid.

Juliette went downstairs and into the street. Nothing and no-one. She heard laughter from the brothel and opened the door. The Madam was counting the takings. She saw Juliette and smiled.

'Ma chéri, where have you been all my life?'

'Pardon Madame but I am looking for my friend Edith. She lives upstairs.'

The Madam came from behind the counter. 'You may be looking for Edith but I am looking for you. Despite your wild appearance, you are the most ravishing woman in Paris. Trust me, darling, I can make you very, very rich.'

Not quite what Juliette had in mind but when a car roared up and several Gestapo agents rushed past the brothel door heading upstairs, she suddenly had to think on her feet.

'Rich, Madame?' she asked. 'How rich?'

Just then the brothel door opened and a Wehrmacht officer entered. Juliette believed her life was over.

But instead of grabbing the Englishwoman and dragging her off to be tortured and killed, the General ogled her. He chided the brothel owner.

'Madame, you wicked, wicked lady. Where have you been hiding this gorgeous creature?' He took Louise's hand and kissed it passionately.

He was overweight but immaculately dressed in full uniform wearing the Iron Cross, First Class. General Wolfgang Fashingbauer was a General der Panzertruppe in charge of armoured troops.

He excelled in the Battle of France and was currently awaiting re-assignment. His stay in Paris was dominated by fine food, fine wine and deviant dalliances.

Juliette was trapped. Both the setting and man were repulsive. The alternative in the flat above was worse. Smiling, she allowed the General to escort her to the facilities in the rear of the brothel. Could she escape and if so, go where?

Inside his favourite cubicle, Fashingbauer eyed his prey. Fresh flesh was stimulating. Juliette opted for the coy and innocent character. 'Oh Monsieur, I am not certain I will be able to satisfy a Field Marshal.'

He laughed. 'Only a General, my darling, but I'm sure you can rise to the occasion. I know I can.' He laughed and lunged at her.

She squealed as if it was a game. He loved her style. He craved her body. The room was small and she was soon cornered. He pulled her to him and stroked and squeezed her buttocks. He slobbered on her neck growling with delight. He pulled back so as to fondle her breasts and nearly died.

Juliette was holding his Luger pistol and pointing it straight at his belly. In fluent German and with a voice one acquired in drama school, she addressed her client.

'Call out, you die.'

Fashingbauer changed instantly. Blood drained from his genitals at a rapid rate. 'Don't shoot, please don't shoot,' he whispered.

'Where is your car?'

'I, I came by taxi.'

Juliette raised the pistol and aimed at his face. Fashingbauer flinched, shut his eyes and quickly whimpered. 'Outside, outside, my car is outside.'

'We'll take the back door. You lead.'

He looked terrified and fumbled in his pocket. 'I have money. Here, take it.'

She took it. 'Thank you. Now pick up your cap, General and move.'

He picked up his cap and gloves. 'You have no chance. Go now and I'll tell no-one. I swear.'

'This is my final warning,' said Juliette. 'Do as I say without question or I'll shoot you now.' She paused and mimicked him. 'I swear.'

Her eyes supported her dialogue. She was utterly convincing. He turned, opened the door and felt the Luger press into his spine. He flinched again.

'Quietly and slowly, General; I'd hate the gun to go off accidentally.'

They walked along the corridor and he stopped at the rear entrance.

'Open it,' said Juliette, 'quietly.'

The door was opened and she pushed him hard. He stumbled. She followed and closed the door.

'Where is your car?' He pointed. She moved to his side and pushed the pistol into his ribs. 'We walk as lovers. Move.'

They crossed the road to a Mercedes-Benz.

'Keys,' said Juliette holding out her free hand.

He offered them then dropped them at the last moment. She indicated he was to pick them up. Slowly he bent down and with head low felt the pistol press into his temple.

'Do you have a death wish, General?'

'No,' he gasped. 'Please, I have a wife and children.'

'Congratulations.'

She took the keys, opened the door and, pointing the pistol at him, beckoned him towards her. When he was very close she backed into the car and into the passenger seat. Her whole body ached. She waggled her finger and he followed. Once he was in the driving seat, she pushed the gun into his ribs and handed him the keys.

'Drive south. Out of Paris and avoid your patrols.' He hesitated. She snarled. 'Drive.'

The first streaks of dawn appeared. Juliette was not admiring the scenery. Her body sent messages to her brain. Sleep is good. Food is wonderful. Hot bath equals Heaven. She kept staring at Fashingbauer. He was planning to end the charade. He wanted control but not a bullet.

The suburbs of Paris were disappearing. They came to an intersection.

'Which way?' asked the driver.

He waited for Juliette to look to her right. He would grab the pistol and push it away. If she fired, his body would be out of the firing line.

She kept staring at him. He stared back. She spoke softly.

'The sooner we get to the south of France, the sooner you return to your wife and children.'

He'd gone right off this woman. He turned right. There were fewer houses and more farms. They drove through a wooded area where the road veered to the right. Rounding a bend they saw a roadblock about a hundred yards ahead.

Suddenly Fashingbauer had a chance. There were two Wehrmacht soldiers either side of a temporary barrier. Both men had rifles.

Juliette pushed the gun into the driver. 'I am your niece and you are taking me to the station to catch the train to Marseilles. Any tricks and your wife becomes a widow.'

One of the soldiers held up his hand and the car slowed then stopped. The general wound down his window. The soldier looked in, saw the uniform and Iron Cross and immediately saluted. Juliette pushed the Luger into her companion's ribs. It was his cue to chat.

'I am General Fashingbauer. This is my niece. I am driving her to the station for her journey to Marseilles.'

The soldier was aware of the power of the man but had another type of pressure.

'I beg the General's pardon but I have strict orders to check the papers of all females between the ages of sixteen and forty.'

In fluent German, Juliette joined in. 'But surely the niece of this outstanding officer is beyond reproach. Please, I will miss my train.'

Oh the agony of decision making. If the soldier let a wanted woman pass, his life would not be worth living. If he failed to believe a General, his next posting could be to Oblivion. The soldier decided.

'I am sorry, Herr General, but I insist on seeing your niece's papers.'

Fashingbauer and the Luger became even more intimate. He lost his cool. 'Listen you little shit, I am a highly decorated Wehrmacht General and I'm ordering you to let us through.'

The soldier hesitated then suddenly raised his rifle and pointed it straight at the General. Poor Wolfgang now had two firearms aimed at him. Well only one actually. Juliette raised the Luger and fired. The bullet hit the soldier's shoulder. He screamed and fell.

'Drive!' screamed Juliette.

The other soldier raised his rifle. The car took off and the soldier dived to avoid being hit. The car smashed through the temporary barrier and kept going. The second sentry scrambled to his feet and started firing. Fashingbauer didn't need any encouragement to accelerate.

Juliette's heart and the car were both racing. She'd shot two Nazis and kidnapped another and all before breakfast. There would soon be patrols out looking for her in many parts of France.

Having survived the latest gun battle, the General finally spoke. 'You're going to get us both killed. Let me out and you can have the car.'

'What, and lose my ticket to freedom? Drive.'

They passed through the odd village and took what Juliette hoped were back roads. She lived on hope. So far her luck had held but for how long?

They were on a narrow road when around a bend came a farmer's lorry. Both vehicles slowed because passing was tricky. Just as they drew level, the lorry swerved hard and smashed into the side of the Mercedes. It spun the vehicle around. Fashingbauer slammed his foot on the brake pedal and the car rocked from side to side then stopped.

The Nazi panicked thinking Juliette would shoot him but she was dazed and before either could react their car was surrounded by men with rifles. Now was a good time to surrender.

The Resistance fighters were amused and couldn't believe their luck; a German General and his tart. What fun. We'll torture him and screw her.

Juliette and her companion were travelling in the back of the lorry while being guarded by several men armed with guns and lust. The lorry turned onto a dirt road and stopped in a farm yard. The prisoners were shoved towards a farm house. A bearded Frenchman was enjoying breakfast in a huge kitchen and looked up when his visitors arrived.

'Holy Mother of God. What have we here?'

The lorry driver spoke. 'A Bosch General and his French bit of stuff.'

The fanatical Resistance leader, Pascal, hated Germans and collaborators with a passion. Juliette was moving towards surrender. She'd flirted with death many times in the last twenty-four hours and been shot at on three separate occasions. Four might be pushing her luck.

She decided to play the English card. She mentally rehearsed her speech. *I'm really English, I'm an SIS agent, I'm on your side, I've kidnapped a General, shot two Germans and have vitally important news to help the Allied cause.*

It seemed her best response. But she wasn't the first to speak. She didn't anticipate Fashingbauer's tactic. He'd had a perfectly awful day. At his favourite brothel he'd discovered what he thought was a new and delicious French prostitute. She turned into the bitch from Hell and kidnapped him. He was shot at by one of his own soldiers and was now a prisoner of several bloodthirsty Resistance fighters. His career and life were ruined but if this was the end, he decided to go down swinging.

'I am General Wolfgang Fashingbauer. With my French mistress here, I am trying to contact the top man in the free French Army to whom I will surrender. I have valuable information which the Resistance and the Free French Army can use to help defeat my country. I will talk to your commanding officer.' He paused then began again. 'Oh and please do not judge my mistress. As a Frenchwoman, she was never happy sleeping with Germans and only did so to raise money for the Resistance.'

The kitchen erupted with laughter. Juliette's case and reputation were trashed. But she was a fighter and then it was her turn.

Her quandary was mentioning the Hôtel Meurice. If her current captors knew of that Resistance disaster, they would delight in the long and slow torture of the woman who some believed was responsible. Was the Resistance grapevine working? But if she didn't mention the kidnap, what other story, true or otherwise, could she deliver?

Pascal oozed contempt. 'So, fellow French citizen, collaborative traitor, what have you to say?'

Juliet looked at him. 'Nothing.'

The men were surprised, especially Pascal. 'Nothing?'

She spoke. 'If you believe the crap from this Nazi slob, you're obviously thick.' Hatred mingled with lust. 'You cretins wouldn't know the truth if it drove in here on a Panzer tank and bit you all on the arse.'

You had to hand it to the woman, she had guts. She had style too. It was her powerful language plus her vivid delivery that made her look and sound utterly convincing. Her eye contact, the volume and pace of her dialogue was poetry in motion. Just as she'd convinced the Resistance in Paris, here she fascinated the Resistance in central France.

But Pascal was too proud to treat Juliette with anything but contempt. Besides, the evidence of her being caught in the company of a top-ranking German general was, for Pascal, case closed. He sneered at her.

'For any French citizen, man or woman, to collaborate with the Bosch, is unforgivable. My men will enjoy your body and then you will be shot and your tortured remains given to the pigs. Take her.'

Two men grabbed her and began to march her away.

She spoke loudly. 'So nationality doesn't count?'

Pascal was educated and intelligent and something nagged him about Juliette. She wasn't your average collaborator. 'Wait.' The men dragging Juliette stopped. Pascal walked to her. 'Nationality?'

'Am I being judged because I'm a collaborator or because I'm French?'

'Both.'

'Ah, but you see I'm not French.'

Fashingbauer was behind on points so launched a new attack.

'That's true. She's German.' A new bidder. The stakes got higher.

Pascal shrugged. 'French or German, your fate is the same.'

'What about English?'

Pascal was interested. 'English? You sound more French than we do.'

Juliette spoke with conviction. 'Well know this gentlemen, I'm English, an undercover operative fighting for the Allies and I have vital information which could save the life of hundreds of free Frenchmen and women. Kill me and you kill your comrades.' Then in perfect English she spoke slowly and emphatically. 'I am English; English.'

189

Again the message was compelling and when delivered with such persuasive brilliance, everyone was impressed.

Pascal moved closer. 'So what is this information?'

Juliette switched back to French. 'Can I trust you?'

He slapped her face. Juliette withstood the pain. She locked her eyes on his. Two strong men held her arms. She was helpless. She spoke.

'Give me a radio and I'll deliver the information to London and to General de Gaulle himself.'

Fashingbauer began flailing. 'She's lying. She's a prostitute in a brothel in the 16th arrondissement. I know dozens of Germans who pay for this woman. She even slept with me before we fled Paris.'

Pascal was thinking. *She's a woman. All women lie.* He'd heard enough of the "evidence" and put on his judge's wig. He spoke in her face.

'I think you're a liar, a brilliant liar but a liar nevertheless. You were caught as a willing passenger escaping with a high-ranking Nazi. You are condemned by your own actions. So let us see how good you are at entertaining my men. If you do well, we'll know you're lying. If you fail to satisfy the voracious sexual appetites of my fellow Frenchmen, we might re-consider your case.'

The men grinned. Juliette was shattered. It was like the ducking stool for the alleged witch. If she drowned she was not a witch. If Juliette was lousy at screwing men, she'd prove her innocence. She faced an appalling no-win situation. She'd never been so scared or so sad.

'Take her,' ordered Pascal and Juliette was frogmarched to her doom. He called after her. 'Only leave some for me.' His men laughed.

There were stairs at the end of the kitchen. Juliette was dragged towards them. Just as she reached the first step a voice was heard.

'Plum?'

Chapter 26

THERE ARE SUCH things as co-incidence, happenstance and serendipity. One of those took place in that French farmhouse.

Everyone stopped. The English voice, speaking in English, came from a dim corner of the kitchen. Juliette felt she was dreaming. The speaker repeated their enquiry.

'Is that *you*, Plum?'

Pascal moved quickly to the end of the kitchen and spoke in his accented English. 'It is okay, Monsieur. You are suffering from injury. We will soon take you out from here.'

Juliette was tingling. Her pulse accelerated. She peered at the person lying on a makeshift bed. She spoke in English.

'Yes, it's me. Who is it?'

The man had his head swathed in a large and badly applied bandage with his left leg in a crude splint. There was blood and dirt on his clothes. He was clearly injured but now came alive.

'It's me, James.'

The penny dropped. 'Pongo!' exclaimed Juliette and broke free to kneel beside him.

Pascal and his companions were amazed. Fashingbauer was suicidal.

Pongo spoke. 'I thought you were touring Australia as a famous actress.'

Juliette cried. The relief was overwhelming. She struggled to speak. 'I can't believe you're here. But what's happened to you?'

'Bloody Jerry. Shot down last week but these Frenchies have patched me up and I'm flying home tonight.'

Pascal stepped forward. 'You know this woman?'

'Of course I know her, said Pongo, 'and her family. Best man at her brother's wedding and I've been in love with this gorgeous girl forever. My heart was broken when she went to Cambridge; beauty *and* brains.'

'And she is English?'

'Too bloody right, and from the best of families. Her old man fought with you lot in the last war and won every damn bravery award going.'

Juliette died and Louise wept freely.

Pascal was not convinced. 'But she called you Pongo.'

Pongo laughed and winced with pain. 'Yes, it's my nickname, ah, ...'

Pascal's broken English had failed him.

'Surnom,' said Louise, wiping her face.

The wounded Englishman spoke. 'Me Pongo, she Plum.'

Pascal nodded then smiled.

191

Juliette, or rather Louise, was escorted to the table and given food and wine. Pascal apologised profusely. The Resistance crowded around. Fashingbauer despaired. Pascal was gentle but insistent.

'So Mademoiselle, why are you travelling with this German?'

'I kidnapped him. He was my ticket to the south of France and my way back home to England.'

'And this vital information; you say it can save lives in the Resistance.'

'Definitely,' said Louise. 'But I'm unsure if I should tell you.' There was a murmur of concern. 'I need to ask my superiors in England if I am allowed to share this secret.'

Pascal was annoyed. 'You do not trust us?'

'Should I? You were about to rape and shoot me then throw my body to the pigs.'

She had a point. Pascal was struggling and spoke in English. 'I regret that, Miss and again, my 'umble apologies.'

She nodded and continued in French. 'Please, I must use your radio.'

'We 'ave no radio.'

'Well can you get me on Pongo's plane?'

'Of course,' said Pascal. 'But if the plane does not make it then your secret is lost.'

Louise thought hard. 'Let me say this. There's a man in Paris, working with the Resistance, who is a double-agent. He claims to be a British agent but he really works for the Nazis. You must warn your comrades about this man.'

'And his name?'

'I will send you his name when I return to England.' More anger from the Resistance. Louise raised her hand. 'But I will tell you this. I am ashamed to say, he is English.'

There was a buzz then silence. Louise wanted to say the name but had become paranoid. *Is there anyone here I can trust? Is there a friend of Silsbury here in this very kitchen?* The silence lingered.

'I know.' The forgotten General entered the fray.

Everyone turned and looked at Fashingbauer. He shrugged. 'Maybe you will kill me quickly if I do something for the French.'

There was a long pause. Pascal was silent. Of deals came there none. The German had nothing to lose. He spoke quietly.

'His name is Godfrey Silsbury.'

It really *was* a dark and stormy night as Louise and Pongo were driven to a field in central France. A British plane would bring guns and collect any pilots or aircrew who needed a lift home.

All day the English couple discussed their respective war adventures. Louise had sworn Pongo to secrecy before she explained why she'd never been touring Down Under. Naturally some things were omitted.

Being a sort of spy was okay but bearing her breasts on stage was definitely too much information. Spending the night in the hotel suite of a Wehrmacht tank commander was totally redacted.

Pongo had news for Louise. Both her brothers had joined up and when last he heard, Louise's mother was alive and well in Wiltshire.

Louise explained her signing the *Official Secrets Act* and begged Pongo to never breathe a word of what she'd told him and to even forget they'd ever met in France.

He wanted to say, "I'll do anything for you, Plum". He was smitten. To him she was the perfect woman and finding her as he did was the ideal tonic to help him recover. Perhaps this dramatic reunion might see Louise change her mind. He lived in hope.

Louise held his hand as they drove to the makeshift airfield. Every bump was agony for Pongo.

The beauty of the Westland Lysander is its ability to land and take off in a farmer's backyard. A few small fires lit the so-called runway in the modest field and they heard the plane before they saw it. The pilot did well and brought the aircraft to a bouncy landing.

The weapons were unloaded and Pongo was carefully placed in the rear cockpit. Luckily Louise was slim and flexible but even so, squeezing two into such a small space was tricky. As Louise prepared to climb into the plane, Pascal grabbed her arm.

'Good luck, Mademoiselle and again my apologies for treating you the way I did.'

She nodded and shook his hand. 'Vive la France,' she said then climbed aboard.

The Lysander turned into the wind, accelerated and took off. The fires which lit the runway were already extinguished and the weapons loaded in the lorry.

Louise was seriously uncomfortable but cared only for Pongo. She held his hand and he smiled in the darkness.

'Now remember, Pongo,' she said, 'you promised to forget everything I told you today. And a gentleman always keeps his word.'

'I promise, Plum, absolutely. Not a dicky-bird.' He paused. 'You do know I'm madly in love with you.'

She squeezed his hand. Hardship and danger can heighten emotions. She moved close and whispered. 'I think you're rather special too.'

Pongo coughed. The pain in his leg was excruciating and his head was throbbing but the young woman behind him was an angel. He fell asleep. She gently kissed his bandaged head as their plane flew over the Channel.

The pilot had told Louise to brace herself once the plane started to descend. She felt the plane dropping and saw the dim lighting of what she assumed was an English airport. She released Pongo's hand and laid it gently on his chest. She leant against the fuselage. The plane landed, hopping twice and taxied to a halt. England. Home. She was excited.

Louise had tears in her eyes. Am I really back in Blighty?

A ladder was placed against the plane and a man's face appeared.

'Evenin' Miss. Do you need a hand?'

Louise got out. 'No thanks. But please take special care of my friend.'

She jumped to the grass, knelt and kissed the ground. 'This blessed plot,' she said and looked up at the night sky. 'Thank you, Will.'

The airport was busy and Louise found it pleasant to have no responsibility. There was no pressure to perform and nobody to answer to. There was no acting of any kind. Several people attended to Pongo. The pilot came over.

'Cup of tea in the hut, Miss; this way.'

'Thank you,' said Louise and they walked to a building with blackout curtains and basic everything. To Louise it looked like the Ritz. She was given a strong cup of tea, biscuits and a blanket. It seemed incredible she was back home in England.

Now she desperately wanted to tell London about Silsbury. She approached the man in charge and asked to make a telephone call.

'Hubby can wait till you get home, Miss.'

In a calm voice, Louise made her case.

'Sir, I've just returned from France with vital information. Unless I can immediately telephone the War Office, I'll report you to my commanding officer who has the ear of the Prime Minister.'

The man jumped to it. Louise rang the number she'd memorized and Major Bunting was reached at home having dragged himself out of bed.

'Miss Wellesley? How delightful to hear from you.'

'Good morning, Major. May I speak freely?'

'Not really but I assume you're home.'

'I am and with very serious news.'

'Can you come and see me today?'

'I can but I want you to know that someone we know is not really a team player.'

There was silence.

'Are we talking about changing sides?'

'We are.'

'I see.'

More silence.

'Major, how is Surrey this season? Have you been to The Oval?'

Bunting understood. He said, 'Damn war's made a mess of the cricket season I'm afraid. But thank you for asking. And we can discuss those LBW laws when next we meet. Come and see me as soon as possible.'

'I shall look forward to it.'

'Jolly good. Oh, and welcome home.'

Louise hung up. Her thespian trip to Australia was over. She was back in Blighty. Her mother had been receiving news from the Antipodes describing her daughter's grand acting tour. Now Louise would have to explain the finer details of her performances and how and why she came back to Britain. Only Pongo knew the truth and he was Mister Reliable.

She went looking for transport.

'Oh Miss.' It was the pilot.

'How is my friend?'

The pilot's face spoke volumes. 'I'm sorry, Miss. He didn't make it.'

Louise felt ill. The man who treated her with respect and kindness, Henry's pal, her unrequited lover was dead; dear Pongo. The pilot continued. 'But he did say something before he died. I'm not sure he was making any sense; something about a plum job, a wonderful plum job.'

Louise nodded, thanked the pilot, walked away and cried. She was still crying when the officer in charge approached her. She wiped her tears.

'Now Miss, we need to get you sorted. Where's home?'

Louise was genuinely stumped. If Surrey had been sold, it wasn't there. She could try Wiltshire and her mother, and of course the Vesteys would welcome her with open arms.

'That depends,' she said. 'Could you tell me where we are?'

'Teversham, Miss. We're close to Cambridge. Do you know this part of the world?'

Louise nodded and smiled. 'As a matter of fact, I do.

The Detective Joanna Best Mysteries

www.cenfoxbooks.com

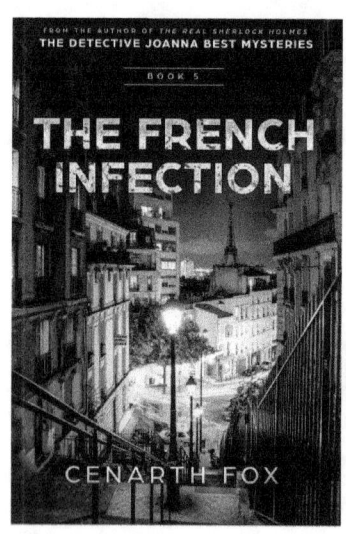

The much maligned and misunderstood father of the famous Brontë sisters led an amazing life. Discover the shocking Brunty (that's right) family tree in Ireland and how this man of sorrows survived horrendous sadness and inspired his daughters to scribble with stunning success.

A splendid story, reading like a Victorian melodrama. **Louise Joy**

Portrays the life of Brontë in remarkable style giving a deeper insight into a famous literary family. **Rev. Philip Higgins**

Cenarth Fox has seized the day to revisit Patrick Brontë, an extraordinary man who encouraged his children to read, to think, and hence to imagine. **Geraldine Starbrook**

Wonderfully evocative. **Steve Stanworth**

(Co-ordinator for the Brontë Bell Chapel)

www.cenfoxbooks.com

NOODLES FOR
SHAKESPEARE

PYGMALION DOWN UNDER

CENARTH FOX

A young Vietnamese woman, Thanh, arrives in Australia speaking little English. Her neighbour, David, is a bitter, retired English Literature teacher. David teaches Thanh not English but Elizabethan English in a love story with a difference.

A beautiful, heartwarming, and brilliant book I couldn't put down with many interesting twists and turns ... a most curious book and very clever with Shakespearean quotes. **Louise Joy**

I have very much enjoyed working my way through your novel and its stage adaptation. It is a very skillful adaptation and the narrative and characters retain their vivid intensity. Above all, three cheers for the Bard, working in mysterious ways to cross cultural boundaries and bring the world together! **John Bell**

Do you have a conscience? Does it work? Melbourne scientist, Bernie Slim, creates a drug designed to kick-start a conscience. Surely this Moral Compass Pill is science fiction. It's secretly given to ordinary people with unexpected results. When a heavy criminal is tricked into taking the drug, serious trouble looms. When a public figure pops the pill, it's no longer a secret. A leading politician, Mafia boss, and Big Pharma CEO fight for the formula. Bernie's in strife. Can the drug and Bernie survive? What would happen if cops, crooks and politicians followed their conscience? Tricky.

Very engaging with laugh-out-loud humour. The characters are well-knit into a complex plot that never loses impetus. **Trevor Blum**

Cenarth Fox's foray into the realm of humour is a departure from his earlier work, and it shows a breadth of skill. The characters are well formed and Mr. Fox does great villains. **Scott Skipper**

This highly funny novel kept me engrossed to the very satisfactory ending. The author's use of word play made it a particular pleasure to read. Characters are well drawn, the pace is rollicking, and the thought of a moral compass pill is quite delicious. **Jay Ayon**

www.cenfoxbooks.com

www.ingramcontent.com/pod-product-compliance
Lightning Source LLC
Chambersburg PA
CBHW071111100726
47908CB00008B/2345